Bachelor Row

Bachelor Row

Desmond Gallagher

Kingford Press
Dublin

ISBN 978-0-9511565-4-4

A CIP catalogue record for this book is available from the British Library.

enquiries to: info@kingfordpress.com

Kingford Press
Dublin
www.kingfordpress.com

CHAPTER ONE

Early 1970s

Do I remember the first time I saw Teresa? Yes – it was in one of my local bars and it was simply because of the way her tongue darted into my surprised mouth. Do I remember what she was drinking? Again, yes – it was rum 'n' coke, which made her an expensive chat-up, but when you are feeling good and you have the money in your pocket, then it doesn't seem to matter. It is peculiar that I can now remember that first meeting, yet the very next day she was gone from my mind – and I must add a lot quicker than my hangover. And it wasn't until some days later when I ran into her in another one of my drinking haunts that she came back into my life. 'Haven't seen you in here before,' I said. 'Following me around?'

'It's a free world,' she said, tossing her head back causing her fair hair to resettle on her shoulders like a full-length curtain that's lifted, then dropped back into place. 'But would it bother you if I *were* following you?'

'It might break me.'

'Skinflint – get me a drink.'

I studied her. Her mouth was wide, and she had freckles about her nose, a left over from a recent hot spell, but it was her eyes that enlivened her face. How could I refuse her?

I was in company with fellows whom I often met here-and-there and none of them seemed to mind Teresa joining the party but as the night passed, I noticed them slip away to other stools and cling like satellites to new centres of conversation, after all, that is what they had come for, not to look at a man slowly becoming intoxicated by something stronger than a pint.

Teresa and I were nearly last in the bar, which wasn't unusual for me, then the barman said, 'Have you no home to go to, Mark?' It was because I knew him well, that he couldn't disguise the trace of grumpiness in his voice, and I wondered was he still having problems with his piles, and as the man moved from behind the counter to collect the empty pint tumblers I glanced at his walk and guessed I was right.

I turned back to Teresa but didn't comment on the barman.

'Well,' she said, 'where to now?'

'I've work in the morning, so I'll be hitting the sack soon.'

'I'll come home with you.'

'The Mother wouldn't approve.'

'We could go to a club?'

'I'd never be able to get up if I did that.'

'Will I see you again?'

'Why?'

'Why?' she echoed. 'Are you thick or something?'

And that's how I got tied-up with her, a moment when I could have told her to take a running jump, but I didn't.

Yet it still didn't feel like I was getting into something big, and I told myself it was just a casual thing. When the mother remarked one day that she was washing more socks and underwear for me than ever, I knew she was fishing for information. At that point, it still hadn't entered my head that I could be in trouble.

On the nights I didn't meet her, I could run into some of my regular buddies and most times they never mentioned or hinted about Teresa, except at the end of the night they would say, 'Maybe we'll see you around at the weekend?' And you knew they were thinking that I was beyond rescue. One night soon afterwards, Teresa persuaded me to leave the comfort of my own district and cross the river Liffey – it wasn't that I didn't know nor had never worked on the north side of the city, for I had painted many a house there, it was just that I like to socialise on my own patch, within the sound of Saint Patrick's bells. Anyway, we were there that night, in a pub I didn't know, when my friend Jimmy, whom I hadn't seen in a long time, came in with a girl.

Teresa didn't know Jimmy but seemed to know the girl. 'Celine, fancy bumping into you here!'

Jimmy landed an arm on my shoulder, then bent as if he were going to give me a slobbery kiss on the cheek, and I shoved him away. 'Get off, you messer!'

'You know one another?' Teresa asked.

'Never saw him before,' Jimmy answered, and turned to the girl with him. 'Celine, I want you to meet this waster! This is Mark.'

I shook her hand. It was indecisive, like she was afraid I would crush it or infect her with something. She looks a bit like the girl at the library that stamps my mother's books when I do that weekly task. But if life teaches you anything it teaches you that even librarians may not be beyond a bit of conniving.

I called for a round, pints for Jimmy and me and – I remember it well – two rum 'n' cokes for the females.

After a while I had forgotten that I was on the north side, and the night was as pleasant as any night in a pub can be. The girls sat side-by-side and Jimmy was next to me, and in this way two conversations could happen without hindrance. However, every so often, Teresa would turn to me and give me a report on something important that had been said in their conversation. 'Celine says her granny lives close to where you live.' – 'Celine says her union might ask them to go out on the street and she doesn't want to.' – 'Celine says Jimmy's taking her to the Isle of Man.'

I paid attention to that last bulletin. 'That sounds serious,' I said.

He had a pained look. 'I promised her, the tickets got and all.'

'Boat?'

'Yeh, good drinking time on the boat.'

'Why don't *we* go with them to the Isle of Man?' Teresa suggested.

'No way,' I spluttered, the drink going against my breath.

'That's a great idea!' Jimmy said. 'You need company for fun!'

'Thanks very much for that,' Celine said, acting as if she were offended. 'Am I not enough for you?'

Teresa became excited. 'We'd have a blast! Anyway, what do you have against Mark and me coming along with you? We wouldn't cramp your style if that's your problem,' she said.

I felt it was time for me to say my piece. 'There'll be no problem because there'll be no Isle of Man, not for me anyway.'

Jimmy looked perplexed. 'Why not?'

'Because it's just…just too serious.'

'What's serious about it?'

I shrugged my shoulders and stared at my pint. I didn't want to tell them that I saw the Isle of Man as a place where only engaged couples went, or couples who saw it in their stars that they were eventually going to be engaged.

Teresa looked disappointed. I didn't elaborate and the company went quiet, like we had suddenly been told that the pub had run out. Just then a man with an overcoat draped over his arm came along and tried to sell it to us. 'It's real Crombie; here, feel it,' he said.

I didn't bother to look up, and Jimmy said that he wasn't interested. 'It's brand new,' the man insisted. 'A cousin of mine in London had to close down his shop.'

'You'd look the part in that, Jimmy,' Celine said. 'See if it fits.'

'It probably fell off the back of a lorry.'

'It's legitimate,' the man said. He attempted to put it on Jimmy.

'I told you I've no interest in the bleedin' coat – now get lost!' he said.

'Don't tell me to get lost,' the overcoat man said. 'I'm just trying to make a living.'

'Well make it elsewhere and don't be annoying us!'

'Come on,' the man said, 'I'll make you a good price.'

Jimmy suddenly took the coat from him and threw it across the floor. 'I told you we're not interested!'

He stared at Jimmy for a moment, then seeing the barman approach, picked up the overcoat, dusted it down and hurried towards a different group, as hawking dodgy goods wasn't welcome, even in a northside bar. In a way, I was thankful for the interruption, as it had broken the silence.

Teresa turned to me. 'Mark, you'd have looked good in a smart overcoat like that.'

I felt my well-worn anorak slung at the back of my stool and wondered what she meant.

Two days later I met her again and she told me that Jimmy had been beaten-up after leaving the pub. 'Two of them were waiting for him. He made Celine run off and she stayed at a safe distance and only returned when they'd gone. She says it was terrible.'

'Was he hurt?'

'He wouldn't hear of going to the hospital, but she thinks he *was* hurt. Now, he won't go outside the door and doesn't want to go on their Isle of Man trip either. It's made him nervous.'

I told her I didn't believe that Jimmy could be nervous.

'Celine says if they cancel, they won't get their money back. However, she also thinks that Jimmy would go to the Isle of Man if you and I were to go, as well. Especially you, Mark. He thinks a lot of you.'

I was thinking that if I'd been with him when he was attacked, I could have helped him. Now I had an opportunity to make amends.

'Find out for definite that he'll go,' I said. 'If it is the case, then get the tickets.' I gave her money to cover it, and some more. 'What'll we do for a place to sleep?' I asked, a practical afterthought.

'We're not going to the Isle of Man to sleep,' she said, throwing me a suggestive look.

As she headed off with the money, I realized that I now had to make up a story for the mother as to why I would be packing a suitcase, so I dropped into a pub to spend some time contemplating the problem.

That night, as she watched television, I volunteered to make her a cup of tea, then served it on a tray with a doily, but she wasn't impressed for she knew it for what it was – a softening-up tactic.

Halfway down the cup, she turned to me and asked, 'Well, what is it?'

Before answering, I was conscious of the array of photographs around us, as if the rest of the O'Brides had been sworn in as a jury. They ranged from my siblings who had left the home, some of them many years before, to my father who occupied pride of place on the china cabinet – Mother only had to angle her head slightly from the line of sight of the television to bask again in his smiling face and usher happy times past into the living room of our tight-for-space apartment. It had been designed in the nineteenth century when a working man's family was not expected to need breathing space for its individual members, and where if you looked for privacy, you were shot down for having notions about yourself; although, small as the apartment was, it had seen the rearing of four of us, the O'Brides. But it was still tight on account of an overlarge sofa the mother had miscalculated; it had been such a job getting it to our second level place that she hadn't the heart to go back to the shop to get it changed.

It's now or never, I decided. 'Mother, I'm going to the Isle of Man.'

I could see a question grow on that round face of hers, a face still free of the heavy lines   to be seen on most of the mothers I knew of her age. She tipped the bottom of the brown frame of her glasses to reposition them on her nose, always a sign that she was getting excited. I waited for it.

'Oh! Who with? Or need I ask?'

'Don't jump to conclusions, Mother. I'm going because of Jimmy Culmane. You remember Jimmy Culmane? From the flats?'

'I remember.'

'I'm doing him a favour.'

'Need I ask if there'll be girls on this trip?'

'Yeh.'

'Mark, we didn't send you to elocution to say 'yeh.'

'Yes, Mother. There will...'

She looked to the photograph on the china cabinet, as if she were waiting on Da to speak, to support her in this latest aggravation. 'You know, me and your father – God rest him – never went anywhere together like that until we were married.'

'Times were different then.'

'What's different? It's still the same world, the same right, the same wrong.'

'There's no wrong in it, Mother. God, I'm only going to the Isle of Man!'

'There's no need to get hot under the collar with me nor to bring God into it,' she said. 'And the females. How come I've never met this new one of yours? Is she too good for us that you won't bring her home?'

'There's no need to "bring her home", as you put it, because there's nothing serious.'

'I hope you're not leading someone up the garden path?'

'That's not my form,' I said.

'That's what I'm afraid of. It's more than likely the other way round. How old is this new girl of yours?'

'I never asked.'

'But you know her birthday?'

This was like a game of draughts. As I admitted to knowing Teresa's birthday, the mother was eyeing up a move. 'She'll make sure she gets her present though.'

There's a king gone, I thought. 'As long as I don't forget yours, Mother, all's well.'

'Son, I don't see any resemblance in that.'

'You're right, Mother.'

Later, as I packed a suitcase in my bedroom, she came in with freshly ironed shirts. 'You'll need these for your trip.'

CHAPTER TWO

The TSS *Lady of Mann* was docked at the North Wall. As it was high season, we made sure to get there early and were not far from the head of the queue when the boarding began and we rushed to claim out seats in the saloon, close to the ship's bar. I had been surprised that Jimmy hadn't a scratch on his face from the assault but figured that he must have suffered blows to the body. Teresa and Celine wanted to go on deck to wave goodbye to the people gathered on the quays, and Jimmy asked me to mind the belongings while he went up after them. 'I'll have the drinks in by the time you get back,' I said. It seemed wiser to get in a double round, as someone said the trip could take up to four hours.

I soon had a forest of drinks on the plastic-topped table. Surprisingly, for me, it was the first of the day, even though it was past 5pm (along the quays, if you had a thirst on you, you could find a dockers' early morning house that opened at 7am). I looked about me. There was a family unwrapping their own sandwiches and the father had gone off to fetch lemonade for his orderly children. I was sure he'd come back with a pint for himself and a mug of tea for herself. An elderly couple across from me were already staring into their drinks, the man smoking a pipe, the woman holding a cigarette at arm's length as if she were disowning it. A young couple had come in, almost shyly, and headed for a corner. They sat hand in hand, looking about them. From where I was sitting, I could almost sense the tenderness between them. I felt a vibration through the saloon's floor and saw that the boat was moving and through the portholes behind the elderly couple I could see the onlookers waving from the quay. I thought of Teresa up on deck, waving back at them. It's happening, no going back now. Anyone would think I was nervous.

A voice cut into my thoughts. 'Are all these seats taken?'

It was my first time to see Paul Sweeney, and at that moment I didn't know his name nor had I any inkling of the role he would play in my life. 'Sorry, friend, they're up on deck,' I said, swinging an arm towards the empty seats and the laden table.

'You're having a party?' he said, nodding towards the drinks. There was an American twang to the voice.

'You're not from here?'

'Wrong. I'm as much from here as you are.' Then he moved away, just as the others appeared.

'Thanks, Mark, you're a star,' Jimmy said at the sight of the drink.

'Don't worry, pal,' I said. 'It'll be your twist next.'

'Have no fears, Celine has my readies, she is our treasurer.'

Teresa looked at me. 'Let's pool ours – then I can be *our* treasurer.'

'I earn it and I spend it,' I answered. 'But don't be shy about standing your round... Women's' lib, and all.'

'What do you think of that?' she said to Celine. 'He invites me here, and now he wants me to buy the drink.'

Celine started to explain her kitty-minding duties 'Well, I'm putting in my –'

Teresa cut her off. 'Wrong answer! What's ours is ours and what's theirs is ours!'

'Communism,' I said.

'We're not communists,' she answered, 'we're girls standing up for our rights'.

'What rights?' Celine looked bewildered.

'The right to be treated as ladies. When we're being brought out, it's the men that pay. At least, that's how it is with me.'

At that stage, I'm only half-listening. The portholes are framing a grey-to-green sea and what I can see of land is getting smaller by the minute. The ship has a swaying motion, and I don't know whether I'm a good sailor, or not.

Suddenly, Teresa says, 'Well, are we going to sing, or something?'

'It's too early for singing,' Jimmy says. 'You need a few bevvies in you to oil the voice.' (I wasn't going to be the one to tell him he was tone deaf.)

Teresa looked irritated and uneasy. 'What'll we do then? Anyone got a deck of cards?' There were no takers for that idea, either, so she stood, hands on hips, and frowned. 'I'm going to find the shop – I need to gorge on a bar of chocolate.' She put her hand out looking for money from me. I pretended not to notice.

'I'll go with you, Teresa,' Celine said, holding her purse. 'Jimmy, if the boat starts to roll, hang on to our drinks and don't let them spill.'

'I'm not an octopus,' he said. 'If it gets rough, I'll just have to drink the lot.'

'You're such a sweet,' she said, disappearing with Teresa.

Alone with him, I said, 'I hear you were badly done-over?'

'*Me*? No. I gave back as much as I got, and more.'

'You weren't hurt, then? I was told you were backing out of the trip.'

'Hey, it's me you're talking about. It was your man from the pub, the one selling the dodgy overcoats, and he'd another ugly puss along with him. I left Overcoat Man screaming on the ground but the other one gave me a punch to the side of the head, and I couldn't see right, and he was able to stick a few digs into me. I lashed out with the boot and caught him in the goolies. That must have sickened him, for he picked up the other fellow and they left.'

I began to think that Teresa had conned me. A set-up, and Celine must have been part of it. But what was I to do? I couldn't get off the ship in the middle of the Irish Sea. Even if I could walk on water, did I really want to leave Teresa? The answer was *no*; I certainly didn't! Time with such a good-looking girl didn't normally come to someone like me, and I decided to wise up and let my annoyance peter out.

'Anyway, Jimmy,' I said, 'I'm glad you weren't hurt.'

The girls came back and for a moment I thought I saw a shadow of worry on Teresa's face, as if she suspected that I now knew the true story of what had happened. I showed her my good face, which is what Mother always said, 'Take off that moody face and put on a good face!' Then, without warning, Teresa gave me a chocolate-flavoured kiss, which I washed down with a gulp of beer.

On time, we saw the Isle of Man and soon the ship approached the dock at Douglas and well-trained deckhands in blue jumpers moved to their positions. The railings on the top deck rattled as the thrust of the engines fought to position the boat and, as the gangplank was hauled into place, the lights of Douglas, not yet fully twinkling in the failing daylight, demoted the lights back home on Bray promenade to a tawdry carnival standard. Teresa came to my side, took in the view, her face serene. We linked arms – it made me feel uncomfortable, yet, at the same time I was happy to be there.

We splashed out on a taxi to the hotel, which transpired to be within walking distance, a glorified bed-and-breakfast, recommended to Celine by some aunt or other of hers – its good point was its position, right on the promenade. There were steps up to the door and inside the carpeted hall we found a small reception counter with a press-for-attention sign; it buzzed and eventually a man with a look that reminded me of a ticket collector on a train came from downstairs. He had a combover, wore a shirt and tie and a fawn, sleeveless pullover, and the sleeves of the shirt were rolled up and held in place by elastic. He slid in behind the counter, adjusted his glasses, and repositioned the bell sign as if we had disturbed it. Celine verified her booking arrangement with him and then she spoke up for us and the man listened without comment as she explained that Teresa and I were last-minute travellers due to my doctor's insistence that I take a holiday to recover from stress. 'You see, he's a prison warden.'

When I heard that story, I wondered what the Painters' Union would think of my desertion from its ranks.

Is it one room or two?' the man asked, looking towards Teresa.

She smiled at him, like a young girl would smile at her father. 'We're *almost* engaged,' she said.

I put up a finger to signify that one room was all that was needed.

'Okay,' the man said, handing Jimmy a key, 'Mr. Culmane you're in room six on the first floor and Mr...?'

'O'Bride,' I said, with a slight cough.

'Mr. O'Bride, I'm giving you our last room, top of the house, room thirteen.' I waited for a key; none came. He said, 'Sorry there's no lock on thirteen, but you've the top of the house to yourselves.' We discovered what he meant – room thirteen was a converted attic. A naked light bulb showed drab greenish wallpaper, a lopsided wardrobe with chipped veneer, and a pedestal washstand with a mirror invaded by spots of brown. I guessed the toilet was outside on the landing, somewhere. Teresa went to the small window and said that she could see nothing because of the dark. Then she went to the bed and tested it with a sitting bounce, but before she'd a chance to comment on it, Jimmy bounded into the room, his swim trunks already on, and a towel in his hand. 'We're heading across the road for a swim.'

'It's night-time,' I said, 'and you can't swim in the dark...'

'That's what makes it crazy! Grab your stuff and let's go!'

'What about the pints?' I was looking at my watch.

'They serve pints downstairs, our own private bar, and Celine says there's no limit on time.' I noticed that Teresa was already getting a swimsuit from her suitcase.

We crossed the road to the promenade and, full of holiday giddiness, dropped on to the narrow beach below. The others had changed in the rooms, but I waited until we were at the water's edge. Close to shore, the sea caught the light coming from the hotels across the street; further out it was a dark blanket. I waded in after the others ready for an icy shock but found the water was surprisingly bearable. I reasoned that a raised alcohol level might have something to do with it and, in a devil-may-care moment, I rushed forward and flopped, tasting the saltiness, screaming like a child released from school. Teresa put her arms around my neck. 'This is the life,' she said.

Jimmy and Celine were locked in a rolling embrace like sea creatures in a television nature programme. Teresa and I swam parallel to the beach, my stroke a clumsy overhand that depended on brute strength, hers a gliding breaststroke. It was a moment not easily forgotten, as it was when I walked my first dog, or when I broke a window in the local factory for a dare. When we turned to go back, I saw Celine waist-high in the water, looking out to sea and calling Jimmy. I made for the shore and ran up the beach to her.

'He's disappeared!' she said. 'He just vanished...'

'Where'd you last see him?'

'He went straight out.'

We both shouted at the darkness, 'Jimmy! Jimmy!' Teresa joined in. By now, Celine was frantic.

I remembered boyhood days at the neighbourhood baths and Jimmy flashing through the water like a mackerel. I wondered how he could have got himself into difficulty so close to shore. We continued shouting towards the darkness. Celine's anxiety was now making me nervous. Then we heard his voice.

'What's all the fuss about?' He was behind us, on the wall above the beach, in bold silhouette. I saw what he'd done. He had swum out to sea, then come back in further down the beach and climbed on to the promenade. 'Jimmy Culmane!' Celine shouted. 'You put the heart crossways in me!'

He jumped from the wall on to the sand and bounded over to her. 'Got you that time!'

'I'll kill –'. Her words were stopped by his lips on hers. But she didn't forgive him; instead, she wrapped her towel around her shoulders and hurried away. I thought the night would be ruined by his antics. Nevertheless, we all met later in the hotel bar, which turned out to be a small room at the back of the dining room. From where we were positioned, you could see that the tables in the dining area were already set for breakfast. I remembered a kitchen porter once telling me that once the lights went out, the mice came out. I kept that information to myself. The bar had a small counter with a solitary tap for brown ale and a locked press for bottles of beer and an old red Oxo tin was used as a till. There was no television and the radio on the wall behind the bar was a silent relic of the past. When we first went in, it had the stillness of a small chapel, and the same man who had met us on arrival still showed us only mild interest, only now the sleeves of his shirt were unrolled, revealing the cuffs to be frayed. Three of us sat an a rexine-covered couch with unpleasant springs, with me stuck in the middle, smelling the bath soaps of the females, while Jimmy perched himself on a stool with one arm on the counter, as if he were back home in a Dublin bar.

Celine was still annoyed with Jimmy but, fair play to her, she didn't let that get in the way of us having a good time – after all, we *were* on holiday. When Jimmy and I tasted the beer, we gave each other a knowing grimace; similarly, the girls had to settle for gin with an anonymous label and a splash of tonic but, mind you, the restricted choice wasn't going to stop us. Jimmy tried to get some banter going with the man behind the bar, but he was a canny dodger who didn't even reveal his name. From then on, he referred to him as 'Squire'. At one point, Celine eased herself out of the couch, and went to stand beside Jimmy, and he quickly jumped off the stool and lifted her on to it. He then stood behind her, an arm still on the counter, his hand round his glass, and every so often he nuzzled her back, and she giggled yet pretended to ignore him. When Squire said he was closing the bar and left with the Oxo tin under his arm, I wasn't surprised when they went upstairs before us.

'He's an awful messer,' Teresa said, when we were left alone.

'That's the way he is, was, and probably will always be,' I answered, realizing that my words sounded like something from the Catechism. We sat for a while, spread out on the couch, letting the last of the day unwind from us. Eventually it was our turn to go up, and I climbed the steps behind her, wondering if she could hear my heart hammering.

'This door freaks me out,' I said, pointing to the redundant lock. 'Anyone could come in on top of us.'

She laughed. 'It's kinky!'

I put out the light and couldn't see anything. I used my lighter and saw that she was starting to undress. When we found each other in the dark, she never mentioned anything about the tee shirt I still wore, yet she had removed all. She was warm to the touch. Despite my age, I was still an apprentice in this department. As for her, I wasn't sure if she was equally inexperienced or just pretending to be so. Either way, we managed the act, then fell asleep. During the night, I put on my pants and went to urinate, the foreign beer being blamed. I left the room by the flame of the lighter and switched on the landing light and went down to a shared bathroom on a half-landing which was also for the use of the guests on the floor below us. I turned the brass knob on the bathroom door but was pushed aside by Teresa coming behind me. She flashed past. Had I dreamt what I had seen? I waited for her to come back out. Yes, she had come down naked. She ran past me on her way back upstairs, without a word uttered between us. In bed again, I lay waiting for sleep to return. I couldn't help thinking that the Isle of Man really was a serious place, exactly as I had felt it might be. I must be on my guard, follow my survival instinct.

We had agreed to have breakfast together as a group. Celine arrived in shorts and blouse, but its neckline didn't hide the love bites on her pale neck. A teenage girl came to us to take our order for the fried breakfast then pointed to a counter for orange juice. Teresa was full of energy and hopped up and came back with glassfuls for her and for me. She also made sure that the teapot was refilled so that I could have a third cup. When we'd eaten our fill and were ready to face the day, she asked what our plans were for the morning. Celine produced a Brownie camera and said she wanted to take a snap of a Manx cat with no tail. The others weren't impressed. I was asked what I wanted to do, and I said that I'd be happy with the beach or with hunting a cat, whatever pleased the most people.

'Well, I'm here for a tan,' Teresa said. 'I didn't splash out on the Ambre Solaire for nothing.'

At that, Celine capitulated.

It was a hot day, and the beach was crowded. Among a sea of transistors tuned in to Radio Caroline, we laid out our towels determined to lose the flour colour of our skin and to become exotic, tanned creatures, as promised on the bottle. I kept on the tee shirt. 'The back burns easily,' I said, splashing the oil on the arms and legs.

'Rub some on *my* back,' Teresa said. It was a smooth back, and when I was finished, she slid from under my oily palms and stretched out on a towel. I put the leftovers of oil on my face, dropped sunglasses over my eyes, then settled down beside her and waited for a movie-star tan. It was easy to forget everything, in the sun, with the hits on the radio, the smell of suntan oil. We lay as you would expect, Teresa next to me, Celine next to her, and Jimmy on the other side. With this formation, the females could talk to one another, at will. After a while, Jimmy went for a swim and Celine warned him against getting up to his tricks. I said that I was going for cigarettes and Teresa asked me to get her a packet. Then she turned to Celine and asked her if she needed any.

She raised herself on to her elbows. 'We'll buy our own later.'

'Fair enough,' I said.

I picked my way through sunworshippers and reached the promenade, where I passed a Salvation Army preacher. 'Remember, Jesus died for our sins, yet He still loves you.' He spoke at the top of his voice, competing with Radio Caroline and the bells of the horse-drawn trams. He looked out of place against the holiday atmosphere and all that went with it: sticks of rock with Douglas mysteriously written inside them, a youth renting deck chairs with a money satchel hanging from his neck, loud girls with Kiss-me-Quick hats, and working-class people released from the humdrum of work, free to wear bright-coloured shorts and sandals with or without socks.

I strolled towards a nearby kiosk, painted in red and yellow candy stripes. A young female assistant was framed by a hatch and as I neared, I could see she was in tears. She was being shouted at by a fellow outside with a North of Ireland accent. His tone was caustic, like paint stripper. 'It's the same money as yours, you dope!'

It was clear to me that she'd refused to take a pound note issued by a Belfast bank. The fellow noticed me. 'What do you make of that?' he said. 'The bitch won't take my money, even though it's all in sterling!'

I could have told him that he should have changed it before he came, like we had done, but held back. You come to know that it's fruitless trying to talk to someone who's red with rage and whose eyes have a wild look. Also, I didn't see the point in needless arguing. 'I'll swap your Ulster pound for one of my English ones,' I said. 'I'm sure they'll change it for me back home.'

I could see he was studying me, trying to figure me out. The girl had retreated into a corner of the kiosk and was waiting to see what would happen. Then, like a Jekyll and Hyde figure, his expression changed. He tidied a mop of fair hair with a brush of the hand and thanked me. The notes were exchanged, he paid for a packet of cigarettes, and left as if nothing had occurred. The assistant returned to the hatch, drying her eyes with one of the paper napkins she handed out with the ice cream cones.

'My job was at stake,' she said. 'The boss warned me about torn, marked, or funny-looking notes.'

As I returned along the promenade, I spotted the fellow from the kiosk. He was ahead of me, leaning against the railing. Is he waiting for me? I thought. But when I drew level, he offered a handshake. 'We Irishmen should stick together,' he said.

'Sure, pal. I've no problem with that.'

'The day will come you know when we'll be united, four green fields, and all.'

'Sorry. I've no interest in politics.'

'If you only knew your history.'

'I just don't believe in it.'

He was staring at me. 'You're having me on.'

I was to later find out that his name was Hugh. He, also, would play a big part in the way that things would work out. I left him, paused to listen to the Salvation Army preacher. He was introducing a song about the foolish man who built his house on sand, only to see it fall.

Teresa asked what had kept me. 'Politics and religion,' I said, without explanation.

Like she'd never heard me, she wondered out loud what the hotel would be serving for lunch. Nearing 1pm, as if a factory horn were sounding, people around us began gathering themselves to go back to their hotels and guest houses. We were served slices of grim processed ham, made worse by a leaf of lettuce and a soft tomato, and all Jimmy wanted to do was go out and find a chip shop. Celine, the keeper of the purse (his at least) overruled him; we made fun of the food yet made sure to eat plenty of bread and down extra cups of tea to tide us over till evening.

It was too good a day to waste, and we quickly returned to the beach for an afternoon that mirrored the morning. We worshiped the sun, lazed, and swam (paddling for me, though, as I kept the tee shirt on); later, the others surrounded me, ducked me under, and I ended up swimming in the wet top. Later, as we lay on the beach, Teresa said, 'This is the life, the idle rich. What more could you ask for?'

'You'd soon get tired of it,' Celine said.

'How do you know that?' Teresa shot back.

'You read about these things.'

Teresa sat up, as if she wanted to show that she was serious. 'Someone has to live it, and it may as well be me!'

'I couldn't, not on a housepainter's wages,' I said.

She looked down at me. 'You don't get it, Mark, do you? If you were one of the idle rich, you wouldn't have to work.'

'Tell me, Teresa, how do I get to that? rob a bank?'

She wasn't giving in. 'Anyway, this is the life for me.'

'Hear that, Mark?' Jimmy said. 'She's setting a high bar...'

I closed my eyes and wondered about being rich. Never again would I have to face a cold, newly built house on an icy morning in some Bally-far-out estate; never again have to prise the lid off a can and stare at gooey paint; never again have to awaken my fingers by blowing hard on them. If only it were so and not just the stuff of fairy tale. I turned to thinking about the first pint I would down later.

The evening meal was better, for it included chips, good 'soakage' for the night to come. We deserted the little bar at the hotel and moved up the promenade and found a lively place that served more than brown ale. Jimmy and I were on pints of lager, and the girls were happy again on rum 'n' coke. A man played a piano – mostly old favourites – tunes I remembered from hooleys in our place, from before the father died. They ended after that, and Mother wouldn't accept an invite to one, unless one of us, one of the family, went with her. I thought of her and wondered what she would be doing at that moment. Maybe coming home from the bingo with Mrs. Donohue from the next block? You always knew she'd won when she came in the door with a big smile, bursting to tell how much. The piano player was playing a mellow number, and Teresa dragged me to my feet and shoved me towards a small dance area, much to the delight of Jimmy who shouted, 'Up for the lurch!' We moved slowly round the tight space, and I must confess that when she started running her fingers through the hair at the back of my neck, I could have lain down like a dog and had my belly scratched. She began to sing in my ear, a private song, a moment of tenderness. I remembered thinking that the

Isle of Man was indeed a dangerous place but, despite that, I wasn't going to let that get in the way. Then Celine coaxed Jimmy up and, as we were shoulder-to-shoulder with them, Teresa stopped singing and the moment went. However, when the tune stopped, I kept my arm round her waist. We sat down and I searched for her hand (leaving the right one free for drinking) and didn't let go of it. Some of the magic was still there when we climbed to the attic room, and we made love in our cocoon, and never once did I worry that the door wasn't locked. During the night I was awakened by a siren. There was a commotion somewhere; I turned in the bed, lay an arm across her warm shoulder, and fell back asleep.

CHAPTER THREE

Just to remind us that the Isle of Man is in the middle of the Irish Sea and not in the Mediterranean Sea, we awoke to rain and cold. They told us at breakfast that there had been a fire at the kiosk on the promenade during the night and that the fire engine had arrived too late to save it. I went to the front door of the hotel and looked across to where I had bought the cigarettes the day before. The sorry sight reminded me of a burnt-out caravan I had once seen after a traveller's death. Round the remains of the kiosk, rain ran off the pavement, a dirty colour from twisted metal, charred timber, and split concrete. The scene was isolated with yellow tape; a solitary policeman stood guard, rain dripping from the peak of his cap; some hardy walkers under umbrellas looked on, probably swapping theories as to how it had started. Beyond them, a heavy grey sky sat on a grey sea, dulling the horizon line. Teresa came out and stood beside me. 'A day for the ducks,' she said. 'What on earth can we do now?'

I felt like saying that I wasn't the group's entertainment manager; instead, I told her that I hadn't a notion.

'One thing's for sure, Mark, I won't be stuck in all day in this pokey hole!' At that, she went inside, and I had a feeling that a plan of action would soon be hatched by the females. Normally I resisted having my life organised by others, especially by the opposite sex (I got enough of that from the Mother), but this time I was happy to stand idly by. I went in and coaxed another cup of tea from the young girl who was clearing the tables. I sat at a window and looked out at the promenade. The deck chairs for hire were drenched and forlorn-looking, and passengers in the open trams were huddled together against the weather. I lit a cigarette and, as I toyed with my lighter, thought of the fellow with the North of Ireland accent who'd argued with the young girl at the kiosk. He couldn't have, I thought. No, he couldn't have…

I was told soon afterwards that we were all going to a leisure complex with an indoor pool. We rode the tram to near the end of the promenade and, with togs and towel under the arm, ran the short distance to the leisure centre entrance, however, we weren't alone, as many other frustrated beachgoers seemed to have come up with the same idea. The woman at the desk, who looked as if she hated her job, insisted that we buy swimming hats. Jimmy's protest '…but we'll only be here the once!' was wasted on her. Grudgingly, we bought the hats then separated to go to the changing rooms. We saw the girls again at the side of the pool, where I couldn't take my eyes off Teresa. Even with her forehead pulled taut and her hair tucked out of sight, a yellow, rubber swim hat didn't make her any less attractive. In fact, I thought it brought out the shape of her face more. She spotted me staring and held my eyes for some moments. You have heard the expression: To swim in one another's eyes – well, it was a bit like that, until Jimmy roared, 'Last in buys the drinks!'

I was about to leap in when the air was cut by a shrill blast from a whistle. A young male pool attendant ran up and pointed at my tee shirt. 'You can't get in the pool with *that* on.'

By then the others were in the water, and I was already the 'loser'. 'Why not?' I asked.

'Hygiene!'

'But it's just been washed…' (I didn't tell him that Mother had also ironed it.)

'It's the rules.'

'What harm is a tee shirt?' I was arguing, but knew I wasn't going to win. I sensed that many in the pool were looking at me.

Teresa shouted, 'Throw off the tee shirt and come on in! You'll love it!'

Whipping it off would have been easy, an end to the problem. But showing the world that I had three nipples wasn't going to happen.

I stood at the side of the pool, hoping the attendant would change his mind, but his role as an enforcer of the rules seemed to have gone to his head.

'Come on, Mark,' Jimmy shouted up to me, 'you're wastin' good time.'

Automatically, I went to pull the tee shirt over my head but thought again about that extra brown eye on my chest. Teresa was looking at me from the water, and all I could do was hunch my shoulders in feeble apology.

She had a look of disbelief. 'You're *not* going out?'

'I've no choice.'

'Just take off the silly tee shirt and jump in!'.

'I can't, Teresa. I'll wait outside.'

The pool attendant had a smug look. I returned to the changing room and then went to the gallery to watch. The three of them were enjoying themselves without me. I rambled about the building to pass the time, my dry swimming gear under my arm and the unbaptised swim hat stuffed in a pocket. In the entrance area there were advertisements on a notice board, which I read with the suspicious looks of the woman behind the desk boring into the back of my neck. There was an advertisement for coach trips around the TT motorbike course; it had a pick-up point outside on the promenade. As the timing was right, I went to the changing room and stuck a note into the door of Jimmy's locker and left to find the tour.

Within a half-hour, I was leaving Douglas by the same route that leather-clad riders take during the Tourist Trophy races, past small villages and on to the mountain roads, where birds, born to the sound, stay in their cover, undisturbed by the rising and falling revs of motorbike engines, undisturbed by racers squeezing more speed out of the screaming machines between their legs. The blazered tour-guide looked as if he had just come off a bowling lawn in Herbert Park and painted a picture of the TT that made you smell burning rubber and exhaust fumes. He talked of the risks the riders took, going out on a limb, chasing the fruit of success, hoping the bough would hold. The gloomy side was when the coach slowed to a crawl as we passed small memorial crosses where men in leathers had died. Then, as if one death were greater than another, we pulled over on a high exposed road and everyone got off at a marker where a hotshot rider had died. We stood in the rain, and the tour guide fired some statistics at us, one of which was that the number of riders killed since 1911 was nearing the hundred, including a woman in a sidecar.

'Serious shit,' someone behind me said. I turned around and saw the fellow with the American accent, the one who'd been on the boat. He must have been sitting somewhere behind me on the coach, for I hadn't noticed him until now. He was smiling, which didn't seem in keeping with what we'd just heard. 'You're like me, with nothing to do,' he said.

'What do you mean?''

'Only those with time on their hands come on trips like this. Where are your friends today?'

I didn't want to think about, or mention, what had happened back at the swimming pool. The tour guide had finished talking and everyone reboarded the coach. The fellow with the American accent was at my elbow. 'I'll sit in beside you,' he said. When he saw me hesitate, he added, 'And I promise not to bother you.'

I claimed the window seat, like I had a childish right to it, and he pressed in beside me. He put out a hand. 'Paul Sweeney.'

I shook it without enthusiasm, not wishing to encourage him.

'Mark O'Bride,' I said. Then, I made a show of listening to the tour guide, like I'm trying to prove something. After a while, I admit to myself that I have zero interest in motorbikes. I remember the motto *Tempus fugit* on the clock in Madigan's bar in North Earl Street and decide not to waste any further time. I sit back and look out at rain-blurred mountainside. After a while, I said, 'And what's your story, pal?'

'Trying to get my head together,' he answered.

'How come, the accent? You said you were one of us.'

'I went to the States to work, was drafted, and ended up in a jungle. Instead of a bag of carpenter's tools, I'm lugging around an MP5'.

'Vietnam?' I asked. The name drips from my lips as if I were used to using it. You couldn't have avoided the images on television but, to me, they had been just that – newsreel with no substance. After the evening news, the Mother and I would still have our cup of tea in front of the television set, perhaps affected by what we'd viewed, but not overly so. It was strange to meet someone who made it real. Concrete evidence. When he didn't answer me, I returned to gazing out the window, to watching the road back to Douglas, to listening in silence while the tour guide pointed to yet more memorial markers on the way. Back at the promenade, he rose to get off at the stop before mine.

'Maybe I'll see you around?' he said.

Then he was gone, climbing the steps of The Anchor, a hotel indistinguishable from the many others strung along the seafront. As the coach moved on, I realized that I now had to face Teresa. While on the coach tour, I'd avoided thinking about the venomous look that she'd given me as I was leaving the swimming pool. And now, I couldn't make up my mind as to whether it was important to me, or not. But I would soon know.

CHAPTER FOUR

S he was in our attic room when I got back. 'We're all going dancing at the Palace Ballroom tonight. I presume you've no problem with *that*?'

'Sounds good.' I felt like a man on a warning – one more offence and you're for it! – but was relieved that an easy path had opened for me. When we went down to tea, the others were already at the table, and I could tell they were waiting to see if there'd been a major falling-out between her and me; they would do it with slyness, look for clues, anything to reveal if we were still an 'item' or if there'd been a breakup. After some minutes, they seemed to realize that all was normal. Jimmy was anxious to give me some news. 'I gave the lifeguard one for you!'

'You actually hit him?' Celine gasped. 'I didn't know that.'

'You and Teresa had gone in first, and when I was running past him, my elbow banged into his face, accidentally on purpose, like.'

'What did he say to that?'

'He was too busy trying to stem the blood gushing from his nose to say anything. I ran for the showers, before he could see who I was.'

'No wonder you were in such a hurry to get us out of there,' she said.

He was smiling, she was worried. She said that someone from the pool could have seen the whole thing and identified him. It would only be a matter of time before the police would come calling. Meanwhile, I noticed that Teresa didn't seem at all interested in what had occurred, as if it had nothing to do with her. Jimmy's eyes met mine and I gave him a wink. We ate in silence, which was unusual, for ours was normally a noisy table. Around the dining room there was an assortment of accents: English, Scottish, Welsh, and Irish – for me at the time this was as international as you could get. When it was time to go to the dance, we got on a tram that swayed along the seafront. The rain had cleared, and people had escaped their accommodation to take the air. I saw large families licking ice cream cones, the children walking ahead, the linking mother and father hanging back, like they had rediscovered intimacy on the holiday. Other couples kept a distance between them, and I wondered if romance for them had rusted and flaked away. In the windows of the hotels, you could see the guests who had decided to stay put rallied at a piano for an old-fashioned singsong. I thought about the party nights we used to have at home. Each relative had a party piece and they didn't need a glass of stout nor cajoling to break into song. Da was different, he couldn't sing a note – I take after him. The brother and sisters take after the Mother, who could sing with the best of them. When Da died, the party nights went.

My thoughts were broken by a shout from Jimmy, 'Here we are!' He jumped off the tram before the horse stopped. The excitement was catching, and we all ran across the road and up the steps of the Palace as if the Rolling Stones were in town; however, even though it turned out that an obscure band was playing, our spirits stayed high. We occupied a table on a raised level close to where carpeted wide steps swept down to the large dance area. There was only a small colony of dancers on the floor and the band seemed to be playing without energy, perhaps saving themselves for later when, I hoped, the place would get crowded. I got the drinks in, and we sat back in armchairs, doing something that I really don't like to do – people watching. Celine scrutinised every female that came into sight, like someone searching for a long-lost sister; Teresa, on the other hand, seemed distant, and often looked to the entrance, as if she were expecting someone, which, of course, I knew she wasn't. As for Jimmy, he appeared disinterested, however I noticed that his eyes followed any fellow that came in with a 'warrior' air about him. Some experienced ballroom dancers had gone on to the dance floor, the women in beehive hairdos, and shoes and dresses of a matching colour, while the men wore black patent leather shoes, and their gleaming hair was plastered down with oil. They whirled about the floor like exotic spinning tops.

'You won't catch me doing that dancing!' Jimmy said. 'It's from the last century.'

'I can do it. A pal's older sister showed us – she does competitions and all,' Teresa said. Then, she turned to me. 'What about you, Mark, have you got dance moves?'

'I can stand and move my arms like anyone else, but that proper stuff, certainly not!'

'I'm not surprised.'

The barb was intended to hurt me. If she's trying to put me through purgatory, I thought, that's her choice. I wasn't going to let it get to me and I smiled back, as if nothing had been said. At Jimmy's insistence we took to the dance floor for our form of dancing – normal dancing. We swayed to the beat, with shaking limbs and bobbing heads, within tight personal circles that could have been laid out by imaginary chalk lines. The ballroom dancers buzzed our islands of movement, their heads in a haughty position, and you felt they were going to crash into you but, at the last moment, they switched direction, like bats in twilight, and passed without a smile nor a nod. The lights were dimmed for a slow number and Jimmy and Celine moved to the music in a locked embrace. I took Teresa by the hand to draw her near, but she didn't want to dance and walked away in the direction of the toilets, leaving me alone in the middle of the dance floor. My walk back to our seats was a deliberately casual one, reminiscent of John Wayne in a movie. I plonked myself into an armchair and took a long swallow of beer. As I put down the glass, a fellow came along and sat on Teresa's seat; I wasn't in the mood for intruders – 'Sorry, but that's taken'.

'Could have fooled me,' he answered.

At first, I hadn't recognized him; however, when he spoke, I looked again. I remembered him belittling the girl in the kiosk who wouldn't accept his Northern Ireland money. He didn't seem to remember me, and I wasn't going to help him. 'She's on the dance floor,' I said, nodding in that direction.

He didn't move away. By now he had swung his legs across an armrest of the chair and was looking away from me, a hand drumming the side of the seat in time to the music. He opened a fresh packet of cigarettes, dropped its cellophane wrapper and silver paper to the floor and flicked a lighter. I remembered the sorry state of the kiosk that still marred the promenade. No, I thought, he wouldn't have risked that. I decided to wait until the others came back, then it would be obvious to him that the seats were taken, and he would leave.

Teresa was the first to return. Seeing him in her seat, she passed no comment, as if he didn't exist, and took up her drink and occupied Celine's chair. She was looking away from me, and I felt the need to say something but nothing inspiring came to mind. The next few minutes were awkward, particularly with the 'squatter' in earshot of us.

I couldn't stand the silence between us. 'The place is filling up nicely now,' I said, not caring that it might have sounded silly.

She didn't reply.

'A wee bomb scare, and they'd all scatter,' the Northern fellow said. He didn't even bother to look round at us.

Teresa's reaction was swift. 'Who's this *eejit*?' she asked.

Breaking my rule of staying out of politics, I told him that we didn't want to listen to his madness. Meanwhile, she was still demanding to know who he was. I told her that I didn't know him from Adam. He remained unruffled, a smirk now on his red, sunburnt face.

'Don't be so shocked,' he said. His casualness was annoying. 'Anyway, I'm Hugo. What are your names?'

Teresa gasped. 'You're talking about a bomb, you've a North of Ireland accent, and you expect us to be all pally-wally? Do us all a big favour and get lost!'

I looked to where I'd last seen Jimmy, hoping to catch his eye; he and Celine were like two vertical wooden shafts lashed together as they moved slowly on the dance floor, oblivious to others. Two bouncers were talking to the barman at the other end of the room.

'Make a fuss,' I said, 'and the bouncers could fling us all out.'

'So, we just roll over and let him sit there?'

'Teresa, he's only making a fool of himself.'

'I can't see how you make that out.'

I had earlier spotted the Yank from the coach tour sitting at the bar but hadn't felt the need to talk to him. Now he was looking at us to see what was going on. He nodded at me, and I beckoned him over.

'Not another one,' Teresa sighed, 'and where's *he* going to sit?'

He carried his pint from the bar, drinking the froth off the top. The pint was placed amongst our drinks, and he pulled across an armchair from a nearby table.

I introduced him to Teresa, and she smiled at him, like you would briefly smile at a stranger whose toe you have stood on by accident. I could tell he was wondering where the Northerner fitted in. 'That's Hugo but he's not with us,' I said.

'What's up, Hugo?' he said. The fellow raised an arm in acknowledgement, without even bothering to look at him.

Teresa turned her annoyance on the Yank. 'Why did you do that? It's getting rid of him we want, not giving the dope encouragement!'

'You're a friendly type,' he said. 'Maybe you'd like me to move, too?'

'I called you over, Paul – you're welcome here,' I said.

'*Sláinte!*' He clinked my glass. He went to clink hers, and after a brief hesitation, she said, 'Why not?'

She'd become less tense, and I sat back, relieved. 'Paul's a lone wolf,' I said.

She turned to him. 'You're *absolutely* on your own?'

'Lost all touch with pals when I went away.'

'I've never been away – I mean, to live away,' she said.

'Here's your brother,' I said. 'Manchester for a week is the sum of my travels. And, of course, here – but I don't think the Isle of Man really counts. Imagine, an Isle of Man stamp on your passport. How wasteful would that be?'

'You haven't even *got* a passport,' she said.

'It doesn't matter, Teresa, we're only talking. Anyway, neither have you.'

'I've been thinking of getting one … for Spain.'

'You'd love Spain,' the Yank said. 'Never been myself, but I hear it's great.'

'We should book Spain next year,' she said, giving me one of her melt-the-heart looks.

'Then, you better start saving,' I said.

The band stopped and Jimmy and Celine left the dance floor; she was clutching him, making them sway like drunkards as they approached us.

Teresa gave them the news. 'We're all off to Spain next year!'

'Sounds great,' Jimmy said.

Celine's love-soaked face had turned to one of concern, her brow showed lines like you see on sheet music. 'What brought this on?' she asked. I guessed she was figuring out the cost of the trip.

Teresa pointed to the Yank. 'You can blame this fellow. He says great things about the place.'

Jimmy said, 'Celine, you can manage the kitty, just as on this trip. Tell me the damage and I'll give it to you by the week.'

'Hey, hold on a minute,' I said. 'I haven't even agreed to this. Don't we get a chance to talk it over?'

'Mark, don't let me come between you and your friends,' the Yank said. 'I only said the place is supposed to be good. It was just to make conversation.'

'It *is* good, and it's a great idea!' Teresa said. 'And there's nothing to stop us getting on a plane this time next year and heading there unless you're too stuck in your ways to see it.' She was looking at me as she spoke.

'Not only can I see it, ' Jimmy said, 'but I can taste it, feel it – sun, wine, sex. What more could a body ask for?'

Suddenly, the Northerner joined the conversation. 'Hey, can I come too? Sun, wine, and some of the other sounds great!'

'It's that fellow Hugo, again,' I said, 'and he's just going, if he knows what's good for him.'

'Do you want me to shift him?' the Yank said. He stood up, and for the first time, I noticed he wasn't very tall; nevertheless, he looked strong and fit.

'What does everyone think of my idea?' Teresa said. She looked frustrated, afraid that if tempers rose further the dream of a Spanish holiday would disappear.

The Yank was ready for all-comers; Jimmy had gone to his side. The squatter put on a show of leaving of his own accord and moved on. Celine took his place on the seat. Jimmy was agitated, as he'd built himself up for a scrap. 'He's not worth it, Jimmy,' I said. 'Forget about him.'

He took up a pint and attacked it in one gulp, like an industrial drain sucker. He put out a hand to the Yank and thanked him for getting involved. There was a comradely handshake, then the Yank eased himself back into his seat.

'What's the matter, pal?' Jimmy said. 'You are acting like you're sitting on nails.'

'I was shot in the ass. It acts up now and again.'

'Shot in the ass!' Celine gasped. 'Where?'

Teresa said, 'In the arse, didn't you hear him?'

'I think she means *where*, as in what country,' I said. 'He's been in Vietnam. It must have happened there.' At that, I gave him space to tell his own story.

'I don't want to go into it,' he said.

Teresa had but the one thing on her mind. 'Before we forget, what about this trip to Spain?'

Celine was more interested in the Yank's story, and she asked him if it really had been in Vietnam. He looked at her for a long moment, then his thoughts seemed to go elsewhere, outside the Palace.

'Yes. They gave me the Purple Heart Medal for my trouble, but what happened to me was nothing compared to what happened to my buddies.'

Celine was nodding her head, like a confessor.

Suddenly, Jimmy became giddy. 'We have a Sacred Heart picture hanging on the wall at home.'

'Jimmy, you're such a gobshite at times!' she said.

'Only joking, Celine. But we don't have to be serious. We're on holidays!'

'He's right,' the Yank said. 'Let's drop the subject of *me* and talk about Spain, instead.'

'You'd risk going to Spain with this lot?' I said.

'No. The girlfriend in the States wouldn't like me doing that but I can still talk about it.'

'She can come too,' Celine said.

'So, it's all agreed then?' Teresa said with the speed of a mouse trap being sprung.

'I'm not agreeing to any trip without knowing more about it,' I said, hating the feeling of being led into something.

'I give up!' Teresa stood up, tugged on her skirt, and looked for a moment as if she were going to storm off, then instead, she thrust a hand towards the Yank and demanded, 'Dance with me!'

Next thing I knew, they were on the dance floor, and I must confess that I did feel surprised. If she wants me to be jealous, I thought, then she's wasting her time. I'm with her to get what I can out of her, and in return she's getting a free holiday out of me. A fair exchange. I felt the eyes of the others on me, waiting for my reaction.

They got no ammunition out of me, and I rejoined the conversation as if nothing had happened. At one point, Jimmy looked towards the dance floor and informed us that the Yank was a good jiver. I didn't look round but went to the bar and ordered more drinks. Hugo, the North of Ireland menace, had camped himself there on a stool.

'I wouldn't trust yonder man with *my* girlfriend,' he said. He was looking towards the dance floor. 'She's a smashing bit of stuff.'

Being baited was nothing new to me. It could have been over the pitiful football team I followed, or over something as personal as the feeble excuse for a moustache I once attempted to grow. Experience in these matters had taught me to remain calm; however, at that moment, I was a simmering pot ready to boil over. Then, like a wasp that had made its hit, my tormentor moved away. As I returned with the tray of drinks, I couldn't stop myself glancing in the direction of the dance floor, where the lights had been lowered and the band was now playing a slow set. I couldn't make them out. My runaway mind urged me to look again; instead, I fixed my eyes dead ahead and convinced myself that it meant nothing to me.

Jimmy and Celine were no company for me because they had begun a kissing session, leaning across from one seat to the other, right before my eyes. I noticed that Hugo had resumed his position at the bar, his back to the counter, surveying all round him. For a minute or two I felt detached from what was going on around me. I sat there with my drink, left to myself. Shortly afterwards, Teresa and the Yank came back and collapsed into their seats.

'It's a good band?' I asked.

'It'll do, but you'd have heard better in the Kingsway…must be years since I've danced there,' he said.

'Just how long have you been away?'

'I forget.'

His short answer told me I shouldn't have asked.

Teresa had settled into her seat and was relaxed, and this had the same effect on me. She reached over and patted the back of my hand, then let it linger there. Until then, I thought that I had been a good actor, then I realized the front I'd put on hadn't fooled her. All I wanted at that moment was to feel comfortable and happy, like it had been when as a child the Mother had let me back into our cosy home after I had been sent out into the cold street for giving back cheek. That was the one thing she couldn't abide in us. It's a wonder that I still have hair left from the tugs she used to give it when I foolishly crossed the line. Still, there were also the times she stood me at the kitchen sink and washed the same hair, while she hummed an old tune. That had stopped when I got into long pants, although for a laugh she would sometimes threaten to get me to the sink again.

What would she say of this beautiful creature who was working her way back into my good graces? They're so different, she and her. Then I realized that I was racing ahead of myself, bringing her home to be scrutinized. When she and the Yank had gone to the dance floor, I'd felt something which I hadn't recognized, or hadn't wanted to recognize. I saw it now in its nakedness. Jealousy. I looked at the Yank. His company gave me the same sense of ease you got when sitting next to a brother. And her hand was still on mine and every so often she would catch my eye and we would exchange private signals.

As the night went on, the Yank left from time to time to do a reconnaissance of the ballroom, searching for someone to ask up for a dance. Jimmy and Celine were still lost in each other, whether beside us or while on the dance floor. When Teresa and I were left to our own company, we made idle talk, drank, and smoked, and the band played in the background.

'They grow on you,' Teresa said.

'Huh?'

'The band, they grow on you. At first, I thought they were crap but now they're better.'

'Could be the drink. They might still be crap.'

The band's front man announced, 'Ladies' Choice!' She hopped up and almost dragged me down the steps and on to the dance floor (I enjoyed playing the reluctant male). The music was slow, and her arms were thrown around my neck and her smell rushed up my nostrils. At that moment, I didn't need anything else in my life. If a wedding officiant had appeared beside us on the floor, I would have said, I do! There was a tap on the shoulder from Jimmy as he and Celine drifted past. The dance floor was a sea of bodies and a determination had arisen among them to make the most of the moment. There was no need to speak. I had closed my eyes. She was running her fingers through my hair now. The Da used to toss my hair. I was a boy then and thought nothing of it. Not so with Teresa's fingers. In slow, deliberate movements they caressed the back of my ears, and the short hairs of my nape. The music ended. The spell ended. She said she was going to the toilets, and I watched her vanish into the crowd. I made my way back to our table and was joined by the others. Celine looked uneasy. 'Where's Teresa?' I didn't understand her reason for asking.

What followed was an eternity of band music as I waited for Teresa to return. The Yank reappeared, flushed from dancing, rested for a while, then went at it again, but Jimmy and Celine stayed with me until I eventually sent them off for the last dance. It seemed that everyone in the ballroom was now on the dance floor, except the bar staff, who were pulling down the shutters, and yours truly.

As they played 'God Save the Queen', Teresa reappeared and sat next to me as if she'd been away for only a few minutes. I gave her a cigarette and pushed her drink closer to her. When the others returned, no one remarked on her long absence. Meanwhile, the ballroom was closing; the crowd was drifting towards the doors; the Yank took a last gulp of his drink, gave a smart military salute, and left, almost tripping over himself on the way out. We left soon after. At that stage, I was unsure as to where I stood with Teresa. We entered the hotel, saw that the bar was closed, and climbed the stairs to our room, she ahead of me, not saying a word. We left the door slightly ajar to let the landing light in while we got ready for bed. I went back and closed the door, then stumbled across and found her. Still no words passed yet she breathed heavily in my arms. Afterwards, when she was fast asleep beside me, I thought about the day just passed and concluded that her disappearing for a while in the Palace was her way of paying me back for leaving her at the swimming pool. She could be forgiven for that, I thought.

~~~

Next day the young girl serving breakfast told us that there had been a fire in a shop in the town during the early hours of the morning. I thought of Hugo, probably because I disliked him. 'I passed it coming in,' she said. 'It was out by then, but everything was blackened – a real mess.'

Being a painter and decorator, I thought that someone in the trade was going to get some work out of it (there's always an upside). The waitress cleared some dirty plates from our table and went off to the kitchen, delighted to have been the centre of our attention, even if it had been for only a few minutes. From my seat I could see a clear sky through the window. Holidaymakers would soon be spilling out of the hotels with their beach bags and towels, crossing over to grab their places on the sand. The ginger-headed youth with the leather satchel who managed the deckchairs would be anticipating a busy day and the Salvation Army would be assembling for a long, hot time in their uniforms. My thoughts were interrupted by Jimmy talking. He had come up with the idea of hiring two rowing boats and going out to the small island in the bay.

'Sounds like hard work,' I said. His plan caused me to remember one of my teenage summers when a gang of us took the train to Howth, hired a rowing boat but lost a rowlock into the harbour. The boatman made a big fuss over it and demanded payment to buy a replacement. Pockets were excavated but we hadn't enough left between us to buy even an ice cream. He wasn't happy.

'I'll help with the rowing,' Teresa said. 'It can't be that hard.'

'Would I get seasick?' Celine asked.

'We won't be mid-Atlantic, only be a bit off the beach,' Jimmy said.

'We'll be rowing like galley slaves,' I said. 'I don't see the fun in that.'

Teresa reminded me of her offer to row. Her lemon off-the-shoulder top showed promise of upper body strength. Funny, I knew those shoulders well – my lips had run across them the night before – but I hadn't counted on them for rowing.

'Okay. Count me in,' I said.

The man in charge of the boats was suspicious of Jimmy (people were often like that with him). 'You mind them boats now, and no horseplay!' They had been pulled up on to the sand and it took only a slight shove to set them bobbing in the water; we struggled to get into them and then struggled to get them pointing out to sea. Their boat was the first away, and we chopped water as we tried to set off after them. It didn't help that Teresa was shouting instructions like one of those lawdy daw coxswains you'd see on the Liffey at Islandbridge. Finally, we were moving, and urged on by our own groans and shouts we worked like site labourers shovelling clay. Jimmy and Celine were making better progress, and after a while we reluctantly gave up trying to stay with them. We were at our own pace now, and I had time to catch a breath, and look round me. By now we had come out further than the hired pedal boats. I could now see the rising back streets of Douglas, where the cheaper bed and breakfast places were to be found. Between the back streets and the promenade were the shops; it was there that the fire had been the night before. When we reached the small island, the others were waiting. 'What kept you?' Jimmy said. He was grinning like a youngster who'd just come first in the Primary Schools' sprint final at Croke Park.

It wasn't really a proper island, more a large rock; we lay on our towels and looked up at the sky. We weren't alone for other people had had the same idea. Bowie's 'Rebel Rebel' came to us from a transistor radio. Seagulls came in beside us, paced back and forward, looking for scraps of food, then at finding none took to the sky with shrieks of disgust. It was about then that I thought I heard a familiar Northern accent. I wasn't mistaken. It was Hugo from the night before and from the kiosk, the nuisance, and I had this irrational thought that our paths were destined to cross like an unending series of railway points. I didn't look round but closed my eyes and mind to his presence. It didn't work, and I felt that there was going to be no peace. Then, I heard not only his, but other voices, all louder now. They were arguing over something. Then, it became more heated, and Jimmy heard it. He sat upright. 'Someone's getting riled,' he said, looking about him. 'It's that headcase from last night! What's his name...?'

'Ignore him. If he comes over, we'll never get rid of him,' I said.

Then I heard a fellow say, 'If you hate England so much, then you've another thing coming if you think you're coming back in the boat with us!'

'You can swim back!' This time it was a female's voice.

I could hear people gathering up their belongings and moving to a boat. 'Love, mind how you get in,' the fellow said, his offended Englishness quivering with anger. 'We don't want her to tip over.' There was the sound of oars splashing; it was obvious that the Northerner had been left behind. I heard him start to whistle a tune. We remained still, hoping not to be noticed. Then I heard him at the water's edge and had an awful thought; I sat up and saw him at the mooring rope of our boat.

'Take that boat, and it'll be the last thing you'll ever do! ' I cried.

He recognised me, retied the rope and came our way.

'We're choosy about our company,' Teresa said.

'What's happened between you and your friends?' I asked, nodding towards the couple rowing away.

'They're not *my* friends. We split the cost of the boat, but I don't even know them, and don't care to, either.'

'You must have said something to get up their noses?'

He gave me a mischievous smile. 'I told them Bloody Sunday would have to be paid for. But that was before they told me their son was on active duty in Derry!'

'It's no wonder they were annoyed!'

I heard Jimmy say, 'You know, our union protested over Bloody Sunday. All the unions were involved. It was a massive march from Parnell Square to Merrion Square. It ended in the British Embassy going up in flames.'

I felt a need to correct him. 'The unions weren't responsible for the fire. The crowd may have cheered, but the protest had been hijacked. Ordinary working-class men don't throw Molotov Cocktails.'

'Did all you boys march?' the Northerner asked.

'Not everyone; I painted a house,' I said.

'You didn't protest?'

I didn't feel the need to answer him.

'Why on earth are we wasting time talking about what happened in Derry?' Teresa said. 'We're supposed to be on holiday.'

All of us agreed with her, and the Northerner took off his shirt and lay on a rock some feet away from us. I sat for a while, looking at a passenger boat arriving at the pier, and wondered where it had come from. Liverpool, Belfast, Glasgow? Not Dublin, because I knew its schedule. I imagined a fresh consignment of pale-faced holidaymakers waiting to rush down the gangplank. Later, the people whose holiday was over would go on board and return to their towns or villages with sunburnt faces and sticks of Douglas rock. It seems like it was only yesterday when we arrived – it'll be no time before we also will be going up a gangplank to head home. I lie back with the eyes shut, search for her hand, and press it. It seems an eternity before she presses back. This is now the life, I am content. There's the music from the transistor somewhere behind us, there's heat in that sun. I doze. I know that Teresa is sleeping, in fact, I sense that all of us are submerged in a clawing laziness. That is, until the Northerner floats a question towards us. 'Is it dancing for us again tonight?' he says.

'What do you mean by *us*?' Jimmy says. 'What we're doing and what you're doing is a completely different matter.'

'We're like castaways on an island and should stick together.'

I felt Teresa snatch her hand from mine and realized she was getting to her feet. 'I think we should go back,' she said.

Jimmy and Celine agreed, and while were going for the boats, Hugo sprang up and reached the water before us. He began to untie the rope securing our boat. 'What are you up to?' Teresa screeched.

'I've no other way of getting back,' he said.

'You're not coming with us! Ask *them*.' She pointed to another couple on the rock.

'I don't know them, but I know you.'

It was one of those moments when the head says 'no, don't do it' but something inside you relents. 'We'll take you back, then we don't want to see sight nor sound of you again,' I said.

I'd hardly spoken when he got into the boat and took up both oars. 'You two relax and I'll get her across.' We sat side by side in the stern. From pictures I'd seen, I felt we were like passengers in a gondola being ferried by a boatman. Oarless, I now had one arm against the small of Teresa's back and the other dangling over the side, fingers dragging through the water. She settled into my arm and gazed into the distance.

'You're good at this rowing lark, Hugo. You keep her going there, lad,' I said. By now, I was giving him the benefit of using his name.

The others came abreast of us, Jimmy also in charge of the oars. Typical of him, the challenge came – 'Beat you back to the beach,' he cried.

The Northerner pulled harder in reply, and his face got redder. The oars banged together when the boats got too close, then separated, then closed again. Celine was Jimmy's slave driver. 'Come on – don't let him get ahead!' She and Teresa were whooping and swapping insults like schoolgirls. Neither boat was getting the advantage, until I heard the Northerner say, 'Take up that arm or you'll lose it.' I pulled it up just in time. It was a sneaky yet skilful manoeuvre. One oar was stalled, and full strength put into the other. He'd made our boat veer, causing it to crash against theirs, then he had brought it back on course and we raced ahead, leaving Jimmy floundering, his rhythm broken. Every curse he knew followed us to the shore. The boatman had seen what happened and when we reached the beach, he was only short of taking a magnifying glass to his property. He threatened to call a policeman if we dared to move off; however, he found no damage and scowled in disappointment and let us go on our way. I turned to talk to the Northerner, but he'd left. Already, he was picking his way through the sunbathers, heading for the promenade. Jimmy and Celine calmed down and we all sat on the sand and waited for lunchtime.

After lunch, Teresa suggested that each couple go their separate ways for the afternoon. 'We should give each other some space.'

Celine seemed baffled by her proposal; Jimmy put his own slant on it. 'Can't you see? The lovebirds want to be on their own.'

'What'll *we* do with ourselves, then?'

'Don't be putting bad thoughts in me head,' he answered, putting an arm round her waist, and lifting her off the ground.

'Put me down, you messer! People are watching!'

For me, it didn't matter whether it was the four of us or just Teresa and me. Not at this time of the day, anyway. We walked along the promenade, and she linked my arm and remarked that it was nice to be on our own for a change.

'Celine wasn't too pleased,' I said.

'She's okay, a good friend, but sometimes she'd wear you out just listening to her.'

'She and Jimmy make a good match.'

'Mark, they're probably saying the same about us.'

~~~

We crossed the road and started along a street parallel to the seafront. Through the large window of a shop, we saw a man in a brown overall operating a machine for making sticks of rock. As if by magic, a length of the confectionary was extruded from the machine and it was carefully landed on to a table in the form of a long thin pole, rather like that of a pole vaulter that I would sometimes see if I took a shortcut across the sports field in Trinity College. It was chopped into smaller lengths; smiling customers came out of the shop with bagfuls. Further along, like a blackened tooth on the row of neat shops, we saw where the fire had been – a clean-up crew was already on the job. Next door, a fish shop offered to post Manx kippers to your home in Dublin, or wherever you lived, and next to it a record shop listed the Top Twenty in the window. The names were handwritten, with 'Rock Your Baby' at the top of the list. We strolled on, until Teresa stopped outside a jewellers, and like a dog smells a tree she refused to budge as I tried to move her on. 'Look at that beautiful watch!' she said.

As I pretended to be interested, I remembered the Mother's remark – 'I bet you know her birthday!' She had warned me, now I was trapped in front of an Aladdin's cave of a window.

'Mark, it's exactly what I've always wanted,' she said, pressing her face against the brightly lit glass. 'Let's go in and have a gander at it!' I was steered into the shop, and we stood in front of a woman who was probably as old as my sister Cora. She was elegant in a black sweater and wore spectacles with a gold-coloured frame. I wondered whether she was the shop owner or a highly paid sales assistant. I made every effort to stay in the background, but Teresa pulled me forward to the counter. The woman hoisted a tight skirt at the back and leaned across the window display and fetched the watch. She held it as if it were a communion pyx containing a host. I caught sight of the price tag – it was the equivalent of a full week's wages. She asked Teresa if she would like to try it on. In a matter of seconds, the woman was making a ceremony of draping it across the outstretched wrist, deftly fastening the strap. She stood back to admire the adornment, as if Teresa had royal blood in her veins. 'Made for you,' she said. Then she looked at me. 'Don't you agree, sir?' She'd guessed that I was the money fountain.

I continued to look disinterested. Rather than stopping her, it made her more determined. 'It's more than a timepiece, it shouts good taste. Of all the watches in the store, the young lady likes this one. Is it a present, a special occasion?'

Teresa turned to me. 'It could be my holiday present.'

'Such a romantic gesture,' the woman said, adjusting the spectacles on her powdered nose. 'It's at a good price and I will throw in a nice presentation case – to protect it when not in use.'

I looked at Teresa. 'I've never heard of such a thing as a holiday present.'

'You've never been on a holiday with me before.' She slid an arm beneath mine and snuggled up to me, her free arm still adorned by the watch. 'Am I not worth it?'

'Have you seen the price? I'd need a bank with me.'

'Go on, Mark. Splash out...'

The woman reached over to unfasten the watchstrap, but Teresa withdrew her arm. 'I was only going to put it in the presentation case for you,' she said.

'Will I let her wrap it?' Teresa said. She was looking up into my face. Her breath was sweet. I reached for my wallet, and I could imagine the Mother's look of disapproval.

'Oh! He's getting it for me!' she said.

The woman hurried to complete the transaction.

We left the jewellers and I had to find a pub.

Back at the hotel, Teresa wasted no time in showing the others the 'holiday present'. Celine looked at me, as if I'd suddenly gone up in her estimation. 'Mark, you've been very generous there.'

I resisted the urge to say, 'tell me about it!'

Jimmy stayed quiet, as if he knew what was coming next.

'You'll *have* to get me a holiday present, Jimmy!' she said.

'No bother. You're the treasurer – see if you can squeeze it out of the kitty.'

'You know as well as I know that we've just enough to last the holiday,' she said, frowning.

'I leave the money matters to you, Celine. Everything I have is pooled with yours; that's how it works, isn't it?'

She looked embarrassed, and I felt for her. She shouldn't have set herself up for a refusal, at least, not in front of us.

Then Jimmy backtracked a little. 'Listen, I'm sure between us we can manage something small...' It had been a tactic.

Her smile was like weak tea, being controller-of-the-purse had its downside. She disappeared upstairs with Teresa, and I said to him, 'Sorry I landed you in it.'

'Don't worry about it – but you splashed out *big* time.'

'She caught me.'

'I suppose Celine will have me haunted till I get her something.'

'Let's slip out for a pint,' I said. 'Just the one before tea.'

'What about the girls?'

'They'll manage. They'll find plenty to talk about.'

Outside the sun was shining and on the seafront holiday life was in full flow. We searched for a bookies shop, knowing that there would be a pub close to it. We found the ideal spot and relaxed for a change in the company of men. Some types in everyday clothes we took to be regulars, for there was a similarity between them and the men to be found in my locals back home. Other types in bright slacks and open-necked shirts had to be refugees from the beach. They had come with their newspapers and pencils to study form. Every so often they would leave their pint on the bar and disappear into the betting shop next door and then return to take up their drink again. They would check their watches, watching that time didn't slip away from them, for they would have promised to help the wives return the hired deck chairs and to help them herd their sand bucket-carrying children back to their hotels or guest houses for tea. For Jimmy and me, even though we were in fully relaxed mode, it was also stolen time, as we too had to be back in time for tea.

CHAPTER FIVE

Teresa wore the new timepiece to the Palace that night, and I noticed that Celine couldn't stop glancing at it. We sat in the same place, across from the bar and beside the steps leading on to the dance floor, camped around a table of drinks. Hugo the Northerner was there, and he parked himself among us, as if he believed we were all one family. We knew he had the thickest of skins and that it was pointless trying to get rid of him, so we tolerated him, like you would put up with a work colleague whose whistling drove you crazy.

Whenever the band struck up a song that she recognised, Teresa dragged me on to the dance floor. For slow numbers, she hung her arms around my neck, the watch visible to any other dancer who cared to notice it. Dancing, slow or fast, was hot and thirsty work and, after one exhausting session, we came back to our table and discovered that Hugo had been in trouble again for swapping insults with a bartender. The bouncers had come but Jimmy had stepped in and fed them a story, saying that Hugo had suffered head damage in a car crash. 'Give him a break, lads. Since the accident he can lose the plot in seconds. When he's right again, he can't remember a thing!'

They had given Hugo a warning. 'One more time and you're out!'

'Where's he now?' I asked.

'He went off in a huff,' Celine said. 'You'd think he'd be grateful. He was going on about fighting his own fights and told Jimmy to butt out in future.'

Shortly afterwards, I spotted him on the other side of the dance floor talking to a group of girls that looked disinterested; then he merged into the crowd, and I didn't see him again that night. As for me, all was well. Teresa by my side or Teresa dancing in my arms. It ended when she sprung from her chair and went rambling, without saying a word. I like to think I'm as cool as a chilled beer, so I wasn't going to let myself down and show the others that I was surprised, even disappointed. Jimmy and Celine were probably used to Teresa's 'flights' by then and passed no remark. How long was she away? I can't be sure. Maybe a half hour or maybe an hour. She came back with the Yank in tow and collapsed into her chair as if she had only been away for a couple of minutes.

'Look who I found,' she said.

He sat close to me. 'That girlfriend of yours danced the feet off me.'

'She does the same to me.'

She leaned across me and playfully asked him, 'What's he saying about me?' The wrist was raised to show the watch. 'I can't be all that bad if he splashes out on me.'

'That reminds me, I must get something for my *own* girlfriend,' he said.

'She didn't travel?' I asked.

'No, she stayed in the States. She knew I wanted to be on my own.'

'But you've fallen in with us?'

'This is different. I've already spent a week in Dublin doing nothing, walking the streets to clear the head. I stayed in a B&B, although I've plenty of cousins who'd have put me up. I looked up no one, spoke to no one. By the end of the week, I was bored. I came here on impulse, just to kill time before my flight home.'

'You don't come across as someone who'd get bored.'

'At the moment, I'm not. Running into you guys has made all the difference.'

Teresa suddenly lay across me, her elbows digging into my lap, and I could see that she had quickly passed into a space where the drink had totally relaxed her. I figured that she must have drunk more than I thought she had.

'What are you two saying about me?' she said.

I stroked her hair, like I used to stroke the setter we once had, but the Mother never wanted the dog and the Da eventually gave away his best excuse for going out for a walk. Teresa suddenly straightened up and looked directly at me. 'Hey...hey, did I thank you...?"

'You did, a couple of times. I'm happy when you're happy.'

She fell back again across my lap. The Yank looked amused. I was intrigued by something he'd just said – 'She knew I wanted to be on my own.' I asked him how it was that a Dubliner ended up fighting in the Vietnam War.

'When the war came, they gave me a random number within my age group. When my number came up, I didn't try to dodge it. It seemed a good idea at the time, like emigrating had seemed a good idea to my father and mother. I never thought that I'd end up spilling my blood for America. Okay, they gave me the Purple Heart, fine, but it ties you to the place.'

I had read of the medal and said that I would like to see it.

He told me that it was back in his hotel, hidden in a dirty sock in the suitcase. 'There's nothing to see, really; it's just a medal,' he said. At that, he gave me a thumbs-up and rambled back towards the dance floor.

I leaned across Teresa to lift my drink, but before it reached my mouth, she sat up and some of it spilled over her and over my lap. We both hopped up and laughed. She wanted to dance and instead of going down the steps to the dance floor, I held her, and we moved in a circle, around and around, on a floor space not far from our seats, her head on my shoulder.

Next morning, I awoke with a thirst. I drank water from the sink and wondered where Teresa was. She'd already been to the sink, because the top was off the toothpaste, and I presumed she'd gone down for breakfast without me. I was feeling rough, and it was on mornings like this that the Mother used to say, 'You never saw your father in a state like that!' I looked in the mirror and cringed. My hand was unsteady as I shaved. Then I looked for a toothbrush, not caring whether it was hers or mine. I was brushing my teeth when the door opened, and Celine came in. She stood halfway between the door and where I stood. 'What's up?' I asked, through a mouthful of toothpaste.

'Teresa's gone to get her hair done. She went straight from breakfast and asked me to tell you.'

'That's okay. What's Jimmy up to? Have we plans for today?'

'He's on about the beach again, but he's waiting to see what you want to do.'

I had a towel to my face when I realized that I was stripped to the waist. I went to cover up, but she came over and stopped my tee shirt in mid-air. She was looking at my chest and put her hand on my third nipple. Mother had always said it was nothing to be ashamed of, but as a young fellow there'd been times when I wanted to take a penknife to it.

'Is this what all the fuss in the swimming pool was about?' she said. She was studying the rest of my chest.

What's she looking for now, I thought, a fourth nipple? I pulled the tee shirt over my head, but she left her hand against my chest, preventing it from falling into place.

'It doesn't seem important,' she said. 'Not to me, anyway.'

I felt uneasy. 'What's this all about?'

'What?'

'You, acting in this way. You've seen it now, so please take your hand away.'

'Mark, it's a nothing thing.'

She's looking straight at me, and my mind is racing. 'What about Jimmy?' I ask.

'He doesn't own me,' she says.

'But you two are … unless I've been reading it all wrong?'

'Jimmy's a messer, you're different.'

Since meeting Celine, I'd only seen her as Jimmy's girl. Now I saw a different person. It took only seconds, and in those seconds, I noticed the shape of her lips, her china-like teeth, the shape under her clothes, a slight growth of hair between the eyebrows, things that hadn't registered with me before. A door was open. I could walk through if I wanted.

'He's nuts about you,' I said. 'What would you do if he walked in now? I know he'd be destroyed. And he'd try to destroy me, and I couldn't blame him.'

'You're afraid of him?'

'Afraid nothing – he's a pal.'

She looked at me for a moment, then her hand slid away from my chest and hung by her side; I stuffed the tee shirt into my waistband. She sat on the edge of the bed and stared at the floor. 'Mark, how will I ever know if Jimmy's the right one?'

'I haven't a clue,' I said. 'How does everyone else decide?'

'That doesn't help me.'

'Celine, at least Jimmy is a joker and makes you laugh. That has to stand for something.'

Suddenly, her expression changed. 'Listen, you wouldn't say I was here?'

'I never saw you.'

'Forget all I said, Mark. I think I've made a fool of myself.'

'No, you haven't.'

She smiled in relief and rose to go. 'Oh! I nearly forgot to tell you. Teresa needed money to get her hair done and took money from your wallet.'

'Women have to look their best,' I said.

When she was gone, I realized the breakfasts would soon be stopped and hurried downstairs.

Later, with Jimmy and Celine stretched out on their beach-towels, and Teresa still getting her hair done, I took a tram along the seafront and got off at the hotel where I had seen the Yank climb the steps a few days before. I asked for him at reception and a chambermaid was sent upstairs to knock on his door but there was no reply. 'Look on the beach,' the receptionist said.

When I saw the beach was as crowded as the one that I'd just left, I thought it would be impossible to find him. Fortunately, as I started to search, he came out of the water, almost in front of me, and ran to a spot to pick up his towel. I followed him and called his name and he spun round, a tension in his face, then he recognised me, and it quickly went.

'Paul, I've come to see your medal. Remember, we talked about it.'

He dried his body with vigorous strokes of the towel. Without speaking, he gathered up his clothes from the beach and we crossed the road to the hotel. We passed a large dinner gong in the hall and climbed to the first level. He had been given a good room overlooking the seafront, with its own bathroom and toilet. I looked out the window at the promenade, the beach, and the sea beyond, while he went into the bathroom to dress. A radio was playing somewhere close by. Dusty Springfield. He came out of the bathroom and swung a suitcase up on to the candlewick bedspread, snapped it open and drew out a stuffed sock. Inside the sock was a presentation box, which he placed on the bedspread and opened to reveal the medal. He handed it to me, and I rubbed my fingers along the purple ribbon. I was sorry I hadn't brought my Brownie camera with me – he could have snapped me posing with the medal. A photograph like that would be a great talking piece in a pub back home. There's nothing like introducing an unusual item into the conversation when a bar is quiet because everyone in the company has nothing to say, is bored to the point of reading the bottle labels on the shelf behind the bar for the umpteenth time.

I was surprised when he asked me if I wanted to know how he got wounded and told him that he could if he wanted. He seemed determined to talk about it.

'I'd been there only about a week. Our patrol walked into a trap; shots coming from jungle cover; they seemed to be on all sides of us. They'd caught us with our pants down. Men fell all around me. The jungle was so thick, you couldn't see who was shooting; the noise was tremendous. We were returning fire more in hope than anything else. Marines began to buckle and fall, some screaming as the bullets hit them. And then it was my turn, only I didn't scream, couldn't scream. The impact of the bullets had pushed me face down into the ground. I was chewing mud and couldn't move. I turned my head to one side but hadn't the strength to spit out the dirt. Someone fell on me, his leg across the back of my helmet. Then another fell on him, and the second marine's face came to rest close to mine. From the corner of my eye, I saw his unblinking eyes. Then I thought I would suffocate, for the weight of the two men was on me. I wriggled until I was able to breathe freely. Then the firing stopped, as suddenly as it had begun. I passed out at that stage.

'I came to, I don't know how long after. I heard more shots, this time they were intermittent. The shots got louder. I couldn't see what was happening because of the bodies over me. Then I realized that the Vietcong were executing anyone that was still alive. I shut my eyes and held my breath. The men above me were being roughly shoved and prodded. Something hard was pressing against my nose. I glanced and met the staring eyes of the marine above me. He wasn't pretending to be dead, not like I was. For what seemed a long time I heard the voices of men moving back and forward. A pistol shot rang out. Then, everything went quiet. No groans, no agitated voices, no bird noises. An ant walked on my face and then there were the flies. And I passed out again.

'I was found like that. The choppers came but it was too late. The medics thought we were all dead; I was only found when the bodies above me were lifted away. I was hit with a jab of morphine, loaded on to a chopper and taken away.'

'You were steeped in luck,' I said.

'I was saved by the ones who fell on top of me.'

'Do you know who they were?'

'Sure, I know who they were. Don't I owe them, big time?'

I handed back the medal. A silence followed, a form of reverence. The radio close by was now playing the Supremes. The medal was put away. I heard the dinner gong ring up through the building, calling all to the dining room. 'I better be nifty, or there'll be no chow left,' he said, closing the case and shoving it under the bed.

Teresa looked stunning. Her hair was short, in the pixie cut, and I couldn't stop looking at her. I knew better than to expect change from what she had taken from my wallet, and she never brought it up and neither did I. Nothing is surer, I thought, this new hairdo will get her more admiring looks than normal. She wouldn't go to the beach that afternoon, wanting to keep the hair right for the Palace that night; instead, we walked along the seafront, and I was proud that she was on my arm.

'What did you do with yourself this morning?' she said.

'I met up with Paul Sweeney, you know, the Yank, and he showed me his medal from the war.'

'Is he a hero, or something?'

'He doesn't say it, but in my opinion he is.'

'Doesn't look it to me. You'd pass him in the street.'

'Fellows like him don't shout about themselves.'

'Yet he showed his medal to you.'

'Only because I asked.'

We walked on in silence, passing old folks on the seafront benches, their heads together in conversation. Suddenly, she stopped and looked at me. 'You never said you liked my hair.' She gave a playful tilt of the head.

'I thought you could tell from my face.'

'It would be nice to hear you say it.'

'*I love the hair*,' I said, exaggerating each word.

She posed theatrically against the seafront railings. 'You should take my photo!'

I had left the camera in the room. Looking around, I saw a photo booth outside an amusement arcade on the opposite side of the road and we crossed over to it. We read the instructions outside, and Teresa adjusted the height of the seat in the booth, then with one last glance in the mirror to check the new hair style, she gave me the signal to insert the money. I listened to her giggling while she waited for the machine to start. She shrieked as the first flash went off, followed by a second flash, and then she put an arm out from behind the curtain and pulled me inside. I squeezed onto the seat beside her and gave up my best face to the final two flashes. When the strip of photographs was spat from the machine, she snatched it up and ran to one side. She studied the photos, grinning, frowning, then grinning again, while I waited for her to pass them over, but she held them away from me. 'I wanted them to be perfect,' she said.

'*You're* perfect; the pictures don't have to be.'

She was holding the strip by the edges waiting for the surface to dry. 'You're still not seeing them!

It didn't bother me, but I was surprised to see them being slipped inside her blouse.

That afternoon, Jimmy and I managed to go to the pub that we'd discovered, an escape from the thronged seafront, and from the girls. We sat in a quiet corner and gave our drinks priestly attention. It was a quiet period, or it was so until he gave a little cough of hesitation and said, 'Do you see anything different about Celine?'

'What do you mean? I haven't noticed anything different – is she sick or something?' I said.

'No, nothing like *that*'.

'Like what, then?'

'It's hard to talk about it…'

I could see that he was having trouble spitting out what he wanted to say and, even though I was curious, I gave him the space to make his mind up.

'Okay,' he said. 'There's no point in me dancing around this; it's our in-bed stuff.'

'Jimmy, I don't want to know your private business.'

'That's just the problem, there isn't much private business, if you get my meaning.'

I watched a low-sized man return from the bookies and swing himself on to a high stool. He drew a folded newspaper from his pocket and laid it out on the bar. I was buying time and didn't know what to say. No friend had ever talked to me before about his life between the sheets, at least, not with a straight face, it just isn't done in Dublin; nevertheless, I managed to say, 'But you and Celine get on so well?'

'Normally we do, until the last few nights. Now, she turns her back to me and doesn't want to do anything and I'm lying there wondering what's gone wrong. After all, we're supposed to be on holidays.'

'Have you talked to her about it?'

'What if she says something I don't want to hear? I couldn't risk that,' he said.

'I don't see what I can do, Jimmy. Maybe you're making this out to be more than what it is?'

'I could be, and I probably am. Still, that doesn't help me.'

We were both solemn faced; he was struggling with his problem, real or imagined; I was thinking back to Celine's visit to my room that morning, and what she'd said.

Suddenly, he broke the silence. 'I was thinking of asking her to become engaged. I could propose to her here, then get the ring when we're back home, when I've got the money.'

I spluttered into my drink and when I finally caught my breath, told him that I thought proposing to her was an extreme move. He said that sometime in the future he would have asked her, anyway.

'Will she go for it, Mark?'

I looked again at the fellow at the bar who was now ticking off more selections, and he reminded me of men back home going into the local betting shop and writing out their dockets in polished handwriting. Not alone was it a place of handwriting, for sometimes the names of the horses were in French and the punters could pronounce them correctly, because they heard them come across the radio system. Also, there were the mathematical geniuses – sums done in the head by punters who had never showed any promise in school. Thinking on these things was my way of buying time before I would answer Jimmy's question. Again, I could see Celine, sitting on my bed, sharing her doubts over her future with him. I felt he could get hurt; I didn't want that to happen.

'You know, maybe you're going about this the wrong way,' I said.

'What do you mean?'

'You could surprise her so much that you could shock her. She could feel that you're putting her in a corner – you've a good chance that she'll agree to it, sure, but you've also a slim chance...well, you know...'

'I don't believe that! She'll accept, no problem.'

'Of course, she'll accept but you might have to give her time. With my way, there's no real risk.'

I knew he was thinking over what I'd said, meanwhile, I tried to be casual, as if the matter under discussion were of no real importance. I strolled to the bar for two more pints, nodded at the fellow with the racing page spread out in front of him. On my return, Jimmy said, 'I think you know more than what you're saying...'

'There's nothing to know. It's just the way I see it. You do as you planned if that's what you really – '

'I would have but now you have me worried. You've always been smarter than me, staying longer in school and all, and I know I should listen to you. But how do I do this?'

'Do it in a gradual way,' I said. He looked disappointed, as it was clear he was looking for concrete ideas. 'You could start by saying something like, "Sometime in the future we should get a house with a garden, grow our own veggies." You paint a picture for her.'

'Mark, that's corny and she knows I detest vegetables.'

'Okay, let's think of something else. But you get my drift? you see what I'm trying to do? You paint a picture in her mind. She sees the two of you living in the future in a neat little house, with a garden. Even if later, you were to build a pigeon loft in the same garden!'

'A pigeon loft, now, you're talking sense, Mark!'

I was now inspired, in full flow. I told him he should show her that Jimmy Culmane was someone with a future who wanted better things. There followed a long silence, and I began to wonder if I'd crossed the line, maybe insulted him, and I cursed my big mouth. What he said next took me by surprise.

'There's nothing worse than needing someone. I mean, needing someone completely. It's now driving me crazy.' He stopped and took in a deep breath, like a swimmer about to dive into a pool, then in a burst of words, he asked me to give him more ideas, to tell him what to say.

I glanced at the clock; it would soon be time to head back to meet the girls. 'Listen I'm not an agony aunt, and ideas just don't spring to mind like that. But finish up your pint and we'll try to think of some on the way back.'

In truth, I felt like a signpost erector who didn't know the way himself. Who am I to tell him how to live? I've enough trouble organising my own life.

We took our places in the dining room that evening. For no reason, Jimmy was opposite Teresa, and I was facing Celine, which I feared was going to be awkward, but she looked me straight in the face, as if nothing had occurred that morning. A large teapot was slapped down on the table, and she undertook to pour for the rest of us. I hoped that she didn't notice that Jimmy was unusually quiet. It was one thing to ask him to cut out the messing, it was another thing to expect a personality change. No one wanted that, not even Celine, I imagined. She was pouring the tea. I tried to get him to speak, to start him on the road of giving her a good impression. But he became a boxer in the ring, weaving away from my attempts. Meanwhile, the girls talked across the teapot to one another, discussing various other women in the dining room.

Later, the waitress who two days earlier had told us about the fire at the shop, told us that there'd been another fire, this time it was the clubhouse at the bowling club. 'The radio says that they think it could be the same person doing it.' She lifted a laden tray and went shakily towards the kitchen.

I instinctively thought of the Northerner, Hugo (even though I'd no real grounds for it).

We went to our rooms to get ready, and I watched Teresa put the finishing touches to her makeup and dab perfume behind the ears. I was proud that she was with me, which I knew was a stupid feeling, as it was based on the notion that she was mine, a sort of ownership thing, and I didn't want that – a claim that would have been as secure as the house built on sand by the foolish man.

'How do I look?' she said, standing away from the mirror above the sink.

'A knockout!' I'd struggled to think of a better word. She smiled in a teasing way, glanced back in the mirror, gave the new hairdo a slight caress of the palm, and declared, 'I'm ready.'

I buttoned up a white shirt, the sharp edges on the sleeves reminding me that the Mother had ironed it perfectly. I ran a comb through the hair, placed my wallet in the back pocket and we headed down to meet the others.

CHAPTER SIX

It was Friday. It would be our final, full day in the Isle of Man, as on the next day at noon we would be going home. A decision was made between us to take a coach tour to Peel on the other side of the island, then return for a session of sunbathing on the beach before heading out for a last night at the Palace. Teresa and I sat up near the front of the coach, and Jimmy and Celine went farther back. At a point in the journey, he came forward and suggested to Teresa that they swap seats for a while. He swung in beside me and Teresa went back to sit with Celine.

'It worked!' he said. 'She didn't turn her back to me last night.'

'That's good. What did you have to say to her?'

'I can't remember it line by line, but it was like we'd said – the little house with a garden, a place within walking distance of her ma's, and everything else you and I had spoken of. Little seeds in her mind. Now, I feel ready to pop the question.

'No, wait a few days more. But now that things are better between you, why bother asking her at all?'

'I couldn't do that. I'm ready now.'

I was looking out the coach window at the passing green countryside. 'Well, at least now if you ask her, there's more chance she'll accept.'

'What about you and Teresa? How do you see that going?'

'I don't look that far ahead. Right now, I'm not complaining.'

'She's a strange one, though, isn't she? I saw how she disappeared again last night. How can you let her wander off and dance with every fellow in the place? She must have been gone ages.'

'If she wants to go off for a while, I don't mind as long as she comes back.'

'Not many fellows would feel that way. I certainly wouldn't.'

We fell into silence. For me, there was something strange about the way the conversation had gone. He should be grateful to me, I thought, for putting his sex life back together; instead, he's now telling me how to run *my* business. I went over the previous night in my mind, how when Teresa had returned to the table – a high colour from dancing – and I hadn't passed any remark, rather, had been glad to again have her sitting next to me. Was I a fool for doing that? Suddenly, she had returned from the back of the bus and was standing over Jimmy. 'Your time's up,' she said. 'Celine's lonely without you.'

'What's wrong?' he said. 'When you two get together, you usually can't be parted!'

'She's back there waiting. Do you want me to go and tell her you're still yapping? can't be bothered?'

He slid out of the seat and headed back to Celine, then Teresa collapsed down beside me, stuck her arm beneath mine and cuddled against my shoulder. She fell asleep, leaving me free to study the outline of her face, without embarrassment.

Peel has a small harbour, with fishing boats and yachts. It was in complete contrast to the hubbub of Douglas. We found a bar and settled into a corner seat and knew we wouldn't be left behind as the coach driver was also there. It was like a small country pub back home and we were not inclined to leave it to go exploring the town. Irish accents floated across the bar from men at another table; they were dug into fried breakfasts and pints. From what I heard of the conversation, I gathered that they were yachting types. One of them stood up. He was tall, with a faint stubble, maybe two days without seeing a razor. 'We're off,' he said. One of the other men got up to join him.

'You're mad,' a man sitting down said. 'Wait for a better forecast.'

'Not possible,' the tall one said. 'I must be in the office in the morning.'

The two men passed close to us on their way to the door. Jimmy had been watching them as well. 'Are you men heading back to Ireland?' he asked.

'Why?' the tall fellow said, eyes twinkling. 'Do you want to join us?'

'Do you think I'm bleeding mad?' Jimmy said. 'I'd be spewing up before I even left the harbour.'

'Well, then, maybe the girls will come? We'll have them back in Dublin in no time.'

'Maybe you would, or maybe you'd sink!'

'No, they'd be dead safe with us,' said the other, a shorter man with veiny cheeks.

'Trusting you with a boat is one thing but I'd be mad to trust you with the girlfriend.'

'You don't have much faith in us,' the tall one said.

'I'd have more faith in me granny!'

Teresa said, 'Give it over, Jimmy.'

The tall one gave her the once-over. '*You* can come with us any day,' he said. His companion had a sly, amused look.

We were two, plus the girls. They had three more behind them at the table who were now paying attention. That didn't stop Jimmy. He jumped to his feet and squared-up to the tall fellow. 'Don't speak like that to our women!'

'Will you sit down for God's sake,' Celine said. 'He didn't mean anything by it.'

I wasn't as sure as she was of that; nevertheless, I stood up, put my arms about Jimmy and pulled him back down on to his seat. Meanwhile, our coach driver noticed the brewing trouble, and he came over. 'What's the matter here?' he said. 'These are my customers and I've to bring them back safe to Douglas.'

'Then, you shouldn't be jarring and driving,' the shorter fellow said, with a sneer.

'I know when I'm able and when I'm not able,' the driver said. 'Anyway, these people have paid good money to enjoy the trip and don't expect it to be spoiled.'

'Who's spoiling anything?' the tall one said. 'We're just being friendly; there's a lift home to whoever wants to come with us. Although, I don't think any of them would be up to hard weather.' The two men turned for the door.

'Good riddance!' Jimmy said, not being one to let things go that easily.

'For heaven's sake, stop it!' Celine said, prodding him with an elbow.

Holding him down by the shoulders, I whispered to him, 'Don't make a mess of this.' He relaxed under my grip and grunting in disgust went back to his drink. As they were exiting, I said, 'Safe journey'. I was trying to be sarcastic, but I doubt if they even heard me. Still, I didn't envy them heading out in a yacht, with a bad sea forecast. The fellows who they'd being sitting with went back to talking among themselves. I felt they could have been from another planet and not from the same country as us, for, although they were roughly dressed and wore soiled deck shoes, they had a look and the sound of men with money. The coach driver passed us on his way out and we quickly downed our drinks to head back to Douglas.

Later, the sun stayed behind clouds, ruining our plan to sunbathe, yet it didn't stop us going across for a shivery swim. Afterwards, while Jimmy and I rubbed our goose-pimpled skin dry at the water's edge, the girls complained about the cold and ran back to the hotel, wet towels draping the shoulders. Once we were alone, Jimmy told me that Celine had said that she'd been proud of the way that he had stood up for her in the pub. 'She doesn't want me to change. Not now, not ever.'

I realized that she'd got over having doubts about him. 'I can see comfy fireside chairs in store for both of you.'

~~~

It can be like this, once you think life is great you are often on the verge of it becoming worse, worse than you ever thought possible. On that last night, we occupied our special place in the ballroom, as we'd been doing now for almost a week, yet our claim on the area was temporary, for you knew that in the next week another group of holidaymakers would come and take up the same space and, like us, view it as their own. That night we also saw the Yank, Paul Sweeney, who came and chatted with us for a while, and we also spied the Northerner, Hugo, prowling the edge of the dance floor, and although he occasionally passed us on the way to the bar, he never looked our way and we weren't going to call him. Then, as usual, Teresa went walkabout – I called it that because I'd seen a programme where the Aboriginals practiced it – and as I was no longer upset by her dancing with others, I was sure she would be back, her face a high colour from her exertions. An hour went by, then two, then three, then they played 'God Save the Queen', and the lights came on and people began to leave, making it easy to see who was left on the dance floor and who was lingering at the bar. Like the stout friends they were, Jimmy and Celine sat with me until finally there was no one left but us and the workers ready for home. We'd missed the last tram, so we walked in silence towards our hotel. Every time I heard a female voice behind us, I would wheel around expecting to see Teresa running up to us, laughing and joking, but she never came. Still, I couldn't help but look, even though each voice was nothing like hers.

My spirits lifted as we got closer to the hotel, as I'd convinced myself that she would be either sitting on the steps waiting for us or be upstairs in our room, in our bed, ready to whisper beautiful things in my ear. I quickened my step and the others pushed themselves to keep up with me. The man at the small reception desk said she hadn't come in. Despite what he said, I took the stairs two at a time and checked our room, but the bedspread was flat and unruffled, exactly as she'd left it that morning. I went back down, where Jimmy and Celine were in the hallway waiting for me, loyal but helpless.

'We should call the police, anything could have happened her,' I said.

'I wouldn't do that,' Celine said. 'You're not certain.'

'She could be lying somewhere, injured, anything...'

'Mark, I didn't want to tell you this, but I saw her dancing with the Yank,' Jimmy said. 'Later I saw them together in a corner and they looked –'

'She's a bitch,' Celine said.

'Did *you* know about this?' I asked her.

'No, but I hear what Jimmy's saying.'

'So, there's no point in going out looking for her?'

'She'll turn up,' she said.

Jimmy said, 'If you want to wait up for her, I'll sit with you in the bar. Where's that man with the key to the drinks?'

'No, you go on up with Celine. I'll be alright.'

'What'll you do?'

'I'll wait here, just in case.'

Celine reminded him that they had to go upstairs and pack their suitcases. I was surprised when she said that, for with all that had happened I had completely forgotten that our sailing was – I looked at my watch – in fact, the sailing was today.

They disappeared up the stairs, and I envied their closeness. There was a wall clock with a barometer, and I sat in a chair placed beneath it. It wasn't a case of trying to appear casual, as I knew that I wouldn't be able to hide my feelings when she came in and saw me waiting, like a father after his young daughter's first dance.

Other couples came through the hallway, showing no sign of noticing me. They disappeared upstairs, with giggles and belly laughs. I felt like a witness to the lives of others, a lonely place to be. The clock chimed one in the morning and the man who'd met us on the first night came and went to lock the front door (guests should have read the notice in the dining room, giving them no excuse if they found themselves locked out). He looked at me, curious as to what I was doing there.

'I'm waiting on my roommate.'

'You mean, the girl you're with?'

'Yes, the girl I'm with.'

'When will she be in?'

'I can't say...could be five minutes or even another hour. Can't I wait here?'

'You can wait, but the door will be locked.'

I got up and stood in the doorway and looked up and down the promenade. 'Then, I'll wait outside.' On the steps seemed as good as any place to sit and wait.

He came out and stood behind me, and I sensed that he also was looking up and down the promenade. 'I'll give you a key,' he said. 'But when you come in, make sure the door closes properly. And for heaven's sake, go up quietly.'

I took the key and nodded. Then the door was closed, and I was left alone with the silence of the Douglas seafront. Across the road, beyond the railings, the sea lapping the beach, in darkness, where we had swum that first night. I sat on the steps and waited. A police car slowed, and I sensed I was being inspected. It was driven away. I must have been out there for nearly an hour when it started to rain. That was all I needed. The wet was going through my clothes and I retreated up the steps and took cover under a small portico. How has it come to this? I asked myself. Mark O'Bride – always considered to be his own man. One who doesn't follow the crowd, always master of his own leisure time, always money in the pocket for standing his round, a master tradesman. How had it come to this? where I'm standing in the rain for a female who might or might not show? What would the Mother think if she saw me now? I would never live it down. And, yet, even if she were to find out, if she were to miraculously have a vision back in Dublin of what was going on here in Douglas, I still wouldn't be able to go inside and give up on Teresa, regardless of what the Mother would have to say about it.

So, it is easy to stick at something when there is no alternative. No matter the rain, no matter the dread of where she might be, no matter the risk of making a complete fool of oneself. It's too late now to worry over that last bit, I thought; I *know* I'm making a fool of myself. But it can't be helped. The minutes went into hours, marked by the sound of the clock chiming beyond the door, and I honestly don't know what went through my mind for most of the night. Being wet from the rain made me cold and there was no way of heating myself except the cigarettes. It would have been easy to slip the key in the door behind me and run upstairs to change and put on a jacket, but I didn't want to miss her.

The rain eased and a drunk came swaying along the pavement. He stopped at the foot of the steps and pulled a packet of cigarettes from his pocket. Having occasionally been that same soldier, I knew what it was like to fumble with a packet and could have guessed what would happen next. He pulled out one cigarette but brought four or five with it. They lay on the wet pavement; it didn't seem to bother him.

'Got a...got a light?' he said.

'Sure'. I cupped my hands against the night, and he lit up. He drew deeply and swayed to the point where I was sure he was going to topple. For a moment, it seemed that he was going to say something else, then it was as if the thought had escaped him, and he shook his head and went on his way. I could say merry way, however, he didn't look at all merry. Again, I thought of the Mother, and could hear her call from the bedroom on nights when I had come home late in a bad state and was on my knees at the toilet bowl. 'Clean that sick up after you!' By now the drunk was halfway along the street and I went back up to my post under the portico. It started to get bright, there was a mist on the sea, and milk bottles clattered as they were being placed outside the hotels by a ruddy-faced man in a white coat who leaped in and out of a milk float looking like Benny Hill singing 'The Fastest Milkman in the West'. A black cat came along and sniffed the bottles. I realized it had no tail. Celine should be here for this, I thought, seeing as she'd wanted to see one. It moved its back against my wet trouser leg, then it padded back down the steps and went from view, searching for something more interesting.

Then, I heard a movement behind the hall door, and it was swung open. The man from last night came out and sucked in the sea air and I guessed that this was part of his morning routine. Then he collected the milk and looked up and down the promenade. I held out the hall door key. His hands were taken with the milk, so he nodded in the direction of his trouser pocket, where I placed the key. He didn't say anything, which could have given the impression that a guest spending the night on the doorstep was normal. I was relieved that he had nothing to say. The new day gradually unfolded, people appeared on the promenade and the first tram went by. A smell of bacon cooking came from the inside. The girl we knew who served in the dining room came up the street and went past me in a hurry. Early risers would be coming down from their rooms, looking for breakfasts.

Then Jimmy appeared. 'She didn't turn up?'

'Got a fag, I'm all out?' The butts round my feet told of my vigil.

We lit up and looked aimlessly across at the sea.

'What time is the boat?' he asked.

'Noon, I'm sure.'

'Celine is just finishing off the packing. She does for both of us. I'd be lost without–'

We were interrupted by a cleaner who had come out to sweep the steps and my butts vanished. In an instant there was no more sign of my long night. I looked up and down the street and across at the promenade, more in habit now than anything else.

'Mark, you go get cleaned up and I'll watch for her. Don't worry, I'll call you...'

'I couldn't do that.'

Celine appeared, and I told her that she had missed the Manx cat. It didn't seem to bother her. She suggested that we should organise a taxi for 11am. Again, Jimmy wanted me to go up to the room to freshen up. I realized that I also needed to pack. Then I thought of Teresa's clothes. 'Right, but what about *her* stuff?'

'You get ready and when you come down, I'll pack her case for her,' Celine said. 'Then we'll wait and hope she turns up in time. Otherwise...'

I climbed the stairs, remembering the times I had followed her up to our attic room. Some of her clothes were on a chair, mixed with mine, and my hands lingered on the soft feel of her underwear. I placed her clothes on the bed so that Celine would see them. When I had washed and changed, I stood at the door holding my case and took one last look at the room and I could see her there. My chest tightened, and I had a choking sensation, then I let out the longest sigh that my body had ever known and carried my suitcase downstairs.

'Celine's inside having breakfast,' Jimmy said. 'You go and join her.'

I was too tired to argue. She fussed over me when I went in and made sure the waitress brought everything I needed. I hadn't realized I was hungry until the fry appeared. She sat opposite me in silence, cradling a cup of tea. I had no words to say, either. I then brought my cup of tea outside, and she went upstairs to pack Teresa's suitcase.

'Don't worry, she has to show,' Jimmy said.

'Thanks, pal. You go in and eat before they clear up'.

He headed to the dining room, and I took up my usual position on the steps. It was becoming a normal day on Douglas Promenade, every class of a person heading for the beach, all carrying every type of necessary item to ensure that they would have the happiest of times. Celine reappeared and placed Teresa's suitcase in the entrance hall. It is true, she does exist, I thought. But where is she? Jimmy came out, carrying a cup of tea. We all sat on the steps and waited. It was after nine. The taxi would come at eleven, regardless. The clock in the hallway signalled every passing quarter hour. No one said anything; we waited.

Then, suddenly, Jimmy grabbed my arm and I looked to where he was pointing. A taxicab had come to a halt nearby, on the promenade side of the road. The engine was running, no one got out. It made a U-turn and, as it sped past, I caught sight of Teresa in the back – there was someone with her. It came to a halt on our side of the street, maybe a hundred yards away. I saw movement in the rear window. Two heads coming together in what seemed to be a parting kiss. The rear window was narrow, I couldn't tell who was with her. Then the nearside door was opened, she stepped out and the cab quickly left.

At first, Teresa stood in the centre of the pavement, seemingly unsure of her bearings. When she started walking towards us, I felt that I was watching a scene from a movie, in slow motion. I was sure that Jimmy and Celine had seen everything that I'd seen, yet they passed no comment. She was getting closer, and I couldn't look away, even though I wanted to look nonchalantly at my shoes and appear indifferent. It was the ordinariness of the moment that caught me off guard – she looked the same as always. There was no sign hanging from her neck that read: Stone me! There was a moment at the bottom of the steps when I thought she was going to speak, offer an explanation, instead, she picked her way past us and went inside. Celine stared after her. 'I'll ring for the taxi,' she said.

'Did you see who it was?' Jimmy asked me.

'Does it make a difference?'

I sat up front during the ride to the pier and resisted the temptation to glance backwards at Teresa. I walked up the gangplank, keeping ahead of her. We headed for the saloon area; however, I watched where the other three went and sat at the other end of the room. Jimmy came over to me, looking guilty. 'I can't leave Celine and she won't leave Teresa. It kills me that you'll be drinking alone. Come and join us.'

'You know I can't.'

'Okay, whatever you want. No hard feelings then?'

'No hard feelings.'

It felt strange going to the bar and ordering for myself. My table was positioned so that I was looking away from them. I tried to relax and wished that I had a book or something to read, even an old newspaper – anything would have done. The boat left the harbour and met a swell. The floor began to sway, drinks spilled, and tray carriers found it hard to stay on course. Then it was calm, and I sat back, sipping my drink, and I thought about how I would make changes in my life from then on. For one thing, women were out – that phase was now truly ended. All right, the Mother and the females in the family would be exceptions, but those floating around in the mix that could be called 'of interest' would be ignored. I was determined to go back to the way things were before I'd met Teresa.

A familiar voice said, 'Can I join you?'

It was the Yank, Paul Sweeney. I pushed a chair towards him with my foot, and he sat heavily on it, spilling the head of the pint in his hand.

'You look rough, what happened? he said. Did you guys party all night?'

'Did *you*?' I asked.

At that moment, he noticed the others at the opposite end of the saloon. 'What's this separate tables lark?'

'Like you didn't know.'

As if he hadn't noticed my remark, he said, 'Let's drag some chairs over and join them!'

'You go – I prefer it where I am.'

'I get it now,' he said, releasing a low, whistling sound.

He was waiting for me to say more. My silence would speak for me, I thought. However, it wasn't easy, like holding your breath under water; I was about to break to the surface and blurt out something nasty, when Teresa came over to us. I watched for some signal or secret look between them, but they weren't giving anything away. I waited for her to speak.

'Jimmy's clean out and needs a loan for the bar,' she said.

I couldn't believe what I was hearing. 'And what do you expect *me* to do about it?'

'You're his pal, aren't you?'

'Sure, I'm his pal. That's why he hasn't asked me himself. He doesn't want to insult me.'

'Are you going to give it or not?' she said.

'Not a chance in hell.'

'Okay, Mark,' she said, 'if that's the way you want it. But I never thought you could be so small-minded.'

I wanted to tell her that now she knew but, instead, I just stared at her. She moved her hand through her hair and there was a look in her eyes that was pulling at my resistance – I didn't cave in. Then she tossed her head back and marched off.

'It must be serious when you'd turn Jimmy down like that,' the Yank said.

'For your information, Jimmy and I haven't fallen out. But you, you've some neck!'

'What are you on about?'

'You spend the night with her, then you sit there acting all innocent.'

'Who? What are you talking about?'

'You know very well who; I'm talking about Teresa. My supposed girlfriend, correction, my ex-girlfriend. And you can have her now if you want her!'

'Mark, I don't get this. Do you honestly think that I'd go after *your* Teresa?'

'That's what I said. You were seen...'

'I don't understand...'

'Listen, I don't have to explain myself. You were seen and that's all there's to it.'

'Mark, let me tell you this to your face. I've never touched your girlfriend, never mind spent a night with her!'

'How can you dance with someone and not touch them?' I knew that sounded childish.

'Jeez, you know what I mean! I never *touched* her. Not in the way you're talking.'

'You were both seen having a cosy chat, then she never came back to our table.'

'Well, it wasn't me that kept her away.'

'Others think different,' I said.

He replied, *'Semper Fidelis.'*

'*Semper* what?'

'*Semper Fidelis*, it's the motto of the marines: Always Faithful. You took me into your group at the Palace. I thought we'd become good buddies, and in the marines you never let down a buddy. That's the way it is. How could I ever betray you by going off with your girl? Anyway, I told you I've a girl of my own in the States.'

I remembered him showing me the Purple Heart medal and the story of why he had been awarded it and I began to think that he was telling the truth. 'Then, *who* was she with?'

'Mark, I can't help you there. I didn't see her afterwards with anyone out of the ordinary. But I'm glad you're believing me.'

'I'm still not one hundred per cent sure.'

'Why don't you ask her? Just go straight up to her and ask her who she was with. It's the only way you'll find out.'

'She could say anything. Anyway, I don't want details. I guess you're sound, Paul... Sorry for the mix-up'.

'There's no need to say sorry to me. You're the one that's been hard done by, not me. Here, let me go to the bar and get you another.'

He had gone from being my worst enemy to becoming a friend again, all in a matter of minutes. He was right, I should go straight over and ask her where she'd been and who she'd been with – but my fear was that she *would* tell me, and I didn't think I could take that. Some holiday this has turned out to be, I thought. He returned with the drinks and for the rest of the crossing did his best to distract me with stories from his time in Vietnam. Even in the darkest of times there are people who will see the lighter side of things and during that sailing back to Dublin he was one of those.

When the boat docked, we made our way to the quay and avoided coming face to face with Teresa; I figured Jimmy might also have steered their group away from me. Paul Sweeney wanted to keep in touch with me and we swapped addresses. We shared a taxi from the quayside; we passed the others on foot heading up the quays (no money for drink and no money for a taxi). Paul got out at O'Connell Street, and I asked the driver to drop me off at a pub on Camden Street, a final drink before heading for home. I drank a pint, glad to be back on familiar ground. The walk home took me along streets I had known all my life – with a suitcase in hand, a strange sensation, and I imagined how the emigrant men must feel when they come home for Christmas or during the builders' holidays.

Mother was setting the table for tea. 'You're home,' she said, wiping her hands with a tea cloth. I thought she was getting ready to shake my hand, but we are not really the contact type. If I had moved to embrace her, she probably would have become all flustered. I would, in all probability, have been no different; instead, I just said, 'Home safe and sound, Ma.' I went into my room and opened the suitcase. On the day I had walked back from seeing Paul Sweeney's medal, I had slipped into a souvenir shop and bought a small figurine of a black cat – it hadn't cost much, however the girl in the shop had taken the Made in Japan sticker off the base and wrapped it in tissue.

I placed it on the table beside her plate and sat opposite her. She began to unwrap it and before she even saw it, she was already saying, 'It's lovely, you shouldn't...' She stood the ornament on the table and looked at it.

'Don't you like it, Ma?'

'I like it, but where's its tail?'

'It's a Manx cat – they don't have tails.'

'I knew that fact,' she said with a mischievous smile. She moved it to one side. It was one step away from being buried in the china cabinet. 'You got a bit of a colour, son. You'd good weather?'

'We couldn't complain.'

'And your friend, how did she get on?'

'Fine.'

'Only "fine" – *that* doesn't sound good.'

'Mother, do we have to talk about it?'

There was a long silence, and I fixed my eyes on the souvenir – an unlucky black cat. Suddenly, I could see Teresa and the others trudging along the North Wall, an image that made me feel rotten and, despite everything, I now regretted not stopping the taxi and helping them out. Particularly Jimmy. He was a mate and shouldn't have been left to walk as if he were out of work and hadn't a tosser. The Mother got up to clear the table and I stopped her. 'You watch the television, and I'll do that.'

'Thanks, son. I could do with resting the legs. Any washing you have, throw them in the basket in the bathroom and I'll do them in the morning.'

Later I lay in bed, back in my own comfortable surroundings. I'd closed Teresa out of my mind, but if I dropped my guard, she would sneak past and plant herself in a corner then spread herself out until my thoughts were only of her. I realized what was happening and became annoyed with myself. I eventually drifted off, unaware of the further part that she was to play in my life.

CHAPTER SEVEN

It was good to be back. Perhaps I had needed a break from Dublin to remind me of how much I loved the place. Within a mile radius of home, I knew every shop, pub, betting office, market stall, church, taxi rank, picture house, chipper, undertaker, and the places on the streets where the local women gathered in the morning for their chats. It was mapped on my brain, and I felt that I could walk the streets and laneways with a blindfold and still know my way. Many faces I knew to see, others I knew very well. There were nods of recognition aplenty, some slight, almost not there, and others big and cheery, asking how life was treating me; salutes from people I knew were returned with a mention of their name, something I had copied from the Da.

When the boss said that he wanted me on a job in Terenure I didn't mind, as it was on a bus route. Because I don't drive, he seldom gave me work that was difficult to get to, unless none of the other lads wanted to do it, then he would moan over having to drive me there and back. However, Terenure was no problem. I rose early and was in the house raring to go at eight on the dot. The owners were on holidays, and I had the place to myself. I found a radio and went about whistling and humming while I worked, renewed by the weeklong break. That evening when the boss came by, I could tell he was pleased with the progress of the job, but he was not the type who would throw you a compliment; however, he paid me well, which, in my opinion, was far more important. And, so, I settled back into normality. A work routine, a home routine, and a drinking routine – life was good.

Months passed, and then one Friday evening the boss springs it on me that on Monday I would be painting a house on the Clonliffe Road on the northside of the city. As I've said before, I had often worked on the northside, but I hadn't since Jimmy had been jumped on. I couldn't say to the boss that the river Liffey was a frontier I didn't like crossing. Anyway, the job was at least on a bus route, and I decided there was no way out of it. As jobs go, it turned out to be an easy one. I'd been given a nipper to help with the preparation work, and a real bonus was that the woman of the house was at home all day and was quick to make a brew of tea for us without even asking.

It was my third morning on the job, and I'd got off the bus at the usual stop and was waiting on the pavement for a break in the traffic when I saw Teresa come out of a house across the road. It had a small front garden surrounded by black railings. The lid had come off a dustbin and some of the contents were lying on the grass, which gave the house a neglected look. She came down the path only so far then stopped and looked back at the still open hall door, as if waiting for someone. I didn't want her to see me, and I moved behind a phone kiosk and watched her through its cracked glass. Then a man came out, pulled the door behind him and they came arm in arm across the road in my direction. I jumped into the phone box and pretended to make a call. They passed within feet of me, talking and laughing. Until then, I hadn't paid attention to the man, but when they passed close to the kiosk, I got a shock. It was Hugo, the Northerner. They went from view, and instantly it all became clear to me. It had to have been him that I'd seen in the rear window of the taxi in Douglas. I took my time leaving the phone box. My legs felt weak, and I crossed the road towards the house where the job was, not heeding the traffic. A car horn was blown; a driver glared at me from behind a steering wheel. I was in a fluster. I couldn't believe that it was *him* who'd been with Teresa that night. I also couldn't believe that for the last few days I had been working a few doors up from where she lived. It took all my willpower to stay on the job that day and not go to the pub.

When I got home that night the Mother asked, 'Why the long face?'

'Nothing, Ma.'

'Don't give me that. There's something eating you.'

'Can't a fella have a bad day without an interrogation?'

'Is that what you call it? An *interrogation?*

'Sorry...you know I didn't mean it that way. I'm just out of sorts.'

'Aren't we all,' she said, and slapped my dinner onto the table.

Later when I'd washed and shaved, I went to the pub with the intention of drinking myself numb, but I knew after three pints that sitting on a bar stool wasn't going to help me that night. I took to the streets with my coat collar up against the cold, the hands deep in the pockets and walked and walked. The more I thought about it, the more baffled I became. Hadn't she made it clear that she'd no time for him? What had changed? It's history now, I thought. All in the past.

The next day on the way to work, I walked briskly, the head down, past the house they had come out of. We finished up that evening and were tidying after us when the boss came and checked everything, as he normally did at the end of a job. After speaking to the woman of the house he told me that there was another job around the corner to be done. 'We got it on this woman's recommendation,' he said. We would start there the following day.

'Can one of the other lads fill my place?' I asked.

'You're the one they all want, Mark. I can't send someone else there.'

'It can't be that hard to get someone to fill in for me?'

'Mark, I hate saying this in case it swells your head but there's never a comeback when it comes to your work. And it's not my fault you're popular with these housewives.' Then he added with a rare smile, 'Maybe they see something else in you?'

The idea of having to spend more days so close to Teresa and skulking past where she lived had made me determined. He must have seen this in me. 'There's something you're not telling me?' he said.

'All I want is to go to a different job, surely you can swing that?'

'All right, all right... I'll get Tommy to come over tomorrow. He can swap with you. I suppose you *won't* mind going to Rialto, instead?' He hadn't got it in him to make a convincing cutting remark.

'You're a star, boss. I won't forget this.'

'I hope not – Leonardo!'

~~~

On the following weekend I bumped into Jimmy as he was coming out of a bookies shop. I hadn't seen him since the end of the holiday and had been worried that he might still be carrying a grudge over what had happened on the boat. There was no cause for worry, for we fell into easy conversation, as it had always been between us. Despite my wanting to forget the Isle of Man, I couldn't stop myself saying that I had seen Teresa in the distance the other day. 'You'll never guess who she was with?'

'I think I can guess. Listen, Mark, the last thing I want to do is make a fool of you. She's in contact with Celine, and she tells me things, and I'm sorry, pal, but if I'd seen you around, I might have told you...'

'You only *might* have told me?'

'I didn't know how you'd take it. But it doesn't matter now that you've found out for yourself.'

'How long have you known?' I asked.

'Since shortly after we got back – you could have blown me over. Who'd have thought...?'

He had told me that he was on his way to visit his mother – we were now approaching the flats where she lived. Jimmy had grown up there and we'd first met in the local school. I knew that his mother was on her own – not a widow, mind you – and the story was that she'd put out Mr. Culmane because he was an alcoholic. I hadn't seen him around in a long time, and Jimmy never spoke about him, but I guessed a son could find out where his father was, if he really wanted to. We lingered at the gates to the flats. 'I'm sorry how this has all worked out for you, Mark,' he said. His face suddenly brightened. 'Things couldn't be better for Celine and me. We'll be shopping soon for that ring.'

'I'm really happy for you, for you both,' I said, and shook his hand.

'You can take some of the credit for it.'

'Celine and you – as the old people would say – that's a match made in heaven.'

'Anyway, I'd like you to be my groomsman. I can't give you the job of best man, because of Shay the brother. It won't happen for a while because Celine's in charge of the budget and reckons it will take us two years to save enough. So? What do you say?'

I agreed, without thinking. Anyway, it was two years away, no need to give it any great consideration. As he'd said that Celine was regularly talking to Teresa, I told him that whatever he heard about her, I didn't want to hear it.

When I got home, I said to the Mother, 'Jimmy Culmane and Celine are tying the knot.'

'She's not...you know?'

'Ma, the wedding won't be for at least another two years.'

'It's not *that*, then.'

I was glad that now she was pleased for them, for even if Celine had been pregnant, the Mother wasn't one to talk about a girl's misfortune, unlike some of the known pious gossipers on the block. Afterwards, I began to regret my readiness to be Jimmy's groomsman, for, since accepting the role, I had realized the high probability that Celine would ask Teresa to be a bridesmaid. I tried to console myself by remembering it was two years off. Lots can happen in the meantime, I thought. Little did I know then how much *would* happen.

CHAPTER EIGHT

The letter was on the mantelpiece when I came in one day from work, its US Mail stamps adding an exotic touch to the lightweight airmail envelope. 'Well, who's it from?'

'Ma, will you give me a chance to open it.' Once opened and flattened out, I saw it was from the Yank. 'It's from Paul Sweeney', I said.

'I know that much! The sender's name is on the back. But who's *he*, what's it about?'

'He's a fellow we met in the Isle of Man. From Dublin originally but lives in the States.'

'And what's he got to say?'

'I've only opened it, Ma – give me a chance.' I read the letter then had to reread the important part.

I want you to come to New York for our wedding. It's in November, which gives you nearly three months to save. There's plenty of beds here so no need to worry about hotels or anything. Just organize your ticket and get yourself across here.'

'He wants me to go to New York in November for his wedding,' I told her. As I spoke, I was thinking that there must be a virus about, as everybody seemed to be getting married.

'He must think a lot of you,' she said.

'What do you mean?'

'He's invited you to his wedding, hasn't he? You don't do that for just anyone.'

'I guess not,' I replied, wondering if I'd have enough cash for such a trip. What I'd splashed out on that holiday present for Teresa would have come in handy now, I thought. And, she never even offered to return the watch, although, in all honesty, I probably wouldn't have taken it.

'I never had the chance to go to America myself,' the Mother said. 'I would have loved to go there when I was younger but your Da was a home bird. Did you know we have a cousin of some description in Saint Louis? He's not an O'Bride, but from our side – the Kennys. He could be a rich relation.'

'That doesn't mean he'd share it, Ma.'

'You're probably right. So, are you going to accept the invitation?'

'I don't know, it's come as a surprise. I'll need a passport. Is there a visa involved too?'

'I'll go to Molesworth Street and get the passport form for you,' she said. 'The visa, I haven't a notion about one of those things, but we'll find out.'

I told her that I wasn't sure about having the funds for such a trip, however she waved that notion away. 'You just go to that boss of yours and tell him you'll want the time off in – when is it? – November. Also tell him that you'll work all the hours that God sends you.' Surprisingly, she then added, 'And if you're a bit short, I'll help out.'

I normally wouldn't have touched her money; nevertheless, this time, keeping my options open, I said nothing and went to the privacy of my bedroom and read the letter again. In my mind, I could see myself walking along streets that I'd been reared on in the cinemas – Broadway, Times Square, Fifth Avenue. Also, Madison Square Garden, the Empire State Building, the images went on. Later, I put the letter back on the mantlepiece and settled down to watch the soccer on the television, however, every so often I looked at the exotic envelope, just to be sure I wasn't dreaming. The Mother got me an acceptance card in Eason's, and then later got the stamp and posted it. Now, it was up to me – I would have to work hard for the airfare. I cut down on the drink, rose early, and put in the long hours. Often, I came in late, sat down to a re-heated dinner, had a wash and a shave, spent a short time in front of the television, and then fell into bed.

I opened an account at the post office and was given a book to show my lodgements. There was steady but arduous growth on what I called the 'New York account', for one thing about been a painter and decorator is that the only way you get results is by doing the job. There are no short cuts, no simply clocking-in and finding a corner to nod off while at the same time still expecting to get wages for it. You had to produce results. But it was taking a lot out of me; I was working more hours than ever; social life was swapped for essential sleep. In the end all the effort, and not forgetting the sacrifice! was worthwhile and by the time of the trip I'd saved more than enough and didn't need the Mother's money.

She said that I should go in style, so I took a taxi to Collinstown Airport, my case in the boot and my dollars for spending money in the neat plastic wallet they had given me at the bank where I'd changed my money. The teller had been a country chap and we'd chatted about my upcoming trip. He said he was envious, then wished me a great holiday which he wasn't paid to do. I'd walked away feeling privileged. This would be my first flight, for I wasn't one of those who'd already been to the Spanish Costas or taken a sudden flight to a relation's funeral in England. I had a few pints on me by the time a hostess pointed out my seat to me, and I was pleasantly surprised when she later came back asked me what I would like from the bar. The woman beside me seemed slightly deaf, so I gave up trying to talk to her and settled into watching the floating clouds below us. They gave me a tray of food, which I cleared, not that I was hungry, more that it was part of the ticket. I had thought that I would be too excited to sleep; however, somewhere mid-Atlantic, the effects of the drink, the food, and the steady noise of the engines suddenly made me tired. I slept, woke up and found that nothing had changed; beyond the silver wings, the sky was a sharp blue; clouds still blanketed whatever lay beneath us. I allowed my eyelids to fall again, and the next thing I knew the cabin hostesses were running up and down the aisle, busily preparing for the landing. My neighbour welcomed me back with a sweet smile, then she looked out the porthole and stabbed a finger downward. I leaned across her and looked – below me was America.

My mistaken impression had been that everyone on duty at Immigration would be of Irish descent and that a handshake of brotherly hospitality would be waiting for me. Instead, an instruction to queue was barked at me and I had to wait in line; it reminded me of the Labour Exchange back home, which, thankfully, I've had seldom need of. When I got to the desk, an impassive official scrutinised my new passport and then banged a stamp onto its virgin pages and, even when he said, 'Welcome to the United States', he still didn't smile. I didn't care, I was in America.

The airport was full of comings and goings, making it hard to spot anyone. Paul had written that he would meet me, and all I could do was stand at a central spot near the doors and wait. Travellers were met by family or friends and taken out to a waiting car only to be promptly replaced by more passengers who had spilled through from the baggage claim area, equally keen to be on their way. I was lost in people-watching, particularly a black porter with a back-support, who carried the cases of travellers and all the time he worked he also managed to hold a conspicuous bunch of dollar bills – folded on the length – in his hand, and it was obvious to me that he was the king of this busy little kingdom.

I felt a tap on the shoulder. 'Great to see you, buddy!' Paul said. He vigorously shook my hand, and we made small talk, then I followed him out to a car at the kerb. It was long, full of chrome, some of it not so sparkling, had pointed rear wings – rusting at the edges – and the engine had been left running. He sprung open the trunk and my borrowed suitcase was lost in it. The car had an automatic shift, and the only gearbox like it that I had seen before was in a funeral limousine. We pulled away and I sprawled out in the passenger seat and not wanting to distract him from the driving, I decided to keep everything I wanted to say until later. Meanwhile, I marvelled at how he managed his way through the horn-blaring, sharp-braking traffic, reminiscent of the dodgem cars on Bray promenade, except that no one collided. We were on the highway, when he said, 'I don't know how to break this to you, Mark, but the wedding's off.'

CHAPTER NINE

When he thought that I'd recovered from the shock, he said, 'Sorry, but there wasn't time to stop you coming.'

It was funny in a way, but at that moment all I could think of was the wedding present, a white linen tablecloth that the Mother had got in Clery's department store and that was now in my luggage in the trunk of the car. She loved shopping and had gone downtown to trawl the department stores. That was the first outing and she had returned brimming with information on value for money presents. Over dinner she rhymed off the options, and I paid attention, for a while that is, then I left the decision with her which I knew she had really wanted me to do.

'What happened, Paul? Or can I ask?'

'After coming all this way, you've a right to ask. But can we leave it till later? Let's go for a drink – I need an escape.'

'You're the driver,' I said.

After a while, we crossed a toll bridge, the Manhattan skyline now visible in the distance. Because I had seen it many times in films and photographs it felt like a friend that I'd known all my life. The skyline stayed with us until we moved into suburban neighbourhoods, then it dropped from our sight. We pulled up outside a single storey building and I noticed that its brickwork had recently been painted over in a cabbage green colour more suited to an institution than to a bar. I found it dark inside; it was inadequately lit by neon signs behind the bar and by nicotine-stained lamps on the ceiling above it and, off to one side, there was an island of light at a pool table, where two players had taken refuge from the world outside. The bar had a long counter and advertisements for Budweiser were etched into mirrors along the walls, and the Irish tricolour hung alongside the Stars and Stripes and a NYPD pennant. The man behind the bar took his time getting to us.   'Well, what's it to be, Paul? he asked. 'In for the last one before she ties you down?'

'Shut your ugly face, Mike, and just serve the customer,' he said.

'Is that what you're called now, the "customer"? Having to listen to your lip, I'd call you a liability.'

'Forever the charmer – that hospitality course you went on was wasted.'

'You're forgetting I own the place.'

'That's worse. You'll go bust if no one crosses your door, and you'd rightly deserve it.'

'And who's the friend?' the bar owner said, as if he were vetting me for admittance to his circle.

'This is Mark. Now, enough of this familiarity with the customers – set up the shots!'

Mike shook my hand and smiled, showing some gold teeth. 'This poor man's upset because he knows these are his last hours of freedom,' he said.

I smiled back showing agreement yet felt like a cheat because of what I now knew. It was worse when he added, 'First ones are on the house, buddy, see it as a wedding present.'

Paul picked up the whisky and lowered it. When the bar owner moved down the counter, I whispered, 'Guess you haven't told everyone your news?'

'They'll know soon enough, then there won't be any sanctuary for me anywhere.'

'Not in this bar anyway unless you pay him for these drinks.'

'I'm not worried about Mike – he gets enough out of me.'

It was in this way that I passed the next three or four hours in the United States of America, on a bar stool, with a background of sentimental come-all-ye music from back home, in the company of

New York Irish, listening – whenever the bar owner moved away – to Paul Sweeney's story.

'As the day got closer, I was becoming more uneasy,' he said. 'I couldn't blame it on any one thing in particular; it was just a feeling. Mind you, I was still going to do it... I was still ready to go ahead with the wedding. Maria and I have known each other a long time, and I wouldn't want to hurt her. But I hadn't slept for a couple of nights; the nerves were really at me. I suppose it was building up from the start of making the arrangements. You know, Mark, that I owe everything to the dead marine buddies who saved my life?'

'Yes, I remember'.

'I've kept contact with their families, and I wanted to invite just some of them to the wedding. One of the wives I write to her; then there's the parents of another buddy and I've been Upstate to visit them a few times and they're fine people and they love to see me coming; then there's another widow who's got three children, the oldest going to college soon. But later we were told that we'd too many guests for the size of the banqueting room, so we had to trim the invitation list. I wanted to remember my buddies, which I think is reasonable. Maria's from an Italian family and she couldn't see how any of her relations could be scratched off.'

'I never knew you were under pressure for numbers,' I said. 'You could have left *me* out...'

'Your name was on the first list sent out and when your acceptance came, there was no way I'd make you pull out. And Maria is keen to meet you – she calls you a real Irish person – so you not coming was never going to happen. Then, she was on about her cousins, and then it looked as if the axe would fall on the families of my marine buddies. I guess it all made me edgy, and it all blew up when a guest on her side cancelled and I thought that I would get the slot for one of my people; instead, she was adamant that it should still be one of her lot. Words were said, and it got out of hand, then I told her that as far as it went for me, the wedding was off. The words came from my mouth as if…as if they weren't even mine. It got worse when her mother came around and ripped into me, then my own mother sided with Maria which left me with no one to back me up. I couldn't get them to understand that I owe so much to those men...'

'They probably understand but wouldn't feel it the way you do.'

There was a pause. Pool balls collided. Big Tom was on the sound system. A woman came in carrying a large shopping bag. The bar owner uncapped a beer and placed it in front of her, without a word between them.

'You're probably right,' Paul said. 'They don't know, but if I say it's important, then it *is* important.'

'Where does it stand now?'

He signalled for more shots. 'I couldn't have had Maria or anyone else dictating to me over this. Anything else, I could lie to myself over. But over Vietnam, never.'

'That sounds definite,' I said.

We were silent for a while, then he asked, 'Will you do something for me?'

'Sure, if I'm able.'

'When we get to the house, will you back me up? You don't have to say anything, just be a friend, be on my side.'

We finished at the bar, and I grabbed my luggage from the car which he'd abandoned for the night, and we took a cab.

It was a residential street, with small, detached houses with timber siding and the one we were now standing outside looked as though every light inside had been switched on. As we climbed the steps to the front door there were voices from within. Paul stopped and said that we should go in the side door instead. We went down a narrow pathway at the side of the house and a rottweiler in the garden next door growled until Paul snapped 'Shut up!' A side door led us to a small kitchen, and if Paul had expected to enter unnoticed, he was mistaken, for at least a half a dozen people were sitting around a table drinking tea and looking as if they were there for a wake. He hesitated and I stood beside him for moral backup, suitcase in hand. All eyes were on us; Paul switched weight from one leg to another. 'This is Mark,' he said, lowly.

My arrival was acknowledged by a nod here or a gesture of the hand there and although no one spoke up to welcome me no one looked hostile.

'Will you have a cuppa?' Paul asked me.

At that, a man motioned for me to sit at the table. Chairs were shuffled and a space made for me. I muttered a word of thanks and Paul poured tea for both of us. He then went to a giant refrigerator that overpowered the kitchen and drew out a plate of cold ham and made us sandwiches. I ate silently, while he leaned against the counter, studying the others over the brim of his mug. Suddenly, a thickset fellow in a three-quarters length leather coat came into the kitchen from the next room and said something foreign into Paul's face; I took it to be in Italian, for he had the same olive skin as the family that ran the neighbourhood chip shop back home. He had the look of a drunk after closing time who was hungry for a fight. I took it that Paul didn't understand him, however the fellow's anger didn't need translation. He stepped back and made a cut-throat sign. Paul turned his back on him and stared out the window, but I could see that there was nothing for him to look at, except his own reflection in the unlit kitchen-window of the house next door.

Speaking the same language, another man who had the air of an elder, placed a counselling hand on the leather-coated shoulder of the fellow and guided him from the room. I could hear an urgent discussion beyond the door. When the older man returned, he looked at me and must have felt that I needed to understand the situation from their point of view. 'He is a cousin, and he and his mother have travelled all the way from Montecasino for the wedding. But that's not the problem. The tragedy is what your friend has done to Maria, my beautiful niece.' His grey eyes moved from me to the floor and back, like a doll with moving eyelids does when it's tipped. I remembered that Paul had asked me to be loyal to him, so I didn't reply. Although, I sensed that this family saw that his decision to call off the wedding not only as a big disappointment, but also as a major insult. And I could see that they had closed ears. They wouldn't want to know that the root of the problem had been an incident in a jungle in Indochina.

Then I noticed that people were straining to hear what was going on in the next room. I could tell by their faces that someone important had arrived.

'Poor Maria, she is a favourite of mine,' the elder said.

I then understood that the abandoned bride-to-be had entered the house. Paul seemed set to dart for the side door. Then an older woman appeared in the other doorway and came in and stood in the centre of the floor. The people at the table acknowledged her with a nod of the head and a respectful, 'Signora'. She looked straight at Paul and said, 'Son, you've one last chance to save this... I've pleaded with Maria to come here so that you two can talk. She has her pride and coming here wasn't easy.'

'Mother, I don't like being ambushed like this. I know you mean –'

She silenced him with a raised palm, like a policeman would stop traffic, and called back into the other room, 'Maria, do come in.'

Paul reminded me of a fly struggling in a spider's web.

CHAPTER TEN

For me, Maria was a surprise and I wondered how she had ever been attracted to the Yank in the first place. She was small and her face was a perfect shape, rather like a doll's, except for bushy eyebrows. Her skin was pale and flawless, without any trace of Italian colouring, and her dark eyes drew you in as if they were magnetic. She moved like a strong, silent river and, if she were upset, she was doing a good job of keeping it to herself. At that moment, the people around me began to leave the room. As the elder was going out, he gave Maria a gentle pat on the back of the hand, like a priest offering sympathy at a funeral. She smiled sweetly. I was about to follow them when Paul reached across to stop me. His mother pointed to the table, and we all sat down, Paul Sweeney and Maria at opposite ends.

He showed defiance. 'What's all this? a counsel of war?'

His mother gave him a look that would wither a nettle, and he hunched his shoulders and turned his body halfway in his chair, so that he was now looking in the direction of the giant refrigerator. I gave a slight cough and with a casual wave of the arm he introduced me. 'I guessed who you were,' his mother said. 'You're welcome here, and your bed is made up and all's ready for you.'

'You shouldn't have gone to trouble on my behalf, Mrs. Sweeney,' I said.

At that moment, Maria spoke. She had a New York accent, without a trace of Italian influence. 'Paul has told us a lot about you. I'm glad that you could come...'

Then she stopped, as if she'd just remembered the reason why we were all gathered at the table.

Before any more was spoken, I told them that I shouldn't be there and that it was awkward for me. However, Paul declared that he wanted me to stay as his witness.

His mother looked puzzled. 'What do you want a witness for? This isn't the Supreme Court!'

'Just saying, I need him here, that's all.'

'What you need is someone to fix the hole in that head of yours.'

'Here we go again.'.

'Don't you be cheeky. If your father were alive, even at your age, he'd take a strap to you for speaking like that.'

I had heard the same type of remark from my own mother at home, the threat of a ghost returning. Something that the Yank and I had in common.

'Sorry, but I don't want to go over it all again.'

'Well, if Maria is prepared to sit down and talk this through, why can't *you*, son?'

'I've made a decision. Let's leave it at that.'

His mother turned to me and asked what I thought of the situation. She'd caught me by surprise, and I felt like a fraudster. I stalled, and all that came out of my mouth was, 'I wouldn't know...'

I was thrown when Maria came to my rescue. 'It's not fair to put Mark on the spot like this – he has to stand up for Paul, that's what friends are for.'

She was looking at me, full in the face, and those dark eyes of hers were deep and calm. I couldn't stay quiet. 'Paul is troubled, that's all I can say, otherwise it's not my place...'

'And what about poor Maria, and all the good people that are expecting a wedding tomorrow? the mother said. She shuddered, dabbed a handkerchief at wet eyes, and Maria placed a hand on her arm to comfort her.

'I'm not explaining myself very well to you,' I said, 'but for him it's deep. You know? Real deep.'

'I know he's troubled,' Maria said. 'He has to be, or he wouldn't be doing this – he's not like that.'

Paul had heard enough and jumped on her remark. 'I don't need you to be saying what I'm like!'

I told him that she hadn't meant anything by it, and he turned on me.

'Who asked you, pal?' he snarled.

'Right, the mouth is shut from now on!' I said.

Silence descended on the kitchen. Paul crossed and uncrossed the legs. There were gentle tears from his mother. Maria tied and untied her fingers, like she was doing a knitting motion I had seen the Mother do when she was making baby cardigans for the family. I moved to the counter and topped up my mug from the teapot.

'Can we call a halt to this fiasco?' Paul said. 'Mark and I are heading out.'

Maria said that she wanted to say her piece before we left, and he told her that there was nothing left to be said. Then his mother pleaded with him to give her the decency of a hearing, and he backed off.

'I have come here with an open heart and without pride,' Maria said, now looking at Paul who was staring at the floor. 'It's embarrassing, it's hurtful, it makes me look like I'm begging you to marry me. But I don't mind because I remember the day you proposed. I was so happy and accepted with all my will, and I am sure that you also asked me with all *your* will.' (I was surprised at the wooden way she was talking; it was as if she were converting her thoughts from another language.) 'That's what we both wanted. I don't really understand what's happened, but I know that my will is still the same. If yours has changed, then that's sad. But I'm still happy that you asked me to be your wife and I was, and still am, privileged to be your fiancée.' At that, she stopped, as if her train of thought had suddenly been derailed by the moment. She was losing her composure and I felt sorry for her. Mrs. Sweeney placed a hand over hers in support. Paul was shaking his head. I was trying to imagine what he was thinking. To me – someone without any interest or success in this department – it seemed so obvious and easy. However, it wasn't my place to speak. Then the most amazing part of the evening happened when Maria said:

'Paul, I'll make it easy for you. Maybe, at the bottom of it all, you're really feeling that you're not ready for a lifetime of commitment. In front of your mother, I'll swear...I'll sign any paper you might put in front of me that in two years I will agree for us to part, if that's your wish.'

'Jesus, Mary and Joseph!' Mrs. Sweeney cried.

'It's easy to say such a thing,' he said, 'but doing it is a different matter.'

'I told you that I'll sign whatever you want,' Maria said. 'No one will know except us here at this table and God in Heaven.' At that, she blessed herself. 'And if it works out, all will be forgiven.'

'And if it doesn't?'

'It will.'

'How can you be so confident if we couldn't even agree on a simple thing like the wedding invitations?'

'We will agree. Whoever you want; whatever you want; we'll somehow manage.'

'It's too late...it's on top of us, and you couldn't invite the people I have in mind at the last moment. It could insult them, and they're too important for me to risk that.'

'I see that now, and I'm sorry I didn't...'

'Anyway, I see holes in your offer,' he said.

'It isn't meant to be perfect. Tell me please, what holes do you see?'

'What if there's a child?'

She paused a long time before answering. I looked over at Mrs. Sweeney who was hanging on her every word. This 'discussion' was now in territory beyond me, and I stood up to leave. Paul looked at me as if I were a deserter, and I remembered my promise to him and reluctantly resumed my place.

'A mother shouldn't be asked to give up a child,' Maria said. 'You'd have no responsibilities....'

'No! I've already made my decision. There'll be no wedding, and certainly no child!' At that, he turned his back on her and began to hum some piece of nonsensical melody.

'If that's what you want, Paul, that's what you want. There'll be no wedding then but you're too late to say there'll be no child.'

'God forgive us!' Mrs. Sweeney uttered.

Paul didn't even look up but continued with his humming. His mother reached across and thumped him on the shoulder. 'Are you deaf, as well as stupid?' she shouted. 'Didn't you hear what the girl just said?'

'Words are cheap. We always used protection.'

'Protection is only good if it works,' Maria said.

'Poor child, and you've been to the doctor?' Mrs. Sweeney asked.

'Yes… and the hospital, too'

'Glory to God, I'm going to be a grandmother again!'

Paul stopped humming and fixed a look on each of us in turn. When he came to me, he said, 'Well buddy, what do you make of this clever ambush? this trap?'

I looked at Maria; she appeared the same as the moment when she'd come into the kitchen; yet now it was different – now I knew that she was pregnant. Or, at least, she was saying she was, and I had no reason to disbelieve her. 'I wouldn't have a clue,' I said.

'I think she has you under her spell,' he said. 'She's like that.'

'*She* has a name – Maria,' his mother chided. 'We didn't raise you to act this way.'

'Listen, please, I think it's time for me to leave,' Maria said. 'I've laid bare my heart, told you a secret I've told no one else – what more can I do? Paul, we can be happy, gloriously happy but it's up to you, now.'

She stood up to leave the table and I felt guilty about studying her for a sign of a bump. She was still trim and petite.

'If you leave now, child, the wedding is dead,' Mrs. Sweeney said. 'Can't you wait? I'm sure Paul needs time to take all this in.'

He spun round to his mother. 'You make me out to be an idiot.'

'If you don't marry Maria, then you *will* be an idiot!'

'I'm going outside for some air,' he said. ' Mark, are you coming?'

I followed him and we stood smoking on the street. It was a crisp night, and the sky was cloudless, with bright stars watching us. He kept transferring his weight from one leg to the other, causing his upper body to sway.

'What do you think, buddy?' he asked.

'I've said it already, you'll have to leave me out of this one.'

'Don't be like that, Mark. Help me out here.'

He didn't realize it, but all the while I *was* trying to think of something useful to say. Finally, I blurted out:

'It seems to me that you've nothing to lose, and she's even given you a way out. You'll never know unless you give it a try.'

A car with a broken muffler came into the street and was driven slowly. For a few seconds, its headlights shone on Paul's face, and I saw how pained he was. A wind rustled the leaves in the nearby trees, and in the brightly lit house behind us, Maria and all those other people were waiting to find out if there was going to be a wedding. Suddenly, he stamped out his cigarette and placed an arm about my shoulder. I sensed a decision had been made.

'Buddy, let's go back in and get this over with!'

CHAPTER ELEVEN

T he good suit was full of creases and Mrs. Sweeney came to my rescue with an iron. All along I had assumed that the wedding would take place in a Catholic church, and I was surprised when we went to a registry office – it turned out that Maria had once been in a short-lived teenage marriage, still, she wore a white wedding dress, and no one would have guessed it was her second time. As for Paul, he wore a navy-blue suit to which he had added his medals. Photographs were taken by a professional on the steps of the registry office, going in and coming out. There was a prominent notice which would have peeved many: No Confetti! Only small groups were allowed in the civic building, and it was explained to me that we would see the main body of guests when we went to the banquet.

It was held in the local Veterans' Club and, before we went in, we posed for a large group photograph in the car park. Inside, the walls of the modest banqueting room were adorned with regimental flags, old uniforms, and photographs of veteran reunions. There was a bar at one end of the room, where already men were waiting two-deep for service. If I hadn't known about it, I'd never have guessed that the wedding had almost not happened, that it had been saved by a last-minute agreement. There were many speeches, including one from the older man from the night before, the one who had calmed the bloodthirsty cousin from Monte Cassino. The best man had called on the older man and introduced him as Uncle Thiago.

Probably because of overlong speeches and a release from the stress of the wedding arrangements, Paul drank more than he could deal with, which became obvious when the time came for the newly-weds to step out for the traditional first dance; he was leaning against Maria, and she showed that she was stronger than she looked by supporting his weight as they rotated in a tight circle in the middle of the dance floor. He survived the dance and when some people clapped, he made an exaggerated bow with a stupid look on his face and stumbled to a corner to join some American friends, while I sat back and just took everything in. Shortly afterwards, I was joined by the Uncle Thiago. 'I must thank you for the part you played last night,' he said (he had a heavy Italian accent).

'I did nothing.' As I spoke, I was I admiring the elegance of his suit and how it sat comfortably on his slight frame, the jewellery on his hands, the watch and cuff links – a natty dresser, but matched to his age, which was most revealed by the lines on his face, like those on the outside of the walnuts we'd cracked as boys at Halloween, only deeper.

'I think you did a lot. Just being there seemed to calm Paul down and it allowed this wonderful day to happen.'

'Honestly, I did nothing...'

'You're too modest... What is your name again?

'Mark.'

'Ah! I will call you Marco. I am the father figure in this family, a responsibility placed on me when my kid brother decided to run off with a younger piece of skirt and leave Maria's mother, my dear sister-in-law. But now that Maria is wedded, the weight on my shoulders is eased, thanks to you. Today we started to regain family pride.'

'Pride in family is important,' I said.

'For us, it is everything. Marco, I won't waste time. I like you; I like the Irish. You are the same as us.' He took my hand and placed it against his chest. 'We feel it in the heart'.

Almost competitively, I put my drink down and lifted his other hand and put it against my chest. 'Feel a true Dublin heart.'

'Marco, we are so equal...no, that's the wrong word...similar, that's it, similar. I am in debt to you, and I *must* repay you.'

'You can buy me a drink,' I joked.

'No, Marco, I am being serious. Tell me, how do you earn your living in Ireland?'

'I'm a painter and decorator.'

He stood back and looked me up and down.

'I am going to offer you a job in one of my companies. I will be your sponsor and get you a work permit and a union card.'

'I have a perfectly good job in Dublin.'

'You are not taking me seriously,' he said. 'I am offering to establish you, here, in the United States of America. There are young men I know back in my hometown who'd kill their grandmothers for a chance like this. My boy, let me tell you this. Let me tell you that I arrived here with nothing and look at me now. I have more money than I will ever be able to spend in the remaining years that the Blessed Saviour will favour me with, and, let me tell you this, too, that this *is* the land of opportunity. You will discover that for yourself when you come.'

I wasn't sure if he was being serious or if it was the drink talking, so I remained silent and, every so often, nodded politely. He wasn't one to give up easily. 'Irish, I *am* going to sponsor you. I will make sure that you are staying in a friendly home. My cousin Rosa's house will be perfect – her cooking, magnificent! Will you let me do this one thing for you? You will make an old man happy twice in the one day.'

'Let me buy you a drink, instead,' I offered. 'That should make you happy the second time.'

'I will take the drink, Marco, but I know that you are still not being serious. What is it? A wife, a sweetheart? She would come with you, of course.'

'No, there's nothing like that.'

'Then, maybe, family ties? How many in your family back in Dublin?'

'We're four, but I'm the only one at home with the Mother. Now, name your poison.'

'Champagne, I brought a case along and it's behind the bar.'

'That's no good. Then I won't be standing you a drink.'

'It's what I would like you to get me, Marco. Don't be offended.'

At the bar I bought a pint of a beer that was so cold I couldn't get its taste and also asked for a glass of Uncle Thiago's 'free' champagne, then I dropped a dollar on a plate for tips that couldn't be missed and went back to the table. I found Maria sitting beside her uncle.

I congratulated her, and she thanked me, offering her cheek. I leaned over and brushed my lips against her smooth skin. Unlike her new husband, she was sober.

Uncle Thiago declared, 'Soon Marco will be working here in New York.'

'Your uncle doesn't take no for an answer,' I said.

'He normally gets his way – be warned.'

Then, just to make conversation, I asked her, 'Do you newlyweds have a honeymoon planned?'

'We're staying put for a day or two. Tomorrow, Paul wants to take you downtown and show you Manhattan. We'll then head off to call on all the people that he wanted here today. The families of the marines who protected him.'

I nodded to show that I knew the story. Looking across to where he was, I wondered what state he would be in come morning. She followed my eyes and seemed to know my thoughts. 'He'll be fine. It's not every day you get married,' she said.

Uncle Thiago sipped his champagne and looked towards the band. 'I should have a dance with my beautiful niece on her wedding day.'

I watched them go to the dance floor; he looked slightly shaky on the legs; however, when he started to move, he became like one of the stylish dancers I'd seen in the ballroom in Douglas – it was easy to imagine a younger version of him raising a high colour on the cheeks of excited partners. I crossed to where Paul was sitting. He slurred his words as he introduced me to his friends, whose names went immediately from my head. It was one of those moments when everyone knows it's a wasted exercise and nobody really cares.

'You're a lucky man, Paul,' I said, looking back at Maria as she danced with her uncle.

'You're having…good time, buddy?' he said, as if he hadn't even noticed what I had said.

'Don't you worry, Paul, everything is good. I've even had an offer to work here, so that can't be too bad.'

'You're sure…a good time?' he said. There was no point in expecting sense from him, not on his wedding day. There was a pause, a breakdown between his brain and tongue, and we stayed quiet and smiled at any guest that happened to pass and smile at us.

I saw Uncle Thiago escort Maria back to a different table; this one was occupied solely by women, like a knitting circle. The mother of the bride looked as if she were presiding, the table being her little kingdom for the day, and I watched as she ordered someone off a chair so that the bride could take a seat. Uncle Thiago didn't delay, for I later spotted him in a corner, holding court with a group of young women and every so often shrieks of laughter came from them, which didn't seem to go down well with Maria's mother who sent disapproving looks across the banquet room at each outburst of high spirits. Later, I said to him, 'You seemed to be having a good time with the young ladies.'

'Marco, my boy, I make them laugh, they make *me* laugh. What else can an old widower do? But I am missing my dead wife, the other half of me, especially on an important day like this.'

I was sorry I spoke. This was too dismal for me.

The night ended abruptly (compared to an Irish wedding), for the band stopped playing, staff began to clear the tables, and the shutter was pulled down on the bar. It was as if they were trade union members who had agreed to work to a rigid schedule and no more; guests were now nothing but dandruff that had to be cleared from the premises. The Yank and his pals made clumsy appeals for more beer, but staff buzzed past them as if they didn't exist. It was time for the women to intervene. Maria and her mother supported Paul and brought him outside to a waiting taxi; his friends were left behind, stranded like dumb castaways.

Mrs.Sweeney appeared at my elbow. 'It's said that you don't lose a son but gain a daughter. But I think I've gained Maria's mother, as well.'

Her words didn't sound like self-pity, they came across more as respect for a future ally.

The head hurt; I didn't know where I was. Someone had banged at the door, and I could hear voices somewhere below me. The room was small, airless, just the single bed that I was lying on and above my head there was a narrow window covered by a Venetian blind which let in just enough daylight between its slats to show my suit slung across a chair to the side of the door. I eased myself up onto my elbows and looked round. The borrowed suitcase on the floor reminded me of where I was. That must be Paul and Mrs. Sweeney talking downstairs. How on earth did he manage to get up so early?

An hour later, we were driving towards the skyscrapers of Manhattan. He parked on a scruffy street outside a metal fabrication shop in Harlem, the walls of which were covered in graffiti – he said he knew the owner and went inside to talk to him. We left the car and walked for a block and rounded a corner and stood at a bus stop where we were the only white people in the queue. Traffic was heavy on Fifth Avenue and the bus driver kept changing lanes, looking for a clear run, but we were going nowhere in a hurry. The bus kept stopping for long intervals, and during one such stop I watched a smartly dressed elderly couple come out of an apartment building and stand under a canopy while a uniformed concierge was trying to hail a yellow cab for them. Paul was drumming the back of the seat in front of us with impatience. 'This will take too long,' he said. 'I'll show you Central Park first.' We abandoned the bus. It was cold and we walked briskly in the Park – a quick taste – then we came out and I made a promise to myself to come back some time to do it justice. Back on Fifth Avenue, we came to the Plaza Hotel and Paul pointed out Tiffany's across the square. The Mother had loved the film *Breakfast at Tiffany's* and was known to sing the theme song 'Moon River' if called on at a party. We ducked down a side street and entered the first bar which we were to visit that day, the 'first of the stations', as he called it. Later, we hit many bars, and in between them I saw the Madison Square Garden arena where in a recent fight Muhammad Ali had beaten Oscar Bonavena. It took two elevator rides to get us to the top of the Empire State Building, where steel grilles had been erected to prevent suicide attempts by jumping. Obviously, all is not perfect in the land of opportunity, I thought. We went to the construction site of the World Trade Centre, where Paul knew a Mayo carpenter who handed us hard hats and smuggled us into a building that was still heading skywards. 'This will be the marginally tallest of two towers,' he said, in a low-key way, like we were being shown a terraced house in a new housing estate. Later, we met him off the site for a liquid lunch and I nearly fell off the bar stool when he laid his payslip on the counter. How could a tradesman ever be worth that type of money? We parted from the fast-becoming-rich carpenter and ambled down Wall Street and finally arrived at the ferry terminal. I mentally saluted the Statue of Liberty as we sailed close to it, for it somehow summed up for me everything I had known of New York. We didn't disembark and, on the return trip, I took time to fix in my mind the view of Lower Manhattan as the boat rode small nasty waves on the way back to the pier. Ashore, we went to another bar, and it was here that I told him more about the Uncle Thiago's offer.

'So, what's it to be? will you come?'

'If you'd asked me last night, I would have said that I wasn't interested but after today, seeing the city and all, a part of me wants to come yet another part doesn't.'

We were comfortable in the bar where we were, and Paul had already telephoned his friend in Harlem to take the car off the street for the night. It was dark when we came out and we took an uptown subway train. We went to the theatre district and, as it was coming up to show time, theatregoers were drifting out of the bars and restaurants, heading for their seats. Last minute arrivals jumped out of yellow cabs or private limousines and dashed in under the sparkling entrance canopies. He knew another watering hole not far away. 'It'll be getting quiet now and will be like this until the shows are over, then you won't want to be here.'

And in this way, I ended my Manhattan pilgrimage, footsore, yet impressed. Paul rang Maria from the bar, and she came by to pick us up. He gave her a sloppy kiss and made a mock introduction. 'Mark, this is Mrs. Sweeney!'

'Hello, Mrs. Sweeney'.

'It's looks like you guys had a good time?'

'He's a good guide,' I said. 'Knows everywhere and everybody...'

The trip was over, Paul was taking me to the airport. On the final stretch of road, I said, 'Do you remember the day we left the Isle of Man, when I accused you of spending the night with the girl I was with?'

'Yep, the good looking blonde...what was her name again?'

'Teresa. And do you remember Hugo, the mad character from the North of Ireland? You'd have seen him hanging around us at the Palace.'

'You're not telling me it was *him*? How did you find out?'

'That's another story,' I said, keeping it to myself that I'd hid in a telephone box.

We approached the drop-off point. 'When I met you guys, I thought yourself and that Teresa chick were the real deal,' he said.

'What do you mean?'

'Like you were heading for old age together...made for each other.'

'It was never like that. She was there for the holiday – definitely just for the holiday.'

He parked at the sidewalk and with one eye on a traffic cop, came with me as far as the revolving door to the departures area. 'Maybe you'll take up Uncle Thiago's offer, and I'll see you again real soon?' he said.

On the flight home I thought about my visit to New York. I couldn't believe that at one time Paul had seen a long-term match between Teresa and me. Who'd have imagined that? I for one certainly hadn't. The flight was through the night, and my fellow-passengers were now asleep under green blankets. I'll be in Dublin in the morning, I thought. I could see the Mother over the frying pan and could almost smell the fried breakfast.

There was a big decision to be made.

CHAPTER TWELVE

The Mother quizzed me. 'Did they like the Irish linen table-cloth?'
'Of course, they liked it, Mother. Why wouldn't they?'

'Something Irish always goes down well over there. Tell me all about it, Mark. Sit down and give me all the details.'

'Ma, I'm on my way out. Can't we do this another time?'

'Where are you going? Sure, you're only in.'

'Nowhere in particular, just out for a pint.'

'The pint can wait, sit down there and tell me all.'

Surprised by her interest, I gave her a version of the wedding, leaving out that it had almost not occurred; also, there was no point in mentioning that the vows were exchanged in a registry office – there was no benefit to be had there, either. Just when I thought that I was finished, she asked, 'And what did the bride wear?'

'It was different.'

'How different?'

'Well...short, just below the knee, you know, not to the ground.'

'White?'

'White as snow,' I said, relieved that I could be truthful on that matter.

'Was she pretty?'

'Yes.'

'Are there photos?'

'I haven't any…maybe they might send some.' As I was speaking, I was wondering whether I should mention the Uncle Thiago's offer.

No, this wasn't the time for it. Besides, I hadn't given it sufficient thought, which in a way surprised me.

'And tell me, Mark, did you like New York?'

'It was okay.'

'Just, okay?'

'Well, it's more than okay, it's everything you've ever heard about it.'

'Just as I imagined it,' the Mother said. She wore a dreamy look which I hadn't seen on her before.

She was satisfied now, and I left and descended the steps to the street. I pulled my collar up against a cold wind and bent my body in the direction of a pub, any one of them, whichever one took my fancy. There was a certain strength to be had, back on your own turf.

The next day it was work as usual and as I prised open the lid on a new tin of paint, I thought of the New York job and knew I would turn it down. He'd given me his address and I would write and tell him. I would write in a way that might keep the door open for a change of mind. Why I had no real interest in going was a mystery to me. Of course, there was Ma to consider, although, because she seemed to be in love with the very notion of America, I felt sure she would see me off with a blessing. After all, as Uncle Thiago had pointed out, there were other family members to care for her. And I had been impressed by the promise of better times that went with the USA; nevertheless, in the end, I came to no conclusion as to why I didn't want to go.

My life returned to its pattern of work, time on a barstool, an occasional visit to the snooker hall, and living with the Mother. Some would say it was an unexciting life – maybe even an existence – but I can honestly say that it was a comfortable existence, and never wanted it to be anything other than what it was.

Time passed. The Mother's blood pressure started to act up and she was put on tablets. Now and again, Paul Sweeney and I exchanged letters. I wasn't surprised when he wrote that he and Maria had split-up, their daughter Marina going with her. You could easily have jumped to the conclusion that all along it had been an elaborate Italian conspiracy, but I didn't see it that way because I had been deeply moved by Maria's words spoken that night in the Sweeney's kitchen.

On another front, for a short while my pipeline of news of Teresa had been cut-off, as Jimmy had done what I'd asked of him. However, when he restarted the bulletins, I didn't object, as they now didn't seem to bother me. She was back in Dublin; no, now she was in the North again; she had returned to Dublin – she had become a mother. A daughter to her and the Northerner. I wondered if she had fair hair, like Teresa. I couldn't imagine her being a mother, nevertheless, that was the reality and, as they say, life goes on.

Months later, I was in the post again, this time it was Jimmy and Celine's wedding invitation.

'Where's this one being held?' the Mother asked. 'Timbuktu?' (Her notion of a joke.)

I let it slip by and replied, 'It's in Cabra, which is handy, but the reception is in a castle in County Kildare, miles away. I hope there's a bus laid on for us.'

'But you're the groomsman? They'll have to provide *you* with transport. You do know that you'll be at the altar, in a waistcoat and all the getup. I met Jimmy's mother the other day and the poor woman is in a tizzy over her outfit. She says that she's worn-out a pair of shoes traipsing in and out of all the clothes shops on George's Street and Camden Street, and it'll be Grafton Street next and she's dreading the price of clothes along there! She told me your friend Teresa is to be one of the maids of honour. That'll be nice for you. At least you'll be walking out of the church with someone you know.'

As it got closer to the day of the wedding, I became uneasy at the idea of processing the length of the church with Teresa on my arm. It was two years now, and I wondered had she changed. Would we have to talk to each other? What to say? The thought of it kept me awake and I'd have asked Jimmy to find a different groomsman if it hadn't been for a feeling which pushed me to meet her again. In fact, resisting was hopeless. I asked the Mother about a suitable wedding present, suggesting another tablecloth.

'Good God, no! You can't buy one of our own a tablecloth. It's okay for foreigners, but here they won't thank you for it.'

'Will *you* think of something, Ma? You know I'm just useless at that type of thing?'

~~~

A black limousine was to collect me and when I heard a car horn below on the street, I knew it was my signal to go down. The Mother did a final inspection of the hired outfit and readjusted the necktie for the third time. By the time I got down, a crowd had already gathered outside the building, shouting well wishes into Jimmy who was seated in the rear seat, looking pale and anxious. Christie, his brother, was up front with the driver, laughing unnaturally to hide his own nerves. I looked up and gave a wave to the window where I knew the Mother would be and climbed in beside Jimmy. Then the limousine glided away from the kerb, and we were in traffic and Thin Lizzy's record 'Whiskey in The Jar' was playing on the car radio as we crossed the Liffey. We cruised up the hill at Broadstone, the car engine noiseless; then we were at Phibsborough Corner and then into Cabra. A fussy photographer was outside Christ the King, and we posed in the church entrance. There was just about time for a last smoke before we went in.

We took our places at the front, on the right side of the aisle, assured by Jimmy that we were in the correct spot because he'd been told so at a rehearsal some nights before. A singer was practising somewhere up in the gallery, running through her numbers. I was nervous, never mind Jimmy. He had good reason; I was going to see Teresa. The priest came out from the sacristy and introduced himself. He wore scruffy tennis shoes and tight jeans, and spoke to us as if he had grown up among us; however, you cannot conceal a country accent. I was aware that the church was filling up behind us, yet I resisted looking backwards. Not so Jimmy. He kept turning around, checking the door for a sign of Celine's arrival. There was a stir outside, and the priest went back to the sacristy to vest up. When he reappeared, I notice that the tennis shoes had been replaced by black shoes, and his vestments hid his tight jeans. During the previous couple of minutes, the noise that people make taking their seats and the chatter that follows had steadily increased. Then there was a hush, and whispers, and I assumed that the bridal party was at the entrance.

A keyboard was playing the opening bars to 'Morning Has Broken'. The wedding singer's voice filled the church; people behind me made tentative efforts to join in. I sensed that the bridal procession was making its way up the aisle and guessed that Teresa would arrive first. I stared at a point straight ahead, not wanting to meet her look. Then, the priest was speaking to her, directing her to a seat just across from us, on the left-hand side of the altar, and I thought that like myself she had missed the rehearsal. The principal bridesmaid followed her and took her position. Without even looking at him, I could tell that Jimmy was shaking from nerves. There was then an awkward moment for the traditional handshake between him and Celine's father. I vaguely knew the man, having met him years before at their house, a small, strong-looking dockworker, with a weathered face and a swagger. Words were muttered between him and Jimmy. The couple now moved towards the altar steps, where the priest was waiting, wearing a practised smile. At that moment, Celine looked back and gave some excited nods of recognition to guests on our side of the aisle, and an image from the Isle of Man, the time that she had come into our hotel room, stole into my mind and I was glad that nothing had happened between us that morning. By thinking hard about Holy Communion – to receive or not to receive? – I managed to distract my thinking. Jimmy was now looking with surprised adoration at her. I remembered us, boys together, scutting on the backs of horse-drawn carts down Francis Street; in Jimmy's company recklessness came easily.

Now, the priest was chatting with them, relations established, the best of friends. I picked up words of encouragement: 'relax' – 'the best day of your lives' – 'try to enjoy' – The ceremony began, and I noticed that Christie the best man was checking a pocket of his waistcoat, clearly nervous of losing the wedding ring. The hymns came with the regularity of a well-fed jukebox, moving the couple through to the 'I do' moment, after which everyone was invited to clap. During the Consecration, we knelt, unsure of our timing, and bowed our heads; I sneaked a look across to where Teresa was, but Celine's lump of a sister Veronica was in the way. By then, I still hadn't had a good look at her. After the Lord's Prayer, the ceremony was approaching a decision time for me. Holy Communion; to receive or not to receive?

I watched Jimmy and Celine taking the host, and then sip the wine from a shared chalice. Then it was the turn of the principal attendants. Luckily, for me, it was ladies first. Veronica approached the priest, hands pressed tightly together as if she were a nervous first communicant. Teresa was behind her. It was my first time to get a good look at her. She was the same as I'd remembered, maybe even better. But there wasn't time to gaze at her. To receive the host or not. If she has the brazenness to do it, then so has Mark O'Bride, I thought. I swallowed the communion host and went back to my seat and realized my heart was beating loudly from seeing her. The priest said the final prayers, and then it was the time for the signing of the marriage register. The newlyweds disappeared into the sacristy with their witnesses; the congregation would have to wait until their return. I smiled across at Teresa and she surprised me by getting up and crossing the aisle to sit beside me.

'You're not supposed to be on this side of the house,' I said.

'Are you sending me back?'

'I wouldn't dare to try.'

A voice cut in between us. 'You look beautiful, Teresa'. It was Jimmy's mother.

'You look smashing yourself, Mrs. Culmane. I love the outfit.'

'Don't talk to me about it!' she said. 'Such stress for one day's wearing! And look at you, Mark,' she added, like I was an afterthought. 'You look so handsome'.

'It's the clothes, Mrs. Culmane, not the dummy wearing them.'

'Don't talk nonsense; I wouldn't bother saying it if I didn't mean it.'

'There you go,' Teresa said. 'You've a fan there, Mark.'

Mrs. Culmane said, 'Are you down from Derry on your own, dear?'

'Yes, best thing really. Ruth would tire and it wouldn't be right for her.'

'She is probably still a bit young for taking to a wedding. Is Hugh here, then?'

'He's not, Mrs. Culmane. He took Ruth to stay with his parents.'

The information which Jimmy's mother had just gathered using simple, innocent-sounding questions, had answered a particular one for me, as during the ceremony I'd wondered whether the Northerner was present, maybe staring at the back of my neck. At that moment, an elderly couple came along and distracted Mrs. Culmane. I was on the point of speaking again to Teresa, when she moved away to talk with a girl who was waving to her from a pew further back. We hadn't spoken much, yet, in those moments, it had been as if she had never made a fool out of me. How did I let that happen? I asked myself.

The register had been signed and witnessed, and we lined up behind the newly-weds for the recessional. Teresa thrust her arm into the crook of mine and, as we moved down the aisle, people smiled at us as if she were the bride and I were the groom, not supporting actors. I was bewildered to find the Mother waiting outside the church holding an empty confetti carton. Without warning, Teresa detached herself from me and I lost her in the crowd.

'Ma, I didn't know you were coming,' I said, swallowing my annoyance.

'I didn't know either, until the last minute. I decided to hop on a bus and come across. Was that the Teresa girl you came out of the church with?'

'You won't get lost over this part of the city? You'll be able to find your way back, I hope?'

'Mark, I was walking these streets long before you were born. Now, are you going to introduce me to the girl?'

I glanced around the church ground and spotted her. 'She must have left, gone on ahead,' I lied.

'Don't be silly, everyone's still here.'

'Well, I don't see her,' I said. I was looking everywhere but not in Teresa's direction.

She often said that she knew me better than I knew myself, and that day was no exception. 'Well, I see a girl in a long dress over there – that *must* be her. Take me over to her."

'I don't think it's a good idea.'

There was no stopping her. She pushed the empty confetti carton into my hand and hurried away, a dart heading for the bullseye. I didn't wait to watch and stepped away from the crowd and took out a cigarette. Suddenly, Jimmy was at my elbow. 'Give's one of those,' he said. He spotted the confetti carton, took it from my hand and kicked it into the air. 'It's been great, hasn't it?'

'Sure has, pal. As young fellows we never thought we'd be doing this.'

'And the day's only starting,' he said, standing on the cigarette. He saluted someone across the way and dived back into the wedding group.

The Mother cornered me again. 'It was her okay; a nice girl.'

'And?'

'Don't worry, I didn't say anything that you need fret about.' She took a moment to look around her and I had the impression that she was taking everything in, saving the scene for it to be later replayed in her mind, then she buttoned up her topcoat, adjusted her headscarf. 'You have a good time and I'll see you tomorrow.'

I could have been kinder, I thought, watching her wobbly walk as she went to the bus stop.

Wedding receptions have a sameness, whether it is in a Veteran's Club in New York or in a castle in Ireland – there is a sense of been there before. Perhaps, it is the predictability of it? Food, speeches, music, dancing and always the relative who wants to do a turn at the microphone. As the day merges into night and the effects of booze, music and excitement brings everything to a high point, you know for certain that at a certain unknown moment the party will all start to slowly unwind, slide downhill and that it's a good time to have pints lined up on the table in front of you, for you are never sure just when the shutter will come down on the bar. I was in that happy position when Teresa came and sat beside me.

'I met your mother today.'

I pretended to be surprised.

'I didn't know who she was until someone passed and called her Mrs. O'Bride, and I'd earlier seen you and her talking, so two and two…And there's a resemblance, as well.'

'What did she have to say for herself?'

'Well, she admired the dress, she admired the hair – she was great, really. A lovely woman.'

'I'm glad,' I said.

'Why wouldn't you be glad? She's your mother.'

'Jimmy and Celine seem happy,' I said, keen to change the subject.

She became distant for a moment, then said, 'Celine wanted a project, and in him she got a major one.'

I was surprised by her comment; my instinct was to defend him. I told her that I had no fears for them, that they would make a solid couple, just as our own mothers and fathers had been.

'Speak for yourself. My pair are nothing to write home about,' she said.

'I didn't know that... But they're still together?'

'They live under the same roof, yes. That's about it.' She was looking across the dance floor to where Jimmy and Celine seemed determined to talk to every guest that was still able to stand up and form words. 'You know, the children of misfits can also go on and become misfits themselves'.

'I wouldn't know,' I said. 'I guess I'm lucky that way.'

'It's such a random thing. You were lucky with yours; I wasn't. And worst of all, I'm already on the same path, making a right mess of my own attempt.'

'What do you mean?'

'Didn't you know? I'm living in sin, as they say. But it's not easy.'

'Is that the way *he* wanted it?'

'No, he wasn't fussed. I suggested it and he went along. It was no big deal, really. But now that we have Ruth...'

I took a long drink, all the while looking across the room at Jimmy and Celine – past, present, and future seemed to form into one.

'You don't have to worry about it, Mark. It's not your problem.'

'He's not the best, then?'

'Who? Hugo? No, no, you've got it wrong. He's not like *that*! The crockery is all intact and we've no broken furniture.'

'Then, what's the matter?'

'He's a tormented soul. I always thought he was a bit strange but never guessed how bad it was until I went to live with him. Now, that's enough of that! I'll tell you all about it some other time but not tonight. This is a celebration. Are you going to ask me up for a dance, or what?'

Ironically, it was a slow number and holding her brought me back to the Palace ballroom in the Isle of Man, except that this time we kept a space between us, no warm body to warm body, yet, even allowing for that, it would have been easy for me to close the eyes and float along like a cork in a slow-moving river. We didn't talk, and I wondered what was running through her mind. The moment was broken by a tap on my shoulder. Jimmy and Celine were looking to change partners. And, like a magic card trick, she was gone from me and instead I was dancing with Celine.

'Are you enjoying yourself, Mark?'

'Of course, I am. It's been a great day.' While talking, I remembered a similar conversation with a bride in New York and hoped that this marriage would last longer than the Yank and Maria's.

'We really wanted our close pals here, like yourself and Teresa. It's made the day for us.'

'It's been a pleasure,' I said.

'Sometimes you talk like a real gentleman. Teresa shouldn't have let you slip through her fingers, but some other lucky girl will get all the benefit.'

'Don't say that too loud. I'm trying to stay under the radar for as long as I can.'

'How do you think she looks?'

It was an unexpected question, possibly loaded.

'As far as I'm concerned, you're all looking fantastic,' I answered, giving her one of my rare wide smiles.

'That's a nice way of not giving me an answer.'

'Maybe it's not a fair question. Anyway, what's the point?'

'No point, Mark, just female curiosity.'

The band stopped playing and I held her hand (I was surprised at how thick her fingers were) and we walked across the dance floor towards Jimmy. Another fellow, a cousin of his whom I recognised from meetings at the Painter and Decorators Union was talking with him. At the same time, they were looking at a man standing in the doorway to the room; I thought at first that he was a stranger who had come across the wedding and was trying to decide whether to gate-crash the party or not. Then I remembered the face and realized it was Jimmy's father Mr. Culmane, or Joxer, as I had heard him called.

Celine dropped my hand and ran to Jimmy and tried to pull him towards the other end of the room. She was wasting her time, for his face was now white and screwed-up with rage and he broke from her grip. His cousin tried to get in his way, but he swept him aside with a wild sweep of his arm. I ran after him, also trying to block his path.

'Jimmy, don't do anything stupid,' I cried.

He shoved me aside as if I were a shop-window mannequin, then punched Joxer in the face before he even had a chance to speak.

'What are *you* doing here, you toe rag?' he said. His clenched fist was held in mid-air, ready to strike his father a second time.

Joxer Culmane wiped a trickle of blood from the corner of his mouth and stared back at him. 'That's some greeting to give your father.'

'You're not invited!' Jimmy snarled.

'It's a fine thing when I had to find out from others about the wedding. I missed the church, and just about made it here.'

'I said you're not welcome! Go crawl back into the hole you came from before I split you open!

'I've every right to be here. Your Ma and me brought you into this world – don't you forget that.'

'You didn't think of that when you were pissing your wages away!' The suspended fist fell like a pile hammer on Joxer's face.

I was close enough to grab Jimmy and wrap my arms around him. 'This'll get you nowhere,' I shouted. 'Just let it go!'

However, I should have known that Joxer would have a streetfighter's instinct and he used that very moment to strike back, a vicious blow to the head. I felt Jimmy's legs crumple and I supported his weight. He quickly recovered, pushed me away and struck back at Joxer with another punch. It was startling to see a father and son at it like that, and these weren't soft blows but merciless digs that hurt. Mrs. Culmane ran up and tried to pull them apart.

Jimmy roared, 'Stay out of this, Ma – he's had this coming a long time!'

The fight moved across the room, drinks were knocked over as the pair banged into tables and wedding guests scrambled to get out of the way. The fight went out a French window that had been left open to cool the room. I followed them outside into the darkness. I could hear their grunts and the sound of the blows. By the light from inside I could see them now on a stretch of lawn, where a blanket of frost had started to get its grip. There was blood on white shirts, blows as vicious as ever, Joxer, despite his age, giving as much as he got.

Celine was shrieking, saying that the day was ruined.

Teresa grabbed my arm. 'You'll have to end this. They'll murder one another.'

I called Jimmy's cousin; he quickly saw what was needed and gathered more help. It took six men to pull them apart. Celine pulled Jimmy back indoors, her wedding dress now bloodied. Joxer had collapsed on his back onto the lawn and, unbelievably, he was softly laughing and didn't seem to have been put out by the scrap. I knelt to one side of him and Mrs. Culmane came to kneel at the other.

'What got into you at all, Joxer?' she said. 'Coming here like this, where you knew you weren't wanted? '

'I've every right to be here,' he said. 'Stella, you know that I wasn't always like this. You know, don't you?'

'You chose your own path, Joxer.'

'You shut me out. Okay, you were right to do that. Gawd, I deserved it. But I still have a right to be here, here at me own son's wedding.'

'Well, you've made a right hames of this day, and I hope you're proud of yourself.'

We helped him to his feet; he insisted on walking back inside without aid. The band had resumed playing and Celine was washing

Jimmy's face, dipping a bar towel into a pint tumbler of water, which had turned a cloudy red. He was watching his father from out of the corner of his eye, ready and able to use his fists again, if needed. Mrs. Culmane steered Joxer along the other side of the room and coaxed him into the Ladies toilet to clean him up. Teresa came to stand beside me. 'Let's hope that's the end of it,' she said. Then she set about straightening my necktie, which was halfway round my neck. I heard Jimmy saying to Celine, 'Why is Ma looking after him? will she ever learn?'

Celine was too engrossed in making him look presentable to answer him. His waistcoat had been torn almost in half; she delicately removed it, then folded it neatly, clearly hoping that it could be mended, and that the security deposit with the suit hire company could be saved. For the moment, the only way to cover the blood on the shirt was to put back on the suit jacket, which had been shed when the dancing started. Meanwhile, the other guests tried to give the impression that nothing had happened. The staff had jumped in quickly, tables were put back in order, broken glass was collected, the floor mopped. Then drinks were reordered, conversations resumed, and some optimists were even back on the dance floor, but there was a sense that it was all a hollow effort to save the day. The reality was that most of us had an eye to the door of the Ladies, waiting for Joxer to come out.

When he did appear, shadowed by Mrs. Culmane, he looked, apart from being a trifle shaky on the feet, in better shape than Jimmy. She was urging him to go and try to make peace. He didn't want to, but she pulled him along until she had them facing each other. 'I want you both to make up so that the wedding day isn't entirely spoiled. Go on! Shake hands, it won't kill you!'

'Why should I?' Jimmy said. 'He's the one that shouldn't be here, not us?'

His mother glared at him. 'Jimmy, do it for me!'

Joxer had already put out a hand.

Jimmy looked exasperated. 'Ma, doing this is like letting him off for everything he's ever done on you, done on us.'

Celine then spoke up. 'If your Ma is prepared to let it go – at least for tonight – then I don't see how you can't. There's no real harm done, is there? Apart from a bit of tongue wagging, but who cares? *I* certainly don't.'

He studied her, rotated the new ring on his finger and then shook his father's hand. To anyone watching it was clear that it was a half-hearted effort. Joxer surprised us all when he pulled him forward and embraced him. Jimmy released himself and backed off, looking unsure. Then Joxer embraced Celine, but, instead of retreating, she clung to him.

'Isn't that nice,' Mrs. Culmane said, looking content. 'And I didn't even put him up to it!'

Shortly afterwards two grim-faced Gardai arrived, cautiously eyeing everyone in the room, as if they expected to be set upon. They approached the barman, who shrugged his shoulders as if to say he knew nothing of the 999-emergency call. One of the garda produced a notebook and asked some questions. The barman eventually pointed towards Jimmy, and they went over to him. I wasn't close enough to hear what was being said, but it was obvious that he was turning on whatever charm he had. It must have worked, for in a matter of minutes the notebook was pocketed, and the gardai left, smiling. There were no more interruptions. Joxer sat chatting with old neighbours, however, by then the 'party' was coming to an end. The band stopped playing, the bar closed, and a gang of us were directed to the hotel residents' lounge, where an overly smart-looking porter poured generous measures and entertained us with stories from the many years he had spent working at a top hotel in London. A taxi was called for Joxer, and he was sent back to Dublin like a human parcel. Mrs. Culmane was now probably used to having a bed to herself and unlikely to change.

It was an ungodly hour when we finally quit the residents' lounge. Over the period, other guests had drifted in and out. Teresa had come in at a later stage and sat on the floor with a group some feet from me. She and I went upstairs in the lift together. She looked happy and was singing to herself one of the songs that the band had played. We shared the same floor and when we stepped into the corridor she fell over, pointing to a high-heeled shoe that had gone sideways beneath her. I helped her to steady herself while she removed the other shoe. Her hair brushed against my face; her perfume rose to me. Once balanced, she tottered down the corridor towards her room and I went in the opposite direction towards mine.

Before falling asleep, I felt strangely comfortable that nothing had happened between us – or had been said – that would have caused either of us to be embarrassed in the morning.

Back home the following evening, I joined the Mother in front of the television. She asked me why I wasn't going out and I said that I'd no money. There was a mock gasp, an inward grin. Then she began to talk about the wedding and began a post-mortem on what the women had been wearing, even though she'd only been outside the church for a short time. After a while, she finally dug for the information that she *really* wanted.

'Did Teresa enjoy herself?'

'I'm sure she did. I think everybody did.'

'That's nice to hear. Weddings take so much planning. You wouldn't wish it on your worst enemy for something to go wrong, although I heard, and you can't believe everything you hear, that later there was some trouble.'

'Oh! I must've missed that.'

She returned her attention to the television, and I rose to prepare a tray with her supper. Her digging for news about the row at the wedding hadn't bothered me as much as that she'd again mentioned

Teresa. Doesn't she know that that's a finished subject? I brought in her tray and a mug of tea for myself, settled into a state of homely comfort, a time for the body to recover from excess.

I had learned from experience that an unexpected happening could always be waiting for me, like a mugger in a dark alleyway, ready to smash any sense of false security that I may have fallen into. However, for the next two years, all was relatively quiet.

Then, there was an avalanche of events.

CHAPTER THIRTEEN

Joxer passed away and I went to the funeral. It was sudden. A priest said sympathetic words from the altar to Mrs. Culmane and her family, but it was clear he didn't know the family; he wouldn't have been so glowing in his remarks about Joxer otherwise. In the front pew, the latest addition to the Culmane family, Anthony, had nothing better to do than try to wrest himself free of Celine and test his new walking skills. Jimmy and his mother watched the contest with kind looks. I felt it was a pity that Joxer never got to see his grandson, as there had been no contact since the wedding; however, I think Jimmy preferred it that way. Celine passed the child to him, but the child slipped his grip and toddled down the aisle and came to a stop beside where I was sitting. He recognised me – after all, I was the godfather – and gave me have a mouthful of baby talk. I played with his podgy fingers and tried to entice him to sit on my lap, but he was having none of it. Jimmy came up behind him, whisked him off his little legs, and carried him back to the front seat. The boy thought it was a game and wanted to be released again and kicked up when he didn't get his way.

Joxer was given a proper burial, avoiding an anonymous grave, which would have happened if it weren't for a social worker at the homeless shelter that knew the family. After the burial, he was also given the dignity of a session in a pub near the cemetery's gates. It was here that Celine came and sat with me, with young Anthony stretched out and fast asleep on the seat between us. Inevitably, the conversation came around to Teresa. I would have preferred not to talk about her, however, because of the day that was in it, I felt that I'd no choice but to listen.

'She's leaving Hugo,' she said.

'It's been a bit of a yo-yo, hasn't it?'

'This time it's final. The marriage has come to an end.'

'I didn't think they'd gone all the way and actually got married.'

'She did it for the child's sake, schools and all.'

'You hate it when things go wrong like that,' I said.

'Don't say that too loud; Jimmy is touchy on the subject.'

I looked across to where he and his mother were sitting and wasn't sure of what she meant.

'She plans to leave Derry and move in back home. Mind you, I don't think it'll make for a happy household. They don't get on too well.'

'And the child? a girl, isn't it?'

'Yes. Ruth, the cutest thing.' At that moment, young Anthony jerked a leg in his sleep and kicked me. 'I should have had a girl,' she said.

Not really wanting to know, I asked, 'How did the husband Hugo take it?

'Not well, he's an odd one.'

'I could have told you that,' I said.

'We saw it too, but –'

She'd stopped herself from saying more and I wondered if she was afraid that a wrong word here could cause me pain. Doesn't *anybody* know? I thought. Do I have to scream it? *There's nothing left between her and me*. Making an excuse that my drink was getting low, I escaped from the boy's kicks, and joined a small group of male refugees at the bar. Jimmy must have seen me, and it wasn't long before he joined me.

'How are you bearing up?' I asked.

'Oh, I'm doing okay, but I don't know about the Ma.'

I looked over at her. Friends had moved in to fill the gap left by Jimmy.

'You'd wonder why she'd be that upset,' he said.

'I suppose there was a time, like when they were starting out...'

'Yeah, but *you* don't know how it turned out. Nobody knows.'

We sat silently at the bar, as if we were thinking hard on some difficult puzzle, but my mind was blank, and it was probably the same for him. A man in a navy-coloured suit whom I vaguely recognised came up to Jimmy and offered his condolences. When he moved on, Jimmy told me he was the man he paid rent to, and that I should know him. I realized that I *did* know the man. He owned the pub in Camden Street; however, I hadn't recognised him in a suit, for before then I'd only known him as an apron-wearing publican.

'What's it like living over a pub, Jimmy?'

'It doesn't bother me. Mind you, I don't drink in his pub. The flat could be bigger, but it will have to do for the time being.'

'Maybe you could move in now with your Ma?'

'No, that wouldn't work with Celine. They get on all right, but they couldn't live together. You know how it is?'

Later, when the funeral party broke up, I decided to walk home. What Jimmy had said about Celine being unable to live with her mother-in-law had caused me to think of our family, the O'Brides. I knew that the Mother could be a trial at times, and I couldn't see either of my two brothers-in-law or my sister-in-law sticking it out in our place; although, when she took ill some weeks later and was taken in an ambulance, we all flocked to the hospital and the family quickly set up a roster so that she had company at every visiting time. Ma welcomed all comers, whether they were in-laws or her own flesh and blood. Always, when it was my turn to visit, she would ask me how I was managing at home on my own, was I cooking proper meals and not just depending on fish and chips from the chipper on the corner. I would lie to her and tell her that I was becoming a good cook because I had watched her in the kitchen over the years. A fortnight later, we waited for the hospital to release her; but the doctors kept putting back the date – more tests were needed. We were all frustrated by the slow progress, including Ma. Meanwhile the visiting roster held firm and as a family we did everything that could be asked of us, to the point that her bedside locker was crammed with eating and drinking delights to satisfy any craving, and she had more reading matter than a dentist's waiting room.

One warm night on my way home from visiting her, I passed the door of a local bar which was jammed open to ventilate sweating customers in rolled-up shirtsleeves. A beer would have been honey to my throat, but I had an early start the next day and would have to be at my pick-up point at seven or the boss would be thick with me. I had moved further along the street when I heard someone come running up behind me. It was Jimmy.

'I saw you passing and had to talk with you. Come back in with me for a jar,' he said, placing a friendly arm around my shoulder.

I told him about my early start.

'Then, I'll walk with you, and we can talk on the way.'

'Sounds like you're after something,' I joked. He fell in beside me as I walked on.

'Mark, to tell you the truth, I'm slowly going demented.'

'Go on, tell me all about it,' I said, not really wanting to know what it was that was ailing him as I'd enough going on in my own life with the hospital visits. Also, I knew that I was way behind with cleaning the apartment, the sink was full of dirty dishes, and I couldn't be confident that the washing I'd hung from the back window two days ago would have escaped the pigeon droppings.

I wasn't prepared for what followed. 'I'm crowded out by that Teresa one,' he said. 'As if our flat isn't small enough!'

I stopped and faced him. 'What's up now?'

'There was a big fall out with the parents, and she and the kid turned up at our flat. Of course, big-hearted Celine had to take her in. Now, the two women are sharing the big bed, the two childers are in the small one and I'm on the couch and have to dress in the pokey toilet.'

'It's probably only temporary,' I said.

'Bet *you've* never slept on a lousy couch with lumps sticking in your back and work to be faced the next day? I can tell you doing it once is enough!'

'What does Celine say?'

'She can't turn her out on the street. Which is okay for her to say but I'm sick of it.'

I hated cutting him short, yet still I looked at my watch to show him I'd other things to do. (An internal voice was telling me that this was their problem, nothing to do with me.) I made to move on when he grabbed my arm. 'Pal, I need advice here.'

'Advice?'

'I'm desperate and on the point of chucking Teresa out, but I know it'll create murder.'

'So?'

'I came after you because I felt you could help. With no sleep, my head is in a spin... I don't know what –'

'Sorry, Jimmy, I really don't see an easy answer for you.'

I left him standing on the street, looking as if he'd just lost a winning betting docket.

The problem was his and I didn't want to get involved. The apartment was tackled that night and, weary from a busy day, I finally collapsed on the bed. I should have been asleep in record time, but I couldn't help thinking of the two families crowded into that small flat. From where I lay, I could see out the open bedroom doorway, out to the small, dim hall beyond. I imagined the living room with its easy chairs and the china cabinet, the kitchen with the oilcloth on the table, the Mother's empty bedroom and I had a sudden sense that the apartment was roomy, maybe even immense in comparison to the tight space that Jimmy was stuck in. A crazy thought began running through my head.

Two days later it was my turn to visit the hospital. I asked the usual question, 'Any word on getting home, Ma?'

'Maybe next week, but I'll be going to Stella and John's until I get my strength back. The doctors want me to be with someone...and she volunteered her place. Anyways, I couldn't be leaning on you, son, as you're out at work all day.'

'You're right, Ma. Well, then, that's good news; I'm sure you'll be delighted to be getting out.'

'*Me*, delighted? You must be off your rocker. Your man John wouldn't make a cup of tea for you even if your tongue were falling out. But it has to be done and please God it won't be too long before I'll be back in my own place.'

I remembered my idea and knew that if there was ever a time to run it past her, it had to be at that moment. 'Can I ask a favour of you, Ma?'

She had a look of wariness, which was understandable, for, after all, she couldn't do anything practical for me, like buy my favourite shaving cream from the street dealer on Meath Street or collect winnings on a horse from the bookies shop. 'It depends on what it is you're after; I *am* confined to a hospital bed.' she said.

I told her the story of how Teresa and her child had come to be sharing a small, overcrowded flat over a pub. 'Ma, I hope you understand this, but I feel that I can help them.'

'Go on...'

'There's room at our place, and it would only be until you were fit to come home from Stella and John's. Once home, then Teresa and the child would have to leave.'

'Have you already asked her?'

'I wouldn't dare do something like that, not without your say.'

'How can you be so sure she'd leave at the end, and that Jimmy would let her back into his place?'

'That would be the deal. We'd be giving Jimmy and Celine a break and giving Teresa and the child more space – they would either accept the terms or it wouldn't happen.'

'But, Mark, why are you *really* doing this?'

'It is what it is, Ma. No hidden motive. I'm able to help; in fact, it's the two of us, we're *both* able to help. And I feel that we should. From my point of view, that's all there is to it.'

'I hope you're not wishing for something romantic out of this, son. I'd hate to see you hurt or...'

'Mother, how many times have I said it? Believe me, there's absolutely nothing between us.'

'This is so unlike you. Caring was never your strong point,' she said.

'Don't worry, I'm not changing. This is just a once off.'

'I suppose it shows you're finally making something of yourself.'

She was sitting up in the bed, a knitted cape across her shoulders, with a soft look on her face. It was clear that she was permitting me to go ahead and only then did I realize the full importance of what I'd asked of her. I'd asked her to open her door to someone she'd only briefly met.

'There's one condition,' she said. 'That she and the child sleep in my room; there's more space in there.'

'That's good of you, Ma. There's one other thing...'

'Something else?'

'This may not go down well with the rest of the family. They could kick up and say that I've no right to bring strangers into the family home, even though they no longer live there. That's the way they still feel about the place.'

'Leave them to me. I'll explain all when they come up to visit.'

'I'd give anything to see their faces.'

'Don't be wicked, Mark. Now get off with you before I change my mind.'

~~~

Jimmy had carried Teresa's case for her on the ten-minute walk to our building. On arrival, the child was asleep in a battered-looking push chair, and Teresa had to wake her. We had a redundant pram shed at the back of the building, where I took a moment to deposit the push chair alongside the Da's old bike. I hurried back in, and Jimmy carried the child upstairs to the apartment. He was restless and couldn't hide his keenness to be on his way, perhaps afraid that I might change my mind. Left alone with them, I gave Teresa the short tour, ending in the Mother's room.

'I've dusted everything and changed the sheets,' I said. 'I've brought in a small bed for Ruth. It makes the room smaller, but you probably want her beside you.'

'It's the Phoenix Park compared to what we've just come from. I hope that doesn't sound ungrateful – Celine and Jimmy have been such good friends and I appreciate all they've done for me. I'd have been lost without them.'

'This gives everyone more breathing space, for the time being anyway. I'll leave you to get settled in. And I've made space in the wardrobe for you to hang your stuff.'

'I don't want to make my own of the place,' she said.

'Don't worry, my mother insists on it.'

I left her to get settled in and went to put the kettle on. It was Ma who had asked me to move the last of the father's suits to make space in the wardrobe. I had left them with the Carmelites and figured that already they could be on the back of some of the city's down-and-outs; yet, if I had passed someone in the street wearing one of the suits, I probably wouldn't have recognised it. I couldn't believe that she'd asked me to dispose of them, after keeping them for so long and in such good shape. The kettle boiled and I called Teresa for the tea.

'I didn't know what to give Ruth,' I said.

'She'll have tea in her bottle. Occasionally, I give it to her. Nice and milky.'

We moved into the living room where she sat in the Mother's armchair – I passed no remark. Ruth was on the floor with her drink, and I sat in my normal seat. Teresa looked round her at the many photographs of the O'Bride family, then she ran her fingertips along the book spines on the small bookshelf beside her. She looked at the neat pile of old Reader's Digests magazines on the floor (they were the Da's, and occasionally I would still pick one of them up to read). 'It's comfortable here,' she said. 'I can see why you've never left home.'

'It never arose...'

She laughed in a way that I remembered. 'It's more likely that you're spoiled here,' she added.

'Not that I'm aware of.'

She went quiet, looked about the room again. 'I feel I don't deserve this.'

There was an awkward moment.

'I haven't a clue what you're on about. Listen, drink up your tea, make yourself at home and don't bring up the subject again.'

She shot me a quizzical look then – as if my words had had a magic influence on her – she kicked off her shoes and stretched out her legs and tickled the child's back with her big toe. I remembered how the Da used to reach over and massage the Mother's feet through her nylons. It would have been easy for me to reach over and do the same to Teresa, but I had laid down strict rules for myself, including one of no overfamiliarity. After all, going by what I knew, she was still married. If I'm to help her, I need to stick to my rules, I told myself.

'I'm going for a pint,' I said. 'So, here's a spare set of keys, in case you want to take Ruth to the park. It's just around the corner – ask anyone. Do you want me to buy anything while I'm out?'

'Some groceries would be good,' she said. 'I'll cook dinner for us.'

I had just the one drink, stopped by the shop and headed home clutching full bags of food. It was the largest amount I'd bought in one go since the Mother had been taken to hospital.

Later that night, when it was the child's bedtime, Teresa said, 'Now, Ruth, give Mark a hug and thank him for being so good to us.'

I was surprised when she flung herself at me and wrapped her arms around my neck. 'Night, night, Mark,' she said, and clung to me for a long moment. When she broke away, she looked at Teresa, an unsureness in her face. I'd had hugs in the past from nephews, however, as the boys had become older, they had become stingier with displays of affection. And, anyway, their hugs had never been quite like this one, an enthusiastic assault.

'And thank Mark, as well,' Teresa said.

I saw that she was at a loss to understand. 'There's no need of anything else, Ruth – the hug was plenty for me.' She picked up a cuddly toy, then danced at the end of her mother's hand when being led to the bedroom. I heard myself say, 'Night, Ruthie.'

On my next visit to the hospital, the Mother was keen to hear all about my 'guests'. I told her how they had settled in and used an incident with Mrs. Mulligan downstairs as an example. All three of us were on our way out to the park, when Mrs. Mulligan met us on her landing. She made a fuss of Ruth, and at the same time, I saw that she was giving Teresa the once-over. The poor woman's curiosity must have been painful. Purposely, I stayed quiet, and, to her credit, she didn't ask any prying questions. The next day she came upstairs to us and asked if Ruth would like to go down and play with one of her granddaughters who was visiting. Teresa let her go and later, when she was brought home, she was full of talk about making a new friend.

I could see that Ma was pleased; this was a different type of news to the normal hospital visit news. We talked for a long time before she raised any complaints about the food, the nurses or even the doctors. 'It'll be next week before I'm out and then it's out to Stella and John's. She was in this afternoon to tell me that my room is ready. Apparently, she nagged him into changing the wallpaper – but I hope it'll be a short stay.'

On the following night, after I had read a bedtime story to Ruth and she'd slipped into sleep, Teresa said, 'Mark, you'd make a great dad.'

'I'd have to find a wife first,' I answered.

She paid no attention to my reply, her mind elsewhere. 'Her father's a good man, you know.'

I couldn't comment. I'd only met Hugo during our time in Douglas – which at the time was enough for me! – and, since then, I'd only laid eyes on him and that was from a telephone box. If she's now trying to paint him as a good man, then what's she doing here without him?

'He's a frustrated soul,' she continued. 'He beats himself up over things, and lets the world get on top of him. The Troubles have shoved him to a point where he's no room in himself for any type of relationship.'

'I'm sorry to hear that,' I said, unsure of what she was talking about.

'Do you remember the first time he was with us, in the Isle of Man?' she said. 'I couldn't stand him; then later, it just happened. We went to live in Derry and eventually got married in a registry office, and I thought that everything would be wonderful for us from then on. After a while, I realized that I didn't like it there. It wasn't the place; it was the tense atmosphere. I'd never paid any heed to another's religion, there was no need, but in the North, it's a different matter. Even your name is a form of coding that puts you in one camp or the other. In spite of that, I did meet many nice people there and, perhaps, I could have come to like it. Unfortunately, Hugo's problems began to wear me down and, in the end, I felt that I'd no option but to leave.

'As a couple, I'd felt that we *were* a match, but his problems became an acid, killing the marriage. He wouldn't speak about them, which made it worse. A sister of his became a good friend, and she helped me to understand why he'd become the way he was. She put it down to a shooting that ended in some close friends of his being killed. They were in a bar, and he should have been in their company that afternoon, instead he went off and played a football match. He felt guilty because he hadn't been there with them.'

'You never knew,' I said.

'Not until I went to live with him, and his sister told me. She said that Loyalists were to blame for the killings, and Hugo had become so incensed that he'd tried to join the IRA. But they didn't trust him and sent him away, because many years before, an aunt of theirs had crossed over to the other side and married a B Special. It was known that the officer had been involved in the kidnapping and execution of a republican, but this had been back in the Fifties before the current trouble. These things aren't forgotten and even though it had nothing to do with Hugo, the IRA has a long memory. He tried to pester them into accepting him as a member; this only made matters worse, and they finally warned him off. So, now he mopes over something that can't be changed and lives in his own miserable world. And I couldn't see a future in that and left.'

'And having Ruth did nothing to help the situation?'

'For a while it did, then he went back into his old ways. However, Ruth's made a big difference to his parents. I get on with them, to a point. Although, they're forever on about having their grandchild around them, and each time I've left Derry they've pleaded with me to bring her back. This time they don't know where I am, which is good, at least for the time being.'

'What will you do now?' I was immediately afraid that I might have given her the wrong impression and was quick to tell her that I had meant in the future.

'I'm thinking of going to London. I've a first cousin there and she's sure that I'll get work.'

'That's a drastic step.'

'Maybe it is,' she answered. 'But what choice do I have? If I stay here in Dublin, sooner or later he'll turn up, and I don't want to live in dread of that. On the other hand, in London, mine would be one face among millions of faces, and Ruth and I could start a new life.'

I wanted to shout that she could stay in our apartment forever, then I remembered that it wasn't my own place, but the Mother's. And, also, that I would be breaking my own rule on overfamiliarity.

Next day on the job, I was restless, rushing my work. I left early and hurried home. She had prepared the dinner and we sat at the table like a proper family. Later I washed the dishes and she dried, then, when it was time for Ruth to go to bed, I read her a story, the same one as the previous night. She insisted on it, which surprised me as I'd forgotten how strong-willed a child could be. Later, I told Teresa I was thinking of taking a day off work.

'Why?' she asked.

'I want us to go out somewhere for the day. A place Ruth would like, like the Zoo or maybe an excursion coach down the country somewhere. Whatever you think...'

'You don't have to do that for us.'

She was hesitating, so I jumped in before she could turn down the idea. 'It's just a simple thing, no strings attached. It's something I want to do.'

'Mark, I hate imposing on you, however, if you want...'

She stretched out on the Mother's easy chair. 'Aren't you going out for a pint tonight?'

CHAPTER FOURTEEN

I stared into the spare wallet which I kept at the back of my bedroom drawer. There should be more money in there than that, I thought; however, I couldn't swear on it, as I hadn't checked it in weeks. Whenever I was going somewhere special, it was always there to dip into, equally, it was a well to which I regularly added a top-up. I counted the money with care, took some for the outing and, for the first time, wrote down the balance. We were going to take a bus to Enniskerry, then walk up the hill to Powerscourt, where we would visit the gardens. Ruth was excited at the very idea of an outing, even though she really hadn't a clue where she was going. She couldn't sit still during the bus ride, yet, when we got to Enniskerry, she complained of being tired, and Teresa regretted not bringing the push chair. I bent down and Ruth jumped on my back and clasped her arms around my neck, and we tramped up a hill to the gates, singing all the songs she knew.

I was never one for gardens; the Mother always joked that I wouldn't be able to tell a flower from a weed; however, Teresa seemed to know what she was looking at. As far as I was concerned, it was like a public park, except for the major difference of it being privately owned. It rolled out from the blackened shell of a big house to walkways lined with old-looking statues, to a perfectly tailored lake, and in the distance the Sugarloaf Mountain appeared as if it had been painted into the scenery by an artist. Ruth found new energy and wanted to run about and pluck any flower that took her fancy. I was doing all the chasing and my only chance of taking a rest was to bring them to the tearoom at the side of the big house. We sat looking out at the view. I kept one eye on Ruth who was chasing a sparrow across the flagstone floor. She was heading for the door, and I rushed over and brought her back to the table.

'It's quiet here. Too quiet for city people like us,' I said.

'Quiet is good, Mark. Noise can sometimes frighten the life out of you. In Derry, a car backfiring can stick you to the ground and you wait for something nasty to happen, then, by the time you realize the cause of your fright, you're nerves are already in pieces, and you want nothing but to get home. No, I'll take quiet any day.'

Ruth had run under the table, stood up too early and banged her head. She started to sob, and Teresa cuddled her, speaking softly, an instinctive skill rather than one learnt. It was time to leave, and it began to rain – we hurried down the hill to the village. We waited with some other day-trippers for the bus, and sat upstairs when the double-decker arrived, where Ruth had a free run of a front seat. We were directly behind her, and I was ready to grab her in case the driver had to jam on the brakes. I suddenly had a hunger to know more about Hugo, brought on by Teresa talking of her time in Derry. 'What does he do for a living?' I asked.

'He's a teacher, but he hasn't taught for a while now – off on extended sick leave. Officially, it's post-traumatic stress, which could be said of many persons I've met up there.'

'And what does he do with himself all day?'

'Most of the time I never knew and still wouldn't. He'd go off in the morning, on foot mind you, and not come back until it was nearly dark, with a look on his face like that of an aimless dog who'd been out sniffing trails all day to the point of exhaustion. And, if I had the audacity to ask him where he'd been, he'd simply look at me as if I were a stranger.'

The bus had arrived back in the city and was snarled up in evening traffic. She had gone quiet, become distant. I wanted to break into her thoughts and rescue her, lighten her problems. Then, a voice in my head asked, For what? The worst thing about it was that I knew I was again being a fool. We got off the bus and strolled home, with Ruth swinging between us.

~~~

It was now on the cards that Ma would be leaving Stella and John's sooner than expected, which didn't surprise me. All along, everyone else in the family had thought it a good idea, but I for one had never really believed that she would fit in there. Teresa and Ruth would now have to move out, and it all felt rushed to me; nevertheless, there was nothing that could be done about it. I knew the Mother wouldn't have wanted to push them out; then, again,, it was her home, and sometimes you must call a limit to your charity.

Teresa was calm about it – 'It just means England, sooner, that's all.'

'I'll talk to Jimmy,' I said.

'Save your breath. When I left there, I knew he'd never let me back in, no matter what Celine had to say on the matter. No, it's all clear to me now. Tomorrow, I'll get the boat tickets.'

'I'll go with you for them.'

'You're a workingman, Mark. Already you've taken a day off for us and I'm sure it cost you. No, I know where the ticket office is, and I'll manage.'

'Have you the fare?'

'Maybe… I can't be sure that I've enough…'

'I can give you some, just in case.'

'I'll pay you back, Mark. Over there, I'll soon be back on my feet.'

Suddenly, the reality hit me. *Over there!* She would be taken beyond my reach and the very thought of it now sent panic through me. I had been living in a fairy tale world since she had come to stay with me, fooling myself with the notion of us being a 'happy family'. All the charitable motives that I had put forward to myself, to Jimmy and Celine, to my own family, all these suddenly fell away, a mask slipping that I didn't even realize I had been wearing. It all slipped away, and I felt like a man naked before the elements, unable to hide my real feelings for a further second.

'Do you *have* to go?'

She didn't seem surprised at my urgent question. She could have reacted like a dramatic actress in an old black-and-white film, full of emotion; instead, I had the impression that while she was interested, she seemed also to be unmoved. I waited for her answer, more in hope than in belief.

Ruth wanted to show me a picture from the book I had read to her the night before, 'Uncle Mark, Uncle Mark...'

I asked myself, Where did this 'Uncle' title come from? I began to believe that Teresa had used it deliberately, telling me that I had a place in their lives, but not the one that I now wanted. I waited for her to spell it out.

Eventually, she turned to me. 'Mark, you know I have to leave.'

'No. I don't know. You could stay – stay with me.'

'How do you make that out? Even if I wanted to, your mother will be home soon, and she'll want her room.'

'We'll get a place of our own,' I said, surprising myself.

'Mark, have you thought this through? You'd leave the comfort of this lovely apartment, desert your own mother, and we'd probably end up living in some dirty, cramped room like Celine and Jimmy? '

'I would; that's what I'm trying to say. I'm serious, Teresa. If you got a divorce we could marry. Can't you –'

'Mark, you're wedded already; wedded to your comfortable life. You've a mother that dotes on you, money in your pocket and you're free to come and go as you please. You've no idea what it's like in the real world, and you would be absolutely miserable if you were landed with the responsibility of looking after us.'

'I'll definitely be miserable if you take that boat.'

'That's what you say now, and I'm flattered. But it'll pass. You'll forget us, and Ruth and I will get on with our lives in London.'

'You're not listening to me, I'm deadly serious about this.'

'That's too bad, Mark, but you're taking a lot for granted.'

'Like what? Tell me, like what?

'I don't want to hurt you, but you'll have to get this between your ears – *I don't want to be with you.* I'm sorry you got the wrong impression and sorry that I ever came to stay with you. You told me originally that you'd no hidden motive.'

'I did,' I admitted, gloomily.

Nevertheless, I felt that she also had been lying to herself. She must have known all along that it would turn out this way. I knew now that it was final; the boat tickets would be bought next day.

~~~

The evening before they left, I got home early and we went out to an ice cream parlour, a last outing together. Although I wanted it to be upbeat and tried my hardest to smile, the white-jacketed Italian that took our order was annoying me, even though he was completely blameless. I was rude to him and immediately felt sorry that I had let myself down. Teresa didn't remark on it.

We sat silently extracting the ice cream from tall glasses. Ruth was making a mess and Teresa had to make a game out of spoon-feeding her. When she'd had enough, she then began to stab the buttons of the jukebox selection box at our table and to amuse her I put money in and played 'Daisy a Day' because it had a catchy chorus. Teresa sang the bits she knew to her, but the child became bored and wanted to run about. The distraction meant that the record played out without us paying attention to it; anyway, the lyrics would have gone over Ruth's head. It was time to go, and I hoisted her upon my shoulders, and we went out on to the street. 'Ruth, how about we go around to the Culmane's to bid farewell to Jimmy and Celine? And your little pal Anthony will be there, too,' I said.

'It's getting late,' Teresa said. 'I'd rather not go there now if that's okay with you. Ruth should be in her bed soon. Anyway, there's no need. I'll write Celine from London.'

'You know best,' I said.

Walking back, I was aware that a passing stranger could have taken us for a family. As for Mrs. Mulligan downstairs, heaven only knows what she thought of us by now. Teresa helped me to tidy the apartment in preparation for the Mother's return. By the time we were finished, it looked to me as good as the way she would like it – still I was nervous of her inevitable inspection. Later, over a cup of tea, we sat in the armchairs and made small talk. Suddenly, she became serious.

'I don't know how to thank you for all you've done. And I didn't mean what I said the other day about you having a hidden motive. I hope it didn't upset you?"

'Why should I be upset? I was out of order. Now, I want no arguments over this, but I'm going with you to Dun Laoghaire tomorrow. You're going to need some help with Ruth and the luggage.'

'I'd like that, although there isn't much luggage. We'll be travelling light.'

'Nevertheless...'

We tidied up and she went into bed, while I took refuge in the television. I dozed for a while, came to, and checked the door bolt, put out the lights in the living room and went for the bathroom. Just as I got there, I heard it being flushed and she came out; she was barefooted and in a short slip, her breasts loose in the fine material; the shortness of her slip revealed pale legs that had a light growth of fair hair. We faced each other in a moment of surprise. She flicked her hair with a toss of the head, and I felt she was looking at me, as if we were only meeting for the first time. My heart was thumping. *She must hear it!*

'Good night, again,' she said, brushing past me and disappearing into the Mother's room. Later, as I lay in bed, I wondered if I had been mistaken – had she flashed a teasing look at me? I went to sleep thinking of her.

CHAPTER FIFTEEN

The Heartbreak House is located across the road from the railway station. This wasn't the proper name for the inn, but the one adopted by people taking the emigrant trail and their friends and relatives who'd come to see them off. We lingered over a farewell drink while we waited for the boat train. I looked around at the groups seated at their tables, the tell-tale luggage on the floor beside them. At this time of day, there was a sadness about the place, the conversation was stilted, reached for, artificial. We sat drinking, not really having much more to say. If it weren't for Ruth running about, it would have felt like a funeral parlour. When the time to go for the train came, the Heartbreak House began to empty, as parties gathered themselves and crossed to the railway station.

'One single adult and a child to Dun Laoghaire, and an adult return,' I said, handing a bunch of the new decimal coins to the ticket seller.

He pointed at Ruth. 'Is that the child?'

I nodded.

'She'll go free,' he said.

Although roofed over, Pearse Station was draughty, being open at each end. Pigeons were on the platform and Ruth wanted to chase them, and to humour her I held her hand and we walked quietly towards them. We were almost upon them, when they rose in a commotion of wing flapping, and we watched their flight until they came to rest on the roof supports of cast-iron. I looked back at Teresa. She was standing at the door of a carriage, ready to board. The train was nearly full, and we shared a carriage with two men who seemed to be strangers to one another, yet each had brought on similar brown suitcases. As we began to move, one of them let the window down and gave a feeble wave in the direction of the platform, then slumped into the seat opposite us and, as if needing to divert his mind, he began to make playful faces at Ruth. The other man pulled out a pipe and went through the ceremony of loading its bowl and lighting it, then he moved into a corner beside the open window and puffed away. As the train moved out from the station and gathered speed, a chill came into the carriage and the pipe smoker must have felt it too, for he raised the window until there was but a small gap at the top to let his smoke out, but the wind forced it back inside and we hadn't even passed Sydney Parade when Teresa began to give little coughs. I stared at the pipe smoker, hoping he would either stop or let the window down again; however, although I knew he noticed me, he kept puffing away as if it were now a challenge to him. I was on the point of saying something when I felt Teresa's hand on mine, and I read it as a signal to keep silent. She tumbled out into the fresh air when we reached Dun Laoghaire pier.

I took Ruth by the hand and convinced the seaman checking the tickets that Teresa couldn't manage on her own, so he let me go on board to see them seated. We found a quiet corner below deck in the saloon, and I stayed with them until there was an announcement asking all persons not travelling to go ashore. I squeezed a pound note into Ruth's hand and made to go.

'Thank Uncle Mark and give him a kiss,' Teresa said.

I knelt for the hug and kiss, then stood and faced Teresa. It was hard to tell what she was thinking; she looked neither sad nor happy. I bent across and brushed my lips against her cheek, mumbled my farewell and left. When I was at the foot of the companionway, I turned and waved. They waved back and I was surprised at how small and defenceless they looked against the scale of the large saloon. I suddenly had an immense feeling of pity for them, however there was nothing more I could do, and I took the steps in twos, my eyes welling, as though I'd suddenly been guilty of bringing a favourite pet dog to be put down. I broke out onto the deck and made for the gangway. The pipe smoker from the train was leaning on the ship's railings, puffing away, watching the seamen readying the cast off. His suitcase was sitting on the steel deck beside him. I suddenly felt mad and had an urge to stuff his pipe down his throat. I didn't – but while passing him I gave his suitcase a sly kick and knocked it over. At this stage, my vision became blurred. I used the handrail to guide me down the gangplank, then waited on the pier on the off chance that Teresa and Ruth would appear up on deck and wave, but they never appeared, and the boat moved out of the harbour and out of sight. It was a lonely train ride back into the city.

I left Pearse Station and, remembering our parting drink, looked across at the Heartbreak House, and felt worse. It began to rain, and I turned up my collar and hurried away. I wanted a drink but the establishments around Trinity College weren't for me – too many college-scarf types – so, I soldiered on until I came to South Great George's Street, where I found the perfect bar to suit my foul humour and fell into company that cheered me up no end. I was still there at closing time. On the way home, I bought chips and ate them in the apartment, then not bothering to undress, I slept on top of the bedclothes. In the morning, I panicked at the lingering smell of the chips. In a matter of hours, the Mother would be brought home to reclaim her kingdom. I opened all windows and the door to the landing to clear the smell and brought the vinegar-soaked wrapping paper outside to the community bin behind the building. My next stop was the bathroom, where the mirror told me that I had been a bad boy last night (as if I really needed to be told). A bath might have helped, but the gas geyser was temperamental and as slow as a CIE carthorse. Instead, I shaved, wet the hair, and coaxed it into respectability, then I changed into fresh clothes and waited for Stella and John to bring Ma home.

I was reading one of the old Readers' Digest magazines to help me relax, when there was a knock on the open door and a stranger walked in, uninvited. At first, I thought he was with Stella and John, but then realized he wasn't the type to be in their circle of friends. He was pimply faced, about twenty years old, and had a lean, wriggly body that spoke of someone who could outrun a garda.

'What are you doing in here?' I shouted.

'Is the woman here?' he asked, looking round the room.

'Who the hell are you talking about?'

'The blondie one that was here a few days ago.'

'Get out! I said, gripping his arm and marching him to the door.

He didn't resist and, on the landing, he brushed down his grubby jacket, as if it were a Burton best. 'No problem, I'll wait for her out here.'

'You can't wait here, it's private. You've no right to be even in this building.'

'Then, you give me the twenty notes she owes me, and I'll go. No problem. But no duds this time.'

'What are you on about?' I asked, losing patience.

'Your woman that was here pawned this off on me,' he said, producing what looked like a twenty-pound note. It was the new type, blue with a playwright or someone like that on the front.

'So? It's the decimal —'

'I know all about decimal but I'm not a fool. Here, you take a good look at it.'

My instinct was to shove him down the stairs, however, my curiosity made me take the note from him. The paper didn't feel right; the printing was slipshod. I had heard about them in the pub, as the recent changes in the money had created a flood of forgeries.

'She slipped it to me in a roll of notes,' he said. 'Listen, she made the score with me. I'm out of pocket and I'm not going to take a hiding because of her!'

'You're mistaken, mate. No one here would have anything to do with a scumbag like you.'

'Mister, I'm trying to be nice here,' he said, his tone changing.

'Push off! I shouted. 'And take your insinuations and phoney money with you!'

'No, I'll wait. And *you* won't move me. If you try to, I'll be back with a blade and the first person to open your door will get it!'

'Come here again and I'll shove your blade up your skinny arse! Anyway, you're mistaken. You're at the wrong door.'

'Do you think I'm thick, mister, or what? It was here, for certain. A blondie one...a bit of all right.'

'What age?' I asked. Suddenly, I was nervous of what he might say.

'Older than me, but younger than you.'

I was about to question him further when I heard familiar voices on the stairs below. The Mother was home!

'Listen,' I said, drawing my wallet, 'I'll give you the money. Just clear off and say nothing. A deal?'

'That's all I'm here for, pal. It's business, purely business...'

With one eye on the landing below, I passed him a twenty-pound note. He started to examine it; I heard the voices getting closer. They had stopped to speak to Mrs. Mulligan from downstairs and I heard snatches of what the neighbour was saying, 'It's great to see you home' – 'there's nowhere like your own place' – 'isn't that right, love?'

Meanwhile, the young man wasn't going to be rushed. Finally, he seemed satisfied, and he stuffed the money into his back pocket and handed me the counterfeit.

'I don't want *that*!'

'It's yours, seeing as you've just paid for it.'

'Give it to me then and clear off,' I said, snatching it from him.

At that moment, the Mother, holding the handrail and supported by Stella, came into view. 'Mark, will you ever help me up the last few stairs?' she cried.

I scrambled to help, and it was at that stage that I saw the brother-in-law John behind them, carrying the bags. We almost lifted her up the final few steps and paused to rest on the landing in front of my pimply-faced friend.

'Who's this young man?' the Mother asked.

Miraculously, he'd taken on an angelic look, which I figured was well practised. 'He's collecting for a charity,' I explained. 'But don't worry, I've given him something...'

'Which charity is it?' she asked him.

'It's for the old folks, missus.'

She tittered. 'Oh! I'm one of them, so I can't be giving to myself, now, can I?'

'You're fine, missus. The man here gave me plenty.' With that, he smiled at me and bounded down the stairs.

I realized that I still had the fake twenty in my fist and stuffed it in my pocket and helped the Mother inside; she hadn't seen her apartment for five weeks. The first thing she said when she sat in her chair was, 'Will someone make me a cup of tea.' I smiled to myself as I put on the kettle. Little had changed. Welcome home, Mother! I thought.

Stella and John didn't hang around for too long. It was like they'd come to deliver a package and now that it had been safely handed over, they showed no desire to linger. On the way out, John paused at the door and winked at me, as if to say, I wish you luck with her!

It was like old times, Ma in her chair and I in mine, both of us drinking tea. She wanted to watch daytime television and relax. At the same time, she was taking in all around her, quietly reconnecting with her home of forty plus years. I was content to sit with her, but I couldn't stop thinking of the counterfeit note in my pocket and what it all meant. To think that Teresa had been sitting across from me, in the

Mother's place, and I never noticed anything unusual. And the child – how could she have taken drugs while in charge of Ruth? She'd never have done anything like that; definitely, it was impossible. At the first chance I got, I tore the fake note into shreds and flushed it down the toilet.

When I returned to the room, the Mother had spread her old photo album out on her lap. 'When I was in hospital, I kept thinking about this album and I wondered if I'd ever see it again.'

'You should have asked me, and I'd have brought it up to you.'

She considered what I said. 'No, it wouldn't have been the same; this is its home, where it belongs. Anyway, it's falling to bits and some of the photos are barely hanging in place, and you'd have been likely to lose some of them.'

'I should get you a new album and you can transfer the pictures over.'

'It wouldn't be the same. Your Da bought this and laid out most of it. He'd let me look but for years wouldn't let me meddle with it. He loved it when we all sat down as a family to go back over past holidays. Funny, later he seemed to lose interest in it, for no reason... But when I was in the hospital, I used to go through it in my mind, page by page, photo by photo.'

'You've some memory, Ma.'

'Maybe, but only for some things, insignificant things, and sometimes it's a curse to be like that. Earlier on, I went to the cutlery drawer, and I thought there was a tablespoon missing. The drawer just looked wrong. So, I counted them, just to satisfy myself. I know that I should be pleased to be back home, that I should be counting my blessings, and what am I doing instead? Counting tablespoons! Can you believe it?'

'And is there a tablespoon missing?' I asked.

'I'm sure there is, but what matter? It's only a piece of cutlery. Anyway, it'll probably turn up, like the bad penny.'

'I think I know what happened to it,' I lied. 'We took Ruth to the park, and she wanted to dig some clay – sorry, I couldn't find anything else – and we must have left the spoon behind us.'

'Well, that's that, then. Mystery solved.'

'I'll get one tomorrow to replace it,' I said.

'You'll do nothing of the kind. It was doing some good for your visitors and it's gone now, so, we'll do without. Anyway, there's more than enough cutlery in there to do an army.'

'Whatever you say, Ma.'

In my mind I could see a tablespoon held over the flame of a cigarette lighter. It wasn't my scene, but I knew enough about it; a scorch mark on the back would be a giveaway sign. I suddenly had an awful fear that it might still be in the apartment, and later I stole a look under Ma's bed, just in case. There was nothing there. I told myself that I could be mistaken, that I was jumping to conclusions, but my suspicion didn't go away that easily. And, worse of all, I had trusted her.

I ran into Jimmy a few days later. 'You know they've gone to England?' I told him.

'I heard,' he said. 'I don't know whether to be happy or to cry.'

'Why? What's up?'

'She went off without paying her debts. She wanted a loan of eighty pounds, and big-hearted Celine convinced me she was good for it. It's money I need badly now. But she's gone and I think my money is gone too. Forever.'

'Maybe you're wrong, Jimmy. She might post it.'

'And I might win big on the football pools. Mind you, in the beginning she seemed to be well set-up, throwing in her money with us on food and all – but it must have dried-up. Now, I'm going short myself.'

'The plastering job not going well, then?

'Work has dried-up,' he answered. 'I suppose she touched you for a loan, too?'

'No, I just gave her money. You know me, a sad case.'

'Maybe, but you did me a favour by taking her in like you did. I owe you one for that.'

Some days later, I needed to go to the spare wallet in the bedroom drawer for money. Out of curiosity I counted it and checked the figure with the one that I'd written down. It didn't tally, so I checked it again, this time with extra care. I'd been correct on the first count. It was exactly eighty pounds over.

CHAPTER SIXTEEN

When Jimmy ended up in casualty, no one knew who'd put him there, yet we had our suspicions. He never saw it coming; they wore balaclavas and hit him with hurling sticks; there were too many of them, even for him. His arm had been smashed and was in a cast. He couldn't work, even if there were any to be found in the plastering trade at the time, although, just prior to being attacked he had got some part-time work as a helper on a lorry – a big step down for a tradesman. But even that had been taken from him.

I visited him to see how he was faring. Celine had gone out with the boy, and I was glad of the opportunity to talk with him in private. He wasn't his carefree self; it seemed as if his engine had run out of petrol. He refused to go for a pint, not even to the pub over which they lived. The conversation out of him was miserly, so we sat in that small flat with long, silent intervals between our chat, he seemingly preoccupied with a large area of mould on the wallpaper.

We passed a laboured hour that way, then it was time for me to leave. I handed him eighty pounds. 'It's only the money you loaned Teresa,' I explained.

He refused to accept it. 'I gave it to *her*, not to you!'

'Jimmy, I feel responsible for the loan. Look at it this way, you'd never have met her if it weren't for me.'

'I met her before you, through Celine,' he reminded me.

'Whatever... Just take the money!' I put it down beside him and went for the door.

'I'll take it because I need it, but I don't want charity,' he called after me. 'When I'm working again, I'll pay you back. That's a promise, pal.'

'There's absolutely no need. It's your own money, I'm simply returning it.'

The flat had a private hall door at the side of the pub and as I opened it to go out, I met Celine on her way in. She was pushing a go-car that had seen better days. I wondered how she would get it up the stairs. 'Here, let me help you with that,' I said.

'It's fine, Mark. I leave it in the hall, nobody will touch it.'

I went to lift the boy into my arms. 'At least, let me carry Anthony upstairs for you.'

'No, Mark. It's fine, I tell you.' She snapped up the child, and I must have looked surprised. 'Jimmy wouldn't like it,' she said. 'You know what he can be like.'

'As long as you can manage...'

I was puzzled by what she meant. She went inside and I waited on Camden Street until I heard the latch click behind her.

It's hard to keep bad news from spreading, and shortly afterwards the Mother heard from Mrs. Culmane about Jimmy's arm. 'Trouble follows that family,' she said, hinting at happenings from the past. I couldn't take their side because I remembered the fight at the wedding, yet, instinctively, I felt a need to say something.

'Jimmy was attacked, not the other way round.'

She said that 'his type' was a magnet for trouble, and from the way she said it, I knew there was no swaying her from this opinion, and I wasn't going to discommode her by disagreeing with her, for more important to me at that time was her health. Although now that she was out and about – that was how she'd bumped into Jimmy's mother – she was slower on the feet and even short excursions to the shops seemed to take a lot out of her, betrayed by little beads of sweat on her forehead. Also, she would almost collapse into her chair to get the breathing back and I would run to put the kettle on for a cup of tea.

'You're a good son,' she would say, like I was still in short trousers.

~~~

It took me a moment to register who he was, mainly because I never expected Hugo to turn up at our door without any warning. Also, he was different from the last time I'd seen him. He was wearing a suit, and his fair hair was groomed, as if he had just left the barber's chair. He looked uneasy, not like the cocky nuisance I'd come across in the past. 'Do you remember me?' he said.

I nodded.

'Who's at the door, Mark?' the Mother called.

'It's okay, it's someone for me.'

'But who is it?'

'I'll be back in a second,' I shouted back, then stepped out on to the landing and pulled the door over behind me.

'I'm looking for my wife and daughter,' he said.

I studied him; he didn't look like someone who'd come for a row.

'They're not here.'

'Oh!' he said. 'This is the third door I've knocked on. I've already been to her family home, where I thought they were all the time. But they said that she'd left there, and they sent me to Celine and Jimmy's where I was told that Teresa and Ruth were here with you. And now I find out that she isn't here, either. Just who *am* I to believe?'

'All that I can tell you, Hugo, is that they *were* here for a time, but they've gone… As strange as that might sound to you, it is the truth.'

'Perhaps they're just out?' he suggested. 'Waiting is no problem, or I can call back? I just need to talk to her.'

I made it clear that she was gone for good, and he looked like a traveller who had turned up for a train and found that the line had been permanently closed. At that moment, the door of the apartment was pulled open behind me, and Ma put her head out.

'I was sure I heard you chatting,' she said. She looked at Hugo. 'Mark, don't leave people standing outside – it doesn't look right.' At that, she retreated to her chair. The Northerner looked uncertain of what to do next.

'We'll have to go in but keep your problems to yourself. She's just out of hospital.'

The Mother asked me to put the kettle on and, while I was in the kitchen, I heard her launch into the interrogation: 'I can tell from your accent that you're not from Dublin, are you? – How did you meet Mark in the first place? – Are you married?'

When I brought in the teas, I found them in cosy conversation, as if he had been living for years in the apartment across the landing and had just dropped in for a chat. I took a seat along with them and kept my mouth shut, feeling that I had lost control of the situation. It was clear that she had already guessed who he was, for he was telling her that he was worried that Ruth was not in pre-school and mixing with other children of her age. Looking at him, I wondered where was the depressed and rejected soul that Teresa had described? At that moment, he looked quite the opposite; a million questions ran through my mind; however, this wasn't the time nor place for them.

'Maybe you're worrying too much, Hugo,' Ma said.

I was surprised at how quickly she had come to be using his first name.

'A mother knows what's needed,' she continued.

'Aye, but did she do anything about it while she stayed here?' he asked.

They both looked in my direction. 'It never came up,' I confessed, feeling guilty. The Mother studied me, and rather than turn away, I let my gaze wander over her in return. People said that we were similar around the eyes, and I could see it now. I noticed that her hair was now showing more white patches among the grey. Some time ago, long before going into hospital, she'd experimented with one of those new hair colours but got a fright when she saw herself in the mirror and swore that, from then on, she'd let nature take its course. I was surprised when she asked me if I could help him find Teresa and Ruth, restore them to their home.

'I've told him already that I don't know where they are. I really can't help him.'

She looked unconvinced.

The Northerner said, 'I'm going back on the bus to Derry this evening because I've a classful of exam students in the morning. If I give you my address, would you write and let me know if you hear anything?'

It was written in a neat hand on a page torn from a notebook and I put it under the Manx cat ornament on the shelf; he never commented on the souvenir.

'It was a pleasure meeting you, Mrs. O'Bride, and I'm sorry for just turning up at your door with no warning.'

'Don't you mention it, Hugo, and I hope that everything works out for you. And, I'll say a little prayer.'

'A wee prayer would be welcome.'

I went down to the street with him and gave him directions on how to get back to the bus station. He offered his hand in farewell, and, as I shook it, I couldn't resist testing him. 'I'm glad to see you're back on your feet.'

'What do you mean?' he snapped. 'Has she been talking about me? What did she tell you?'

I had unsettled him and for a second, I saw the same fellow that I'd known in the Isle of Man. I tried to look apologetic. 'Sorry, I must have been mistaken... Forget I ever spoke.'

He was calm again. 'That'll do rightly,' he said, lifting the lapels of his suit jacket so that it sat better on his shoulders. Our eyes met for a challenging moment, then he left, and I watched him meet the corner at the top of the street and turn correctly – at least, so far, he was following my directions.

On the way back upstairs, I met Mrs. Mulligan on her landing, washing down her door. 'It's nice to see your mother getting plenty of visitors,' she said.

'Yes. It's a tonic for her.'

'God bless her, and she's doing so well now too.'

I agreed and escaped upstairs. It wasn't that I didn't want to be friendly, it was just that I wasn't in the humour for it.

'Well?' the Mother asked when I came back into the apartment.

'He's gone on his way,' I said.

'That's not what I'm talking about – you know where she and the child are, don't you?'

'What makes you think that?'

'A mother can tell things.'

'Don't I know it,' I said.

'Mark O'Bride, there's no need to be cheeky.'

'It wasn't meant that way but this time you're wrong. I don't know where they are and wouldn't know where to start looking.'

I hadn't told her that Celine would probably have her address, however, at that moment, I'd had enough of dealing with other people and their problems.

One day, completely without warning, Ma said, 'Son, I'm worried what will happen to you when I'm gone.'

'Why, where are you off to?' I answered, trying to keep it light.

'You know what I mean. I won't be here forever, and heaven knows how you'll live on your own then.'

'How did I manage when you were in hospital? when you were in Stella and John's? You'd forgotten about that, hadn't you?'

'You did your best but as soon as I got home, I saw that it had been neglected.'

'That isn't fair, Ma. It was clean when you got home, and don't forget that we'd company here for some of the time.'

'Son, your version of clean and mine are on different planets, but it's not only that. It's the thought of you being left on your own, the thought of the bachelor thing...'

'You're worrying over nothing. To begin with, I can't see you dying for a long time yet, and, as well, I don't see why you're concerned over me, especially when I'm not.'

She sighed. 'That doesn't give me comfort. You're just like your father was. I couldn't get him to talk about the serious things neither.'

I looked to his photograph. Although it was always accepted that I resembled her in looks, she said that in my thinking and actions I was more like him. In many ways I knew she was correct for when it came to serious subjects, I was a bit of a coward. The excuse I always made to myself was that in many cases it was outside of my control, and pointless. I had to go to the pub after talking to her. It was plain that she fretted over me, but did she know how much I hated thinking about what lay ahead for *her*? She was slowing up – not upstairs, there she was still as sharp as ever – but in the gradual and small ways that remind you that nobody lasts forever.

In the pub, I got into the company of fellows from the neighbourhood, and before I knew it, it was closing time. Then I queued in the chipper. The girl serving was a daughter of the owner and she always smiled at me, like she knew me well. Her skin was pale, although that night it was flushed from the closing-hour rush. She didn't have the olive skin look of her father, who always seemed to be standing with great patience over a fryer which was as big as a church organ, waiting for the chips to cook, then he'd scoop them up and bag them and pass them on to his daughter, who was ready to add the salt and vinegar. That night, I wondered if she had the same traits as her father, like I was supposed to have of mine. She was called Maria. I knew that because I'd heard the father use it. I imagined that one night I would surprise her by saying 'Thanks, Maria'. But it certainly wasn't going to be said that night, for I doubted my ability to form the words. I'm sure I had a drunken, dumb smile when she passed the chips across the counter to me.

I was reminded of the Maria in New York, and of her Uncle Thiago, the godfather of the family who had offered me a job, and of my friend Paul Sweeney. It is uncanny that I thought of the Yank that night, not expecting to ever see him again; however, a few days later, a chatty letter came from him, seemingly for no other reason but to keep in touch. He clearly wanted to keep up our friendship.

The Mother looked amazed when I asked to use her writing pad.

CHAPTER SEVENTEEN

The Mother called me. 'Mark, will you slip into the library for me? I'm all out of reading material; you know what I like. Get the large print if you can, but if a book looks a good one, take the normal size – I can squint.' She had already put the consignment for returning into a straw shopping bag and it was waiting for me at the door. I had almost reached the library when I bumped into Celine, wheeling the go-car. She was wearing sunglasses which surprised me, as they would have looked good on a sun holiday, but here in Dublin they made you look as if you were trying to be somebody you weren't, especially on an overcast day that threatened rain. I knelt and talked with young Anthony for a moment, then straightened to face her – I could see discolouration on one cheekbone, a yellow-purple patch extending below the frame of the sunglasses.

She knew I saw it and was quick to say, 'I'm the most awkward person at times…tripped and hit the post at the start of the stairs…'

'You were lucky, you could have lost an eye.'

'Yes, I was lucky.'

'At least, it gives you an excuse to wear your sunglasses – I like the look!'

'You won't believe it, Mark,' she said, smiling. 'The last and only other time I've worn these was in the Isle of Man – that was a great holiday, wasn't it?'

I nodded in agreement. It may have been good for her, I thought. But she appears to have forgotten that it didn't end well for me.

'By the way, how is Jimmy this weather?'

'He's improving but the arm is slow to heal. Sometimes it gets to him... You know, the frustration...'

We stood for a few seconds, both unsure of what to say next, then I remembered the visit from the Northerner. 'You sent your man Hugo over to me?'

'I'm sorry about that, Mark. It was the only way I could get him out of my hair.' She adjusted the sunglasses as though they were irritating her. 'You didn't tell him anything, did you?'

'Why would I have done that? I owe him nothing. Mind you, my mother seemed taken in by him, but I wasn't.'

'I knew you wouldn't tell him anything. However, I sometimes wonder why we're all so protective of her. It's almost impossible with her to know who's telling the truth. I've known her all my life and still don't really know her. But she's my friend and I must stick by her – and, as you say, we owe Hugo nothing.'

'I take it you're in touch?'

'Yes, we write...'

'How are they doing? or does she say?'

'She paints a good picture. And gets on well with her cousin who even has got her fixed up with a job.'

There was a whimper from the boy in the go-car.

'Listen, I have to be going. Jimmy will be waiting for us. I better be on my way.'

'Sure, sure... Tell him I'll drop over some night. Maybe even get him to come out for a jar!'

'That'll be nice, Mark – you're a real pal.' She hurried away.

At the library, while I emptied the straw bag and waited for the librarian to check in the books, I found myself thinking about her story of falling against the banister post. I had to believe her, only because the alternative was unthinkable. As usual, it was the Romance section I was in. This was the Mother's taste, which I'd originally found unusual as it hadn't fitted my image of her, and I would have been surprised if later she changed her taste and asked for a crime novel. I concluded that it was the predictable, happy endings that pleased her, and I was grateful for the library books because it meant that she had less free time to talk, for when she was idle, with no television to watch or romantic novels to read, I was expected to fill in the gaps with conversation. Back home, I laid the newly borrowed books on the table, hoping she hadn't already read any of them. It was a test of my memory, and I was relieved when she read the blurbs, then neatly made a reading stack on the floor beside her chair, without rejecting any.

'Did you meet anyone on the way?' she asked, in her routine manner.

'No one you'd know, Ma, except for Celine.'

'Celine? Isn't she the one married to Jimmy Culmane?'

'That's her,' I said, knowing in my heart that she really didn't have to ask that question. 'She's had a small accident. Tripped and banged her face. She's fine, though.'

'In my day you'd think twice before heading out with a mark on the face. Just in case people got the wrong impression. I bumped into the press door in the kitchen once – you weren't even born then – and stayed put for over a week.'

'That seems excessive to me. Sure everyone knew you and the Da, knew that he'd never raise a hand to you.'

'Perhaps it was, but I wasn't going to give them the chance to talk about me.'

'Sometimes, Ma, you amaze me. I can't believe that you'd think that people around here would think bad of the Da. He was so respected.'

I looked at his photograph and remembered him. You knew that he valued his respectability by the way he dressed. Just as you'd never see a priest or politician looking untidy, so it was with him. Also, he was careful when he came to choosing his company: no men who hung round the corner outside the pub; no men who were last to leave it or had to be ordered out; no men with constant foul mouths;

or, most certainly, no women who drank in the bar and not in the snug. It wasn't that he had airs or graces, it was just the way he was. Times have changed, I thought, and everything is more relaxed now and you don't have to worry so much about what others think of you. But, now and again, the Mother would pick me up on my appearance. 'You're not going out in that scruffy jumper!' And just to please her I would change it.

~~~

Jimmy appeared glad to see me. Anthony was in his bed, and Celine was in a corner of the room at an ironing board.

'Are you any good at ironing, Mark?' she said, laughing.

'The Ma wouldn't let me within a mile of an iron. She says I'd scorch everything. So, I wouldn't have a clue.'

'Any excuse, you men are all the same.'

'Celine even irons the sheets,' Jimmy said. 'I tell her there's no need, no one will ever see them, but she wants to. A waste of time really.'

'They're nicer to sleep on, don't you think so?' She was looking at me as she spoke, but I could only shrug my shoulders, pretending that the question was beyond me. She was standing away from the light and her face was in shadow. The mark could still have been there, but I couldn't see it. Better not to mention the accident, I thought.

'I came round here to drag himself out for a pint,' I said, talking to her, yet – at the same time – looking at him.

'You know I'm a bit short, pal,' he said.

'So what? I'll stand you a few, no big deal.'

We walked further than normal to find a pub for even though it wasn't said, it was better to stay out of our regular places, just in case we happened to run into someone we knew, someone who would drag us into a drinking session. We found a quiet place, took up a small table in a corner, our only company being a bored barman and a distant television, its flickering figures unrecognisable from where we sat, its sound a murmur. '*Sláinte*!' he said, raising his glass.

'Your good health, Jimmy.' We both took our time with the first swallow. There was an opportunity to look around the bar, from the purple-painted timber that went from the floor to a dado rail halfway up the wall, a failed effort at modernisation, to the carpet that was so soiled by spilled drink and vomit patches that it was impossible in the gloom to tell whether it was green or blue.

'It's great to get out,' he said.

'The simple pleasures…hard to beat.'

'Here's to simple pleasures.'

We were like old age pensioners that you sometimes see filling up their time. I didn't want to say anything that would remind him of the injury that had put him out of work. He was looking straight ahead, possibly at the distant television, when he broke the silence, and I knew then that his brain had been clicking away all the time. 'Do you remember when you helped me out in the Isle of Man with that personal matter? when I thought Celine was slipping away from me?'

'I was only a sounding board.'

'I need your help again.'

Oddly, at that moment, the barman moved closer to us, giving me the impression that he was shoving an ear in our direction, but I knew it was impossible, unless he had superhuman hearing. The question of helping Jimmy was hanging in the air and I didn't want to know about it, mainly because I felt unfit to be handing out advice; I was trapped with him at this lonely table in this lonely pub and saw no way out of the situation. 'What's up?' I said finally.

'I feel it again, you know…'

'I don't follow.'

'There's a gap coming between us. She's gone cold on me... Gawd, Mark, I'm terribly bad at talking about things like this.'

'You're both just under pressure, that's all.'

'If it was only that easy,' he said.

'It will end when you're back earning. In the meanwhile, if you're badly stuck, I could help a bit. It would be a loan, mind you.'

'I'd hate that, Mark – it would make me feel like shit.'

'Don't take me the wrong way; I'm just trying to help out.'

'You know, I thought Celine and I could get through anything. I never thought it would change us.'

'I wouldn't know anything about that,' I said.

'She gets narky for nothing; I'm at my wit's end; Anthony even cries more…'

'As I said, all will be right when you start earning again.'

'I hope we can hold out till then,' he said. It was as if he were waiting on the cavalry to arrive.

The barman had disappeared, but the sound of bottles clinking in crates being pulled around told you he wasn't far away.

I changed the subject and asked, 'If someone you knew were doing drugs, doing it slyly, yet, under your nose – do you think you'd be able to tell?'

'You're talking about that bitch Teresa, aren't you?'

'How did you know that?' I asked. Then it dawned on me that he had known all along. 'You knew, and you *let* me bring her into my home!'

'What was I to do? *We* didn't know, not until it was too late. Teresa said it was only occasional and that she could drop it at any time. And Celine wouldn't let me put her out on the street, with the kid and all.'

'So, you used me, instead?'

'It wasn't like that, pal. Remember, you offered.'

'Don't "pal" me, you bolix! You could have warned me!'

'And if I had, you'd have shied away from her. But we had to move her on because the landlord had seen a dealer hanging around the place. He was worried over the reputation of the bar and threatened to put us out on the street. What was I to do?'

'So, you sold me a sob story and I bought it, the fool that I am.'

'It wasn't meant to be like that.'

'Then, tell me, how was it meant to be? You foisted her on me! Some friend you are!'

'Mark, you offered to take her in. I didn't force her on you.'

'I only did it to help out.'

The barman had reappeared and was re-arranging beer mats on tables, watching to see if our row was going to erupt into a fight. I realized that I was shaking, that my heart was thumping. I had to get out of there.

'Don't go, Mark...'

I spat out my parting words. 'You've made a right fool of me!'

He must have looked a lonely sight, the only customer left in that gloomy pub. You could say that I overreacted, but I was sickened by the whole thing and had never imagined he'd pull something like that on me.

Mind you, I never intended for it to be the death of a friendship.

CHAPTER EIGHTEEN

We'd had the telephone in the apartment for some months now. Before its arrival, the Department of Posts and Telegraphs had thrown up every excuse, no lines, no available connections at the exchange, but when the Mother had increased difficulty climbing the stairs and we were afraid of her falling in the apartment due to dizzy spells, the family put pressure on our local politician and eventually a black, Bakelite telephone was given a prominent position on a small table, within her easy reach. It was there in the event of an emergency; however, it also opened a new world to her, as she no longer depended on Stella or any other member of the family to call in to see her, instead, all she had to do was dial a number and talk to them. And could she talk! It was as if the telephone had been invented with her in mind. As for me, I seldom used it, and was surprised when one day it rang and she called, 'Mark, it's for you.'

'Who is it?'

'Don't ask me, son, he didn't say...'

I took the phone, not knowing what to expect.

'How's it going, buddy?'

It was the Yank's voice and I remembered that in my last letter to him I'd given him our number. 'It's Paul Sweeney,' I told the Mother (she was close by, waiting to know who it was). 'You know, my New York friend'. I went back to the call. 'The line's really clear, Paul.'

'It should be clear – I'm here, in Dublin!'

I found out that he'd come on a last-minute charter flight, with a room in a city hotel thrown in, all at a bargain price. We went out that night for a meal, and after eating I took him to a few of my favourite pubs; one of them he knew, of the others he said, 'And I thought I knew Dublin!' He had lost his Marine Corps ready-for-action physique, for even though a stout leather belt was tightened on the waist, it didn't contain the peep of expanding belly; in addition, his hair was longer, and had started to go grey early.

'Mark, I'm here long enough to take a quick trip out of the city, would you come with me? Go one day, back the next.'

'Sure. Where to?'

'I'll leave it up to you. You pick a place.'

'Derry.' (I had said that without thinking.)

'Derry? Why would we go to a place like that? I've had enough trouble in the past, without walking into more.'

'There's a coach,' I said (I knew that from the Northerner's visit), and it's a place we've never been – well, I haven't. Have you?'

'No, I haven't. But that doesn't mean I have to go there. Tell me, why can't we hit Cork, or Galway? Somewhere, where people just do the tourist thing?'

'Someone I knew lived there,' I said, 'and I'd like to see the place for myself.'

He laughed. 'I know who it is. It's your woman from the Isle of Man – the one that went off with that headcase from the North. What was her name?' He was searching for it in his memory, and I wasn't going to help him. Then his face lit up. 'It's Teresa, isn't it? I thought you were finished with her?'

I shrugged my shoulders, like a footballer trying to explain an own goal.

He was now staring at me, as if I were an oddity. 'There's absolutely no way I'm going to waste my short time in Ireland in a place like Derry,' he said.

~~~

We stood on Craigavon Bridge over the river Foyle. It was a hot July day, and we lingered and probably would have felt like holidaymakers if it wasn't for the two armoured Land Rovers that were parked at a skewed angle at one end of the bridge. Minutes before, we had walked past the checkpoint and seen soldiers with weapons trained on the line of queuing traffic. Now, as I looked at the river, the hills rising from each bank, I found that I couldn't enjoy the view, because seeing the soldiers had swept away any sense of relaxation; however, it was my own fault as I had persuaded Paul to come here. But he seemed at ease, and I really shouldn't have expected him to be any different, for, after all, he had done a tour in Vietnam.

We moved along the bridge, Paul following my lead, but I really didn't know where I was going or why I was here. I thought of asking someone for directions, but directions to where? The bridge ended. Do we go straight on? Turn left, or right? Suddenly, we were face-to-face with two British soldiers in combat gear.

'You men look lost,' one of them said. The other one kept looking away from us and towards the distant buildings, and then back to us.

My smile was a weak effort, as if my face muscles were on strike. 'We're visiting,' I said.

'Where did you men come from?' the first soldier asked.

'We came up from Dublin…on the coach.'

The soldier's eyes narrowed, as if the very mention of the word "Dublin" had spooked him. 'When?' he asked.

'An hour ago.'

He looked at our shoulder bags then glanced to check that his backup man was still in place. 'And why are you in Londonderry?'

'We're visiting,' I repeated.

'Who? where?'

I thought of the address Hugo had given me and whipped it from my pocket. Paul looked at me, curious as to what I'd handed over. 'I think we've taken a wrong turn,' I said.

'And who are these people?' the soldier demanded, poking a finger at the address.

When I told him they were relatives, he studied the piece of paper, but it might as well have been a cryptic crossword; then he passed it back to the second soldier. 'Rod, do you know where this place is?'

The second soldier, who had a boyish face, didn't even bother to look at the address. 'I'm as lost in this fucking town as you are.'

'They could be hostiles,' the first soldier said.

The backup man's boyishness left him; he now looked like a dog threatening a postman. I noticed that Paul seemed amused by them, and was standing in a casual way, like a bored corner boy. The soldiers looked unsure of themselves. Suddenly, the first soldier stood out on to the traffic lane and waved down a taxi. The driver looked grumpy, and the soldier showed him the address. From what I could hear, he was checking whether the address was genuine; the taxi man said he knew it. Then the soldier turned back to us. 'This man will take you where you're going. Now get on your way, and don't let me see you again!'

The driver wanted to know if we'd the money to pay the fare. I waved a sterling tenner at him, and we pulled away.

'You never told me that we'd be doing house visits,' Paul said, as we left the bridge behind.

'I didn't know it myself,' I answered.

He was unfazed by what had happened; however, I found that my legs were shaking, and I was beginning to be sorry that I'd ever heard of Derry, or even Londonderry.

The taxi passed extremely steep streets of terraced houses as we moved upwards from the river. Looking back from the car window, the view of the city and its surrounds was like a picture postcard. Derry in CinemaScope, like a film taken from an aircraft; then we lost sight of it and the river. We went two or three more miles and stopped outside a neat bungalow; it had a lawn as smooth as the bowls green in Herbert Park. A man came out, wiry, a suit waistcoat left unbuttoned, the sleeves of his shirt rolled up.

'Robert, I've visitors from Dublin for you,' the taximan said.

'Oh! And who might you men be?' he asked. 'I don't know anyone in Dublin...well, not really'.

'I know Hugo,' I said. 'He gave me this address. I thought he lived here?'

'*I* live here,' the man said. 'How do you know our Hugo?'

'We met on holidays in the Isle of Man, sir. Is he here?'

At that point, the taximan coughed to get my attention and I paid the fare, and he gave me back my piece of paper with the address on it and drove away. The man, Robert, walked out to the road and watched the car disappear into the distance which gave me the distinct feeling that he didn't want to talk with us. I looked at Paul, who was standing to one side, and I wondered what he was thinking. The man rambled back to us, and, on his way, stooped to pick up a child's toy from the pathway.

'No, he's not here,' he said. 'I'm his father.'

'I also know Teresa,' I said. That news didn't seem to impress him. 'And, of course,' I added, 'I've also met young Ruth.'

He looked me up and down. 'How did you meet Ruth?'

'They stayed with me in Dublin.'

'Did they, now... Well, that doesn't change anything. Hugo still isn't here.'

'We can wait. Will he be long?'

He mumbled something about his son having no fixed times to his comings and goings, and walked back to the house and, without going inside, he closed the front door, then returned to where we were standing.

At that moment I heard a familiar voice. 'Uncle Mark! Uncle Mark!'

It was Ruth; she had come running from round the side of the house and was skipping down the pathway. She stopped in front of me, and I bent down to give her a hug. 'Are *you* staying with us?' she said.

Hugo's father looked startled at the fuss she was making over me, and he took her by the hand. 'Don't be annoying the visitors,' he said gently.

'But it's Uncle Mark,' she said, as if he should have known who I was.

'All right, wee darling, I know, I know. Your visitors have come a long way to see you and your daddy. Maybe we should bring them in and make them a cup of tea?'

'Yes, yes, a cup of tea – I can use my new tea set!'

She dropped his hand and, instead, took mine and guided me around to the back of the bungalow and the grandfather and the Yank trailed behind. We went in through the kitchen door where a woman in a pinny met us with a smile. She wiped a hand with a tea towel and prepared instinctively for a handshake, despite clearly having no idea of who we were or what our business was. 'Robert, who are these good people?' she asked.

'We're friends of Hugo,' I explained.

Then Ruth said, 'Uncle Mark, come and look at my drawing!'

The woman had a sudden look of panic.

Maybe an hour or more had been spent in the kitchen, playing with Ruth and her imaginary play friends. A few times, I attempted conversation with Robert the grandfather and the woman – she was either the shiest person in the North or had a problem with her hearing or just didn't want to talk. A large electric clock on the wall clicked the minutes away. Every so often I looked across at Paul, who was becoming fidgety, continually crossing, and uncrossing his arms. Finally, a car pulled up outside. 'That'll be our Hugo now,' the man said. Gravel was crunched underfoot as someone passed down the side of the bungalow, and each one of us looked to the back door.

Ruth ran to him. 'Daddy, Daddy! Look, it's Uncle Mark!'

He lifted her, gave her a hug, spun with her, then placed her back on the floor. He was dressed in pants and shirt, the collar loosened and a necktie dangling. We were given a nod of recognition, then he went to the kitchen sink and washed his hands; the woman handed him a towel and, as he slowly dried them, his shoulder blades were moving like gathering storm clouds. He turned to look at me. 'So, this is what I get for giving you my address,' he said, sarcastically.

'We were stopped by the army, and they wanted to know what we were doing here. It was fortunate that I had your address on me, that's all that was in it. Then, when I saw that Ruth was here, I thought I'd wait to see you.'

'And here I thought that you'd come specially to see me. I am disappointed.'

There was a moment of uncertainty, then, unexpectedly, Paul Sweeney said, 'I'm sure you are, Hugo, but at least you can offer us a drink.'

'This is a teetotal house. You'll have to go elsewhere for liquor. My parents don't approve, and there's no way they'd permit scandal. Isn't that correct, Ruth?' he asked, sitting on a wooden form, and lifting her on to his knee. She didn't answer but played with the necktie. 'But Mammy can offer you a cup of tea,' he added. His mother went to busy herself at the range. There was a pained look on Paul's face.

'You found Teresa, then?' I said, motioning with my head towards the child.

His father spoke from the corner. 'We don't talk about such things in front of wee Ruth.'

'Okay.' I said, 'I can understand that.'

The Yank was standing now and edging his way towards the door. I asked Hugo if he could call a taxi for us. He volunteered to take us back into the city, however, before we left, I stole a hug from Ruth and gave her a fleeting kiss on the head. She wanted to come with us and cried when the grandmother's bony hand restrained her. As we pulled away from the bungalow, the grandfather Robert looked a worried man as he raised an arm in a weak salute. Hugo was driving as if he were in control of a fire tender on callout, instead of being in a Ford Escort. His shoulders were hunched over the steering wheel, and he noisily changed gears without sympathy for the gearbox, and even though I was never a driver myself, I'd seen enough to know that he wasn't a good one. The city came back into view, and he swung the car into corners at speed, sending us, the passengers, from side to side.

I shouted at him over the engine noise, 'So, how did you manage to find Teresa?'

He hit the brakes and the car screeched to a halt. '*You* certainly weren't any help,' he said. 'Anyway, she wrote home for something, and her father sent me the details. I drove over to London, found the house and came home with Ruth.'

'I'm amazed she let you.'

'She couldn't stop me, as we were gone before she knew it.'

'You actually *took* her?'

'Yes, just as she had taken her from me. Ruth belongs here with us, where she has a proper home, not some dump on a grimy terrace. And don't waste your sympathy on poor Teresa, she knows well that Ruth is here, safe, and happy. That's why she hasn't even come after her. She knows we can do better for her here.'

'I find that hard to believe,' I said. 'She must be –'

'Don't you worry yourself over her,' he said. 'I know you've a soft spot for her, but take it from me, she only thinks about herself. I know that to my cost.'

A horn blast from a car coming up behind reminded him that he had stopped almost in the centre of the road. He restarted the car and this time we moved at a sensible pace, as if the need to remove us from Ruth had suddenly become less urgent. I kept thinking about Teresa, and of how she would be demented with worry, despite what he had said. Suddenly, he was more of a mystery to me than ever.

True, he wanted the child to grow up in Derry, but was he also trying to entice Teresa back to this patch of the world?

The road now fell back towards the river Foyle. We passed housing estates that shouted the Northern divide; the loyalists had kerbs painted red, white and blue; the nationalists had green, white and orange; depending on your tribe, graffiti messages told you whether you were welcome or not. We crossed the bridge where we'd been stopped earlier in the day; however, we were waved through, as if the soldiers now on duty were wilting in the heat and had grown tired of the routine. Hugo drove us to a hotel near the river, but had to park away from the building, as waist high concrete cubes stopped him from pulling up to the door. He stayed with the car while we went to check-in. A girl with a sweet smile was on reception and I wondered how she could be in such good form, as I was already feeling down and had only been in the city for a matter of hours. Once a room had been secured, we rejoined Hugo, who'd offered to give us a quick tour of the "sights". We passed more checkpoints and entered the Bogside and he showed us where the Bloody Sunday shootings had happened.

Looking round, I saw ordinary people going about their daily business, doing normal things. And children were playing on the streets. And people looked small against the Republican murals on the gables of end-of-terrace houses. The ordinariness of daily living made it seem unreal.

'I've seen enough, let's go to a bar. What about in there?' Paul said. He was pointing towards a public house with boarded-up windows and a single menacing entrance. 'You can drop us off here.'

Our "guide" advised against it; I was glad, as I hadn't liked the look of the place. He said that he would bring us to another bar and then leave us, as he'd exam papers to correct. We were only in the door of the place when Paul rounded on me. 'You knew all along you were going to contact him, yet you hid it from me!'

'Not really...'

'Not really, my arse. You're obsessed with that woman Teresa, and everything connected with her. That's why we're here, isn't it?'

'Nonsense,' I said. 'If I were, I'd have gone to London, not come here. We're in Derry to see the place, have a good time. Here, let me get a round in.'

'You might be fooling yourself, but you're not fooling me!'

I left him to seethe and went to the bar counter. The evening news came on the television. Everyone in the pub stopped to listen. The announcer said that a bomb had gone off. There'd been casualties. Even though the blast was a distance away – another Northern town shattered – it was too close for comfort. It could just as easily have been here, in Derry, I thought. The announcer moved to the next item, and the bar went back to business as usual. I brought the drinks back to our table; Paul had cooled down by then.

He said, 'When I saw that child Ruth today, I was reminded of my own daughter Marina. I have to fight with her mother for visiting rights.'

'Who does Marina take after?' I asked.

'She's Italian. No contest there. But I'm good at being a father, whenever Maria gives me the chance.'

He was no longer annoyed with me. We drank; companions; not truly knowing one another; unfamiliar with the bar we were in, unfamiliar with the city we were in.

The next morning, we slept in and made it down to the dining room just in time for the breakfast of "Ulster Fry". The hotel's policy on vacating the rooms was relaxed, so we read the newspapers in the residents' lounge and generally took our time. It was an opportunity to telephone the Mother. 'And what time will you be home?' she asked.

'I can't be sure, Ma.'

'I'll keep the dinner for you.'

We paid the bill and, on our way out, we met people on their way in for lunch. Wanting to see something of the city before we left, we went to its centre. Here also it was everyday living; shoppers meeting in the streets, stopping to chat, just as they did at home. We rambled around, stopped at a redundant black cannon on the city's walls. Below us was the river glistening in sunlight, in the distance the hills were green. We could see the Bogside nestling in the valley where Hugo had taken us the day before. I began to feel that I had misjudged the place.

We were on the coach heading back to Dublin when the Yank started talking about the break-up of his marriage to Maria. 'On the outside it looked good. Marina was born, a beautiful baby, and Maria was, and still is, a wonderful mother to her. I was earning good money and we'd moved into our own place, a little house that I was able to do up. I can't explain what went wrong, but I know it was my fault, not hers. Something within me wanted to destroy what we had, even against my own wishes. Can you believe that?'

'I don't understand it,' I said.

'Neither can I,' he answered.

I thought about my trip to New York, the wedding, my wedding dance with Maria; somehow, I remembered her Uncle Thiago, who had wanted me to go and work for him, take me over to the Promised Land. I asked about him.

'He's in jail. It turns out that his little empire was a front for money laundering. You'd a lucky escape there.'

He had given me this information in such a matter-of-fact way that at first it didn't sink in. I then felt a sense of relief, but there was also a sense of guilt which came because at one stage I'd seriously considered the Italian's offer but worse still had even contemplated leaving home, leaving the Mother to live alone. And it all would have come to nought! I watched the countryside pass the coach window. My mind went back to the day before and to seeing Ruth, and to the surprise of it, and to the fuss she had made of me, and I wondered if she really thought that I *was* her uncle.

When we arrived in Dublin, Paul had one more night left in town and that was promised to an aunt – his mother's sister – then he would fly back to the United States on the following day. I had suggested to him that we get together again sometime in the future and travel somewhere else.

'That's a deal, buddy, but on one condition.'

'What's that?'

'That I get to pick where we're going.'

There was a handshake, then a bear hug, and I watched him walk away.

~~~

I knew it was serious when I came down the street and saw the neighbours gathered on the pavement outside our building. The brother-in-law John came forward from the group, and offered his hand and I shook it, not fully sure as to why I was doing it; however, I knew that shock was already gripping me.

'We'd no way of contacting you. The ambulance was called, but...' he said.

'What happened?'

'She rang Stella saying she wasn't feeling well. We found her on the floor. I'm really sorry, Mark.'

'Where's she now?'

'They took her to James's Hospital. Stella and the others are probably still there.'

'But I rang her earlier. She seemed fine.'

He was talking but my mind was elsewhere. I imagined the Mother lying on the floor of the apartment surrounded by her photographs. My only need at that moment was to go to the hospital and see her. John said he would drive me. Solemn-faced neighbours were watching, and I knew that they wanted to say something to me but were bound to silence by the code of respect surrounding a death. They would come to me later. I had been an onlooker myself many a time but today... My legs felt strange as I walked with John to the car. Before we got in, I stopped to smoke, then tossed the cigarette away half-finished.

This couldn't be put off.

CHAPTER NINETEEN

S he was buried with the Da, then everyone went to a pub close to the graveyard. No one had a bad word to say about the Mother, which made it better and at the same time made it worse.

For the family, there were promises of further bonding between us – we owed it to the Ma and Da. And I got well-meaning invitations of a bed from the others, to help me while I was getting used to the fact that the Mother was gone for good; however, I told everyone that I would manage. Over the next few weeks there were letters and Mass cards from people who'd known the Mother, some of whom I didn't know. The letter from Teresa was a surprise.

Dear Mark,

I'm sorry to hear that your mother has passed away. It must have been a big shock for you. I remember meeting her at Celine's wedding and thought she was a lovely woman, and now I feel that it's a pity I never got to know her properly, especially after her letting us stay in her lovely home.

All's well here, but it's not the same as Dublin. Ruth is visiting with her grandparents in Derry for the moment.

Your dear friends,

Teresa and Ruth.

Her address was on the letter. Now she had no need to be secretive because Hugo had already tracked her down. It stood in its envelope on the mantle piece, looking at me, inviting me to reread it but when my sisters Stella and Cora came by to tidy the apartment, I hid it from them, hid it from their curiosity. I felt that they were intruding on my privacy by even coming to the apartment – after all, this was my home, and they had long left to set up their own. In the back of my mind was the suspicion that the Ma had made them promise to care for me. She was gone now, and I didn't have to answer to anyone, except the boss who paid me my wages.

But you don't always have it your own way. I mean, like the day they came in without warning, looking as if they meant business; there was nothing that could have prepared me for what happened next.

'We're going to clear the Mother's bedroom,' Stella declared, 'bag her clothes and give them to charity.'

I told her that I felt they were being hasty.

'What's the problem, Mark?' Cora said. She couldn't help it, but since childhood, she sometimes came across as being aggressive.

'It just seems wrong.'

'What's wrong is that the room isn't right. Ma always liked things to be right. Anyway, into the room and let's see what we can do!'

They were stripping the bed by the time I caught up with them. A pile of laundry was tied up in a sheet and brought out to the hall.

'I want to toss the mattress and air the reverse side,' Stella said.

It was then we came across an envelope. It was open and when Stella picked it up, two passport-size photographs on a strip fell out onto the base of the bed. They were in black-and-white, memories of a giggly moment in a Douglas amusement arcade. One showed a startled Teresa on her own, the one below it was where I'd sat in along with her. Hadn't there'd been a second one of us together? I thought. The photographs were snatched up before I could reach them.

'She's pretty,' Stella said. 'Who is she? And why are they under the Mother's mattress?'

I shrugged my shoulders. I knew the answer to the first question, but the second...

'Go on, Mark! Who is she?'

'Just someone I knew.' It annoyed me that she was playing detective with things that didn't concern her.'

She handed the photos to Cora, who immediately pounced on the truth. 'I *know* who it is. It must be the girl Teresa who stayed here! Where else would she have slept but in the Ma's bed? She re-examined the photos. 'You look like you're having fun, especially her. *Is* she good fun?'

'She was when they were taken,' I answered, 'but, I can't say what she's like now. She's had a messy marriage, problems with custody of the kid, stuff like that.'

'Why were they here under the mattress?' Stella asked.

'That's a complete mystery. Maybe for safe-keeping?' I knew it was the feeblest of feeble suggestions.

'It's looks as if she meant you to find them, otherwise she wouldn't have left them there.'

At that moment, I was back in Douglas and Teresa was laughing and holding the photo strip at arm's length, while she waited for it to dry.

My sister was still waiting for an explanation.

'If she'd meant me to find them, why were they hidden so well? I said. 'And what if Ma had found them? Can you imagine?'

Stella burst out laughing. 'God only knows what she'd have thought. But she was broad-minded, you know. Maybe you never saw it, but she was.'

'At times, maybe,' I said. 'Hey, let's get stuck into the room and finish the job.'

'Now look who's in a hurry,' Cora said. 'Maybe you're scared there's other surprises in here for us?'

There weren't any more, thankfully. The hall was now taken up with the bundle of laundry and a pile of black plastic bags – more of Ma being erased. John would come by later with the car to remove them. When they had left, I looked again at the strip of photographs. I smiled at Teresa's laughing face and inspected the younger version of my own ugly pus. Yes, it had been a carefree moment. The puzzle as to why she had placed them under the mattress saw me go back into the bedroom and stare at the bed, something I was to repeat over the following days.

There was now a new photograph in the apartment. Mother was smiling, a recent shot, used in the memorial card. Her usual pile of borrowed books kept within arm's reach was no longer on the floor; I had brought them back to the library and cancelled her ticket. Her chair stared at me all the time, daring me to disturb it.

~~~

The day I saw Celine pushing the go-car on South Great George's Street, I thought of ducking into the Arcade to avoid her. It wasn't that I'd something against her, rather it was because I was finished with Jimmy, and she was his wife. But I changed my mind at the last second and stopped to talk with her. Anthony's face and hands were a mess from chocolate and while she was wiping it clean with her spit on a handkerchief, she told me that she'd left Jimmy. She'd said it in an ordinary way, like someone commenting on the weather, but it had shaken me. I guess my face showed it.

She was quick to add, 'I thought everyone knew by now.'

'I'm sorry to hear it...'

'There's no need to be. We're better off without him.' As she spoke, Anthony was struggling to get out of the go-car. 'Aren't you my little man now?' she said to him, in a singsong voice. He didn't look impressed.

I couldn't help but steal a brief look at her. She looked more upbeat than the last time we'd met. And she didn't have any mark on her face.

'So, how are you managing?' I asked.

'We survive, we have to.'

'You're at the same place?'

'For the moment, yes, but me ma and da want me back home. If it comes to the worse, I'll probably have to. But I don't relish the thought. You know what it's like – you don't like giving up your freedom.'

Although nodding in agreement, I felt guilty because I *didn't* know, having never lived anywhere but at home. She didn't offer any details as to why she had left Jimmy, and I think she knew that I could guess the reason. 'You're not nervous in that flat on your own?' I asked.

'Never. There's always a buzz coming up from the pub below and the landlord has been nice about it. No, I'm not afraid at all.'

There was a break in the conversation. I was suddenly aware of the traffic on the street; a double-decker squealed to a halt at the bus stop close to us; a woman was selling flowers from a high pram at the entrance to the Arcade; I thought I knew her face and gave her a smile.

Celine spoke again. 'I heard your mother died, Mark. Really sorry about that.'

'Thanks. I'd a letter of condolence from Teresa. It was good of her.'

'I'm delighted she wrote. She can be thoughtful at times.'

'And when she spent that time at our place, I got to know Ruth, the kid.'

'She's a lovely child, not like this terror here!' Anthony had kicked off his shoe and I picked it up. She dropped it into a shopping bag. 'He can go without it now, and he's only himself to blame if his foot gets cold.'

'Tell me, Celine, would you happen to know Ruth's birthday? I'd like to be able to put a card in the post whenever the time comes around…a little surprise for her.'

'Sure, I have it in my notebook, but it's back at the flat. I'll get it to you. Mind you, the child is in the North now, but she hopes that

that'll be sorted soon. He's claiming she's unfit, but she won't take that lying down.'

'It isn't true, is it?'

'No, it's not true. It's the usual nonsense out of Hugo. Yes, she can be a bit wild at times, but she's the mother and would lay down her life for her.'

'I agree. The child comes first, I've seen that myself.' As I spoke, I had an image of the weasel that had come to our door looking for drug money.

'Mark, you sound doubtful. You shouldn't be.'

When we were parting, I pushed some coins into Anthony's fist, glad that I hadn't avoided her. I watched them go along the street until she went into a department store.

She kept her promise. I came home from work one evening and found a note stuck under the door with Ruth's date of birth and, in case I didn't have it, the London address.   On the lower half of the page, she had written, *Ruth's birthday is next month. Good timing on your part! Teresa hopes to have her back home by then. Celine x.*

I wondered how Teresa was going to get her back to London, however, judging by the note, Celine seemed sure it would happen, so a card signed 'Uncle Mark' and a sterling pound was posted in plenty of time, something the Mother had drilled into me. 'What's the point in a card arriving even a day too late? You might as well not send it!'

A few days later I came across Celine's note again, when, for the first time, it struck me as odd that her signature was followed by the kiss symbol. What's this about? I asked myself. The mind was going down all types of paths, then I came to my senses and shrugged them off as stupid notions. More than likely, this was the way she wrote to close friends, and I guessed that I must be one of them. It was as simple as that – or was it?

CHAPTER TWENTY

Celine likes the radio on. She says that it's company for her when Anthony is at school, and I am out at work. However, today is Saturday and we are all at home in the apartment, but I don't mind the music. Thin Lizzy is on now – 'The Boys Are Back in Town'. The title words and the guitar riff run through my head. The washing machine is purring in the kitchen, we're all still in pyjamas and I'm just into my second mug of tea and catching up on the tipster Captain Jinks's racing selections from the Evening Herald. Later, I might put a bet on in the bookies, but then again, I mightn't. Since it looks like being a good day, we could just as easily take ourselves to the local park, or we could stroll down to the market in Meath Street where Celine could ramble, with the boy in tow, and I could slip into a bar and wait in comfort for them. That is how it has been since she moved in, and we all get on simply fine. Mind you, there are rules.

The principal one is that there will be nothing physical. This is a living arrangement, no romance. It gives shelter to her and to Anthony; it gives me company, and my dinner is put on the table. They have the Mother's bedroom; I have my bedroom. These are the private spaces. I stay out of theirs; they stay out of mine. An exception has been that Anthony doesn't understand this concept and sometimes wanders into my territory, which is fine by me. Other rules are minor: there will be no hanging of wet tights or underwear in the bathroom; we stay out of each other's mail (not that either of us gets much of it); no smoking, as the boy can get chesty, and I have no arguments with that, and am becoming used to smoking in the yard behind the building or on the landing. There are other minor rules, some agreed as we go along.

Fellows in the pub have ribbed me over the arrangement. Nod, nod, wink, wink stuff. I never rise to the bait. I have also been jokingly called the Vincent de Paul, because of the way I take in stray families. Some would even hint that I am a soft touch. Again, I pretend not to hear. And as for Mrs. Mulligan downstairs (yes, her, she is still on the go), when I pass her on the lower landing, I feel she must be wondering what the modern world is coming to. It is easy to imagine her saying to herself, 'And that O'Bride family were always so respectable!'

Celine wanders in from the kitchen, Anthony is playing with his cars on the floor. 'Mark, the washing is nearly ready, have you anything to go into the machine when ours is done?'

Saturday is a day of rest, and I was feeling lazy. 'I suppose I must have, but do I have to do it now?'

'Tell me what needs done, and I'll throw it on for you,' she says.

'That's not the deal. We agreed that I do my own washing.'

'It's not as if I'm doing them by hand. It's no bother. Anyway, I don't really want to be looking at your dirty boxers!'

At that moment, my attention was captured by a horse at the bottom of the weights, with good past form. Without looking up, I said, 'Give me a minute then and I'll gather them up for you.' I placed a tick against my selection – it will have to be the bookies now, I thought. Putting the newspaper aside, I gathered the dirty clothes and left them beside the washing machine. 'But it's just this one time,' I said to her. 'I can't have you doing my stuff like this.'

'It's the least I can do. But if you insist, I won't ask again.'

Returning to the racing page, I look for another horse to put in a double with my first pick; however, I'm distracted by what she has just said – 'It's the least I can do'. She says it often and each time I hear it, it makes me feel uncomfortable. I certainly don't want her feeling that she's under any obligation to me; that's the last thing I want. They had been living with me now for three months, ever since Celine had left the flat on Camden Street, where she'd had to leave because the money had run out. Jimmy was no help, as he still had no wage and was at the family home, living off the generosity of Mrs. Culmane.

As for me, yes, you could say I was being a fool again, that after Teresa I should have had more sense. However, this time I saw one big difference – I went into it with my eyes wide open. No one had influenced me.

'Celine, I'm off to the bookies for a while,' I called. 'Will I take Anthony with me?' Her head appeared around the door; her face flushed from housework. 'Maybe you better not,' she said. 'You know how smoky that place can be?'

She was right. A stub of a pencil in one hand, a handful of blank dockets in the other, a cigarette dangling from the mouth, its smoke coming up into the eyes – this was how many of the men in the bookies looked, as they moved fretfully from one list of runners to the next, in the eternal hope of turning a small bet into a big win. Sometimes it happened, giving a happy punter a rare moment in the sun. Most times, it was the opposite. There would be curses of disgust, dockets made into a ball by a taut fist and flung to the floor, then a frantic search of the form pages to see what was running in the next race, hope never died. It was no place to bring the boy. Unfortunately, he heard me and was already looking for his coat, wanting to come; I got out of it with bribery, promising to bring him back a comic. Nevertheless, I felt guilty over disappointing him, and promised to take him – and Celine, if she wanted to go – to the park later.

Just my luck, Jimmy was also in the bookies. I pretended not to see him and wrote out my docket and went up to the counter. When I turned around to go, I saw he had joined the queue behind me. In fact, we were face-to-face; he was blocking my way. He had obviously seen me, for he showed no surprise. 'Any tips?' he casually asked, as if there were nothing wrong between us.

'Hang on to your cash,' I said. 'It's the only real tip, this is a mug's game!'

He forced a laugh. 'You could sing that if it had an air.'

We were holding up a queue of anxious punters waiting to get their bets on, so I moved to one side, out of their path. He followed me, like a shadow. His face seemed thinner than when I'd last seen him and the smile that hung on it was without depth. 'That's *my* bet on,' I said. Then I placed the betting docket in my breast pocket and patted it for luck. 'I'm off to watch them on the television.'

He was throwing shapes with his shoulders, jerky movements, and I noticed that his arm was no longer in a sling. 'And you won't be watching it on your own either,' he said.

The sarcasm was as thick as jam on toast, and I wanted to give a biting reply, yet held back, seeing no point to it. Searching his face, I saw the look of a stranger. I didn't even feel sorry for him. 'My runner is going to post soon,' I said. 'I'm rushing – sorry.' I escaped from the betting office and strode back to the apartment. I had promised the kid we were going to the park, and the park it was going to be.

Anthony burst any bubble I'd had about still being fit and Celine, looking on, wasn't slow with her remarks about my beer belly's performance while I ran, kicked, bent down, puffed, rolled over, and finally gave in – yes, I conceded, he *had* scored more goals than I had. Yes, he *was* the champion! I lay on the grass in mock exhaustion and stared at the slow progress of a cloud while Celine came on the 'pitch' to take my place. Their voices broke the quietness of the park, and every so often I popped my head up to check when a shout of 'Goal!' was raised by Anthony as he fantasized that he was Georgie Best. They stopped playing when the score reached about a hundred goals for Anthony (his count) and five goals for his mother, and he didn't stop talking about it until he fell asleep that night.

I was watching the television before going out for the night, when I told Celine that I had seen Jimmy in the bookies.

'And?'

'Nothing… I'm just letting you know I saw him, that's all.'

'Did your horses come in?'

'Haven't checked them yet.'

After a pause, I had to ask, 'It doesn't bother you?'

'No. We're finished! I thought you understood that?'

'I do…completely. That's why I didn't stay talking with him.'

She'd just made herself a cup of tea, and, while I was preparing to go out, I saw her settle down to watch the *Late Late Show* in Ma's comfortable chair, where Teresa had also sat. Oftentimes, when I came back from the pub she'd have already gone to bed, other nights she could be asleep on the couch, and I would have to wake her. On those nights, she would jump up and insist on preparing a supper, and we would watch a late film, then, later, if I happened to fall asleep, she would switch off the television, leave me as I was and go to her bedroom.

If I had thought that I was finished with Jimmy Culmane, I was sorely mistaken, for he began to appear too many times in my regular bars. When he wasn't in sight, I was able to drink in peace; but, inevitably, by the time the night was over, his smirk would be at the other end of the bar counter. He would nod to me, and I'd have to drink up and leave, either for another establishment or to head home. I'd thought about confronting him, then decided that it would do no good, not with a person like Jimmy. There were times when I thought that I was reading more into it than I should have, then one night he played his cards. He came straight over to me, like in the old days when we were pals. 'How's it going, Mark?'

For the life of me I couldn't guess what he wanted. 'It's okay.'

'Can I get you a drink?' he said.

For a fellow who had been out of work, I wondered where the money was coming from. 'I'm good, Jimmy...just got one in.'

It was clear to me that he was building himself up to say something. The shoulders were jerking again, the eyes looked to the ground, a nervous cough, then it came out, 'Listen, pal, if you're going to take my place, we'll have to come to some sort of an arrangement.'

The appearance of friendliness had been replaced by a hard look.

'What are you on about, Jimmy?'

'You know, pal... I'm giving up an awful lot here, and you're stepping into my shoes...'

'I think you've got this the wrong way round. You didn't give them up; they gave *you* up.'

'She said *that*. What else did she say?'

'You wouldn't want to hear. And there's another thing, I'm not – as you put it – stepping into your shoes because there's nothing between Celine and me. And I don't care whether you believe me or not!'

'And my son? You're seeing Anthony grow up, aren't you? That's more than I can say.'

'I took them in, but would you rather they were out on the street?'

'I know what you're up to – all this playing at happy families.'

'You're a headcase and I'm sorry I even spoke to you!' I was annoyed with myself for losing my cool and imagined people looking in our direction. Taking up my drink, I pushed past him and went to the other end of the counter. He didn't follow me, but stood on the same spot for a moment, staring towards the display of spirits behind the bar. The barman went to serve him, but Jimmy ignored him, shot one final glance towards me, muttered something under his breath and left. I looked around the bar, normality had returned, as if our brief argument had been no more than a glass breaking on the floor.

The barman came to me, wiped my counter space, and stuck a beer mat under my glass. Our eyes met, he said nothing. In my mind I kept hearing Jimmy's words, '...some sort of arrangement'. It sounded borrowed, not like something he'd think of himself. What did he mean by it? And the cheek of him, thinking that I wanted his wife and child. Anyway, it was all his own fault. My night had gone sour, like a bad pint, and I finished up and went home early. I found her writing a letter. When she saw me, she put the writing pad aside and jumped up to make some supper.

Jimmy has accused me of taking his place, I thought. He's wrong; I don't feel anything special for her. 'Stay where you are,' I said. 'I'm making the supper tonight – you just carry on there with your letter-writing.'

Later, she told me that the letter was to Teresa. The envelope was already addressed, ready for a stamp. 'She's taken up with a musician and is to sing with his band at their next gig. Can you believe that? Her singing? She wants us all to go over to London to support her'.

'I didn't know she sang,' I said.

'This guy Johnny has seen something in her that I've never seen either...she's definitely doing the gig.'

'And what have you said to her?'

'The obvious. I told her that money was tight and that we wouldn't make it.'

'Maybe we should do it. It'll be a laugh if nothing else,' I said.

'No, Mark. It's too dear, and you're already too good to us. You go if you like. We'd be happy to stay here.'

'I won't hear of it. You're her pal and you above all people should be there.'

She seemed overwhelmed. 'I'd love to be there! And I can't believe that she's actually going to do this.'

'So, it's settled, we'll go then?'

'What about Anthony?' she said with a sudden look of guilt.

'Stella will take him, I'm sure of it. He knows her now and won't make strange.'

'I'll have to rewrite the letter,' she said, picking up the already-sealed envelope. 'Oh, Mark, I'm so excited! I can't believe it!' She flung her arms round my neck in a strong grip, and I felt a wet kiss on my cheek. Surprised, I lightly patted her on the back, then stepped back to find her crying. She brushed her eyes with the back of a hand, smiled like she'd just blown out birthday candles, then took out a writing pad and began the new version of the letter.

While she was writing, I thought about Jimmy and how he had said '...we'll have to come to some sort of an arrangement'. I now had no doubt that he'd been looking for money. It disgusted me. This wasn't the same Jimmy I'd known. Yes, we'd lost a friendship; nevertheless, I couldn't forget the good times we'd had. In a way, I pitied him but at the same time I didn't want to ever set eyes on him again.

Celine finishes the letter, and I wonder what Teresa will think when she reads that I also will be travelling to see her.

CHAPTER TWENTY-ONE

A Twiggy-like figure wearing an orange dress and heavy eye liner, and pale pink lipstick, bounced out in front of us at the platform gate. 'Hello, I'm Viv!' Her accent was a mixture of Dublin and London, and she spoke breathlessly like there wasn't enough time to get the words out. 'Teresa's cousin – I'm bringing you to the house first, then she'll catch up with us later and we'll all go together to the gig.'

As we followed the orange, bobbing figure through Euston Station, Celine turned to me and pointed to Viv's purple knee-high boots and bandanna of matching colour; she poked me playfully in the ribs and said, 'Welcome to London!' We hurried to keep up with the cousin, especially when she veered into a busy, white-tiled passageway with direction signs for the Tube, and we met a stream of commuters coming against us. While we waited on a platform for our train, I now had a chance to study the cousin. Beneath the make-up, I felt she was still a good-looker, and everything about her seemed modern; however, I noticed that the heels of the purple boots were worn down to an angle, which took away from the overall image. It didn't take long to get to Hackney; the house was a two-storey in an old terrace, with makeshift curtains, neglected front gardens and overflowing bins.

She brought us upstairs to a bedroom. It was a spacious room that looked cluttered, because the only piece of furniture that wasn't untidily loaded with clothes was a double bed with a neat coverlet.

'It's Teresa's room, but she wanted you two to have it, so she's kipping with Johnny while you're here.'

I glanced at Celine who showed no sign of alarm over the bed. We dumped our bags, and on the way out, Viv pointed at another door. 'Hugo's in there. He went up town somewhere, but said he'll be back in plenty of time.'

'Hugo!' I tried to hide my disbelief.

'This gig is a huge thing for Teresa. She's called on everyone she knows for support.'

'And the child, Ruth?' I asked.

'She's back in Northern Ireland with the granny. It's their turn to have her, but she'll be here again next month – she's adorable.'

Downstairs, Viv went into a scullery to make coffee and pointed us towards a couch that was losing its stuffing; presently, she sat opposite us on a winged cane chair – she would have been an exotic creature if it hadn't been for the worn heels of her boots. We were chatting, when we heard a key in the front door and a clatter of activity in the hall. 'Oh, that'll be our singer now!' Viv said. On hearing that, Celine rushed out to the hallway, and I could hear shrieks of delight. My heart rate suddenly quickened. They came into the room holding hands, like two schoolgirls meeting after the summer break. Instead of our eyes being locked together across the room, as in a romantic film, she brushed her lips against my cheek on her way to the scullery and returned sipping a glass of water. 'The throat's been dry all day, and I'm in a panic in case I lose my voice.'

'It's only nerves; they'll disappear when you're up there,' Viv said.

'I know, but *you* tell my body that. I'm in bits. I so wanted to enjoy... Look at me, one minute I'm drinking this stuff and the next minute I'm running to the toilet. I tell you, I'm in bits.'

'Teresa, it's the cost of fame,' I said.

She threw me an examining look, then smiled and said, 'Mark, I'll feel a lot braver now that I have my friends around me.' She glared at the unfinished glass of water, as if it were poison. 'Only for Johnny, I'd murder a real drink!'

Viv must have felt a need to give us an explanation. 'Johnny's all for clean living, no alcohol, no drugs, no swearing in his lyrics. He says his music doesn't need it.'

'I can see that something's doing you good,' Celine said. 'In fact, I think you're glowing.'

'You're such a true friend,' she answered. 'Keep on saying such beautiful things.'

'It's the truth,' Celine said. 'Isn't it, Mark?'

This wasn't a question that I was prepared for. I shrugged my shoulders. 'Clean living, clean liver.' It was a stupid thing to say, and I hoped it went unnoticed. Anyway, I doubted if she was even listening to us, the nervous state she was in.

She looked at her watch. 'The day's marching on! Mark, darling, you don't mind if I use your bedroom to get ready, do you?'

'It's your bedroom, don't let us –' I hadn't finished the sentence and she was already halfway up the stairs.

The talk of preparing to go out had unsettled Celine and she rushed to a mirror to check her appearance. She turned to Viv, 'Do I look okay for this gig? All I have to wear is what I'm standing in.'

'Don't worry, darling, everyone will be casual.'

Suddenly, I felt that someone was behind me. It was Hugo. None of us had heard the front door opening. He tossed the front door key to Viv, took a slow look round the room, then he sat on a floor rug. The teacher's clothes had been swapped for brown corduroy pants, with stains you would expect on a car mechanic's overalls, and even though the weather wasn't cold, a loose, seaweed green polo neck sweater hung from his shoulders. I also noticed that he was trying to grow a moustache. He reminded me of an over-age college student on one of those sit-down protest things. 'What's this about being casual?' he said.

'It's like this, it seems you won't be needing your tuxedo tonight,' I said, trying to be pleasant.

At that moment, Teresa came down in a plaid shirt and blue jeans and stretched her arms upwards in a stage gesture. 'What do you think?' she asked. 'Don't I look cool?'

We all made comforting sounds of agreement and Celine turned back to the mirror to finish working on her hair, then, as if she were competing with Viv, she put on her own version of pink lipstick, a colour I'd noticed that she kept for special outings. Soon we were in the Tube again, the walls sometimes visible in the gloomy tunnels as we sped from station to station. Teresa was standing next to me, going over the words of a song. Celine and Viv had managed to grab a seat and Hugo was close to the door, leaning against the wall of the carriage; he'd changed his pants and put on a white shirt, and he looked more in keeping with the Saturday night crowd, out and about in London. We came to our station, and came up out of the ground in Islington, laughing and joking. Viv was leading again, a bouncing figure – a sight I was starting to enjoy.

The gig was in an old pub which reminded me of similar surviving ones in Dublin. It had a high ceiling – stained yellow from cigarettes – with a ribbon of ornate plasterwork on the outer limits, like icing on the border of a cake; there were two round columns, like tree trunks spaced well apart; the counter was marble-topped, and the beer taps were gleaming brass, with porcelain pull handles. We had arrived early and had a pick of where to sit. The table we chose had a clear view of the small stage; this was set against a back wall and its slightly raised, rectangular shape already appeared overcrowded due to a drum kit and all the paraphernalia of lighting and sound systems.

Looking at Teresa, the way she was fidgeting, her flushed face, I could see that she was now struggling even more with the nerves. Suddenly, she pointed. 'There he is!' She jumped up and dragged a fellow over to us. His hair was long and flowing and looked pampered. 'This is Johnny,' she said. They were dressed like identical twins, jeans with plaid shirt – I felt like saying 'snap!' but held back as I didn't know if Johnny would appreciate my humour. 'I'm happy now,' she added, 'I have the three men in my life around me.'

'Welcome to the club,' I said, and shook his long-fingered hand.

He swept his hair back with a sweep of the free hand and smiled at me, as if he already knew who I was. Then he moved over to Hugo. 'I've wanted to meet you ever since Ruth was last over. She never stopped talking about 'Her Daddy'. She's a great kid, but of course you know that already, mate.'

'Yes, we know it rightly,' he answered, at the same time he gave Teresa a strange look.

Just then a scrawny man in a black tee shirt came into the bar, carrying a guitar case.

'Billy's here!' Teresa said.

Johnny stood up, and I realized he was over six feet tall. 'That's our Mister Cool,' he said. 'Always the last to arrive – I must go and talk with him.'

I glanced at Celine. She had gone quiet, and I worried over her being left out of the conversation. I reached over and patted the back of her hand. She smiled at me and seemed content. Teresa saw us and sat between us. 'I only hope I don't freeze or forget the lyrics or fall off the stage,' she said. 'But it's great having my friends with me.'

Her cousin Viv heard her and gave reassurance. 'You'll be a knock-out. You've rehearsed your number so much that you should be able to sing it backwards.'

'You're singing just the one song, then?' Celine asked.

'One is enough – but I still need all the support I can get. Sure, just look at the state of me!' She held out her shaking hands, like someone casting a spell.

I noticed she was wearing the watch – the 'holiday present' – that she'd inveigled out of me in the Isle of Man and wondered if she'd meant for me to see it.

The bar was filling up now. The sound checks were completed, the lighting adjusted, then the guitars were placed on the stage in readiness. A drummer, Viv said he was Jamaican, was in place, rolling drumsticks through his fingers. Johnny came over to us. 'I just heard that a scout from one of the labels is here.'

Teresa gulped. 'You shouldn't…you shouldn't have told me that,' she said. 'I'll be sick.'

'There's no time for that now,' he said. 'We're on in a minute. You'll sing the second number.' He thrust a tambourine at her and jumped on to the stage.

Viv rushed to Teresa and placed an arm round her. 'You'll be great, darling. Just sing to our group and try to ignore the audience. We know you can do it.'

'Go on, Teresa,' I said. 'Sock it to them!'

Suddenly, I was excited for her. A man with shirt sleeves rolled up came from behind the bar, stepped on to the stage and took up a microphone. When I heard him speaking, I could tell he was well used to the stage. 'This pub has brought you many bands. So, by now I *should* know a good one when I hear one. So, give a rocking welcome to tonight's act, The 4 Courts.' He signalled for Johnny to step up to the microphone, then added, 'Let's get this pub jumping!'

The hubbub of the bar was silenced in a moment of expectancy; on Johnny's cue the band launched into 'Route 66'. He had a voice as strong as a barrow boy's, his shining hair bounced and kissed his shoulders as he moved, and across from him, Billy looked out into the audience with the look of a bored professional, and only glanced down at his guitar for a tricky key change. Behind him, the Jamaican was already sweating, his head moving like a pecking bird to a strong drumbeat. Teresa was like someone in a dentist's waiting room; she weakly tapped the side of her jeans with the tambourine. I looked about the pub. People were listening, feet were tapping, the audience liked it. Johnny lost himself to a guitar solo then returned to the lyrics, and by the end of the number it was clear that the gig was starting well. But now it was time for the second number; it was Teresa's turn.

Our group released a devoted cheer, which almost spooked her. She moved awkwardly to the front microphone, blinked because a spotlight was full on her, looked at the tambourine in her hands and seemed to decide that it wasn't needed and left it down beside her. She ran her hands through her fair hair, then looked to Johnny for her cue to start. He nodded to the Jamaican who started a beat; I could see her counting with taps of her left boot; she put her lips close to the microphone and began to sing the song 'Ode to Billy Joe'. This was the one she'd been going over in the Tube. The guitars slid in, not strident, but gentle. Teresa had her eyes closed, as if she needed to concentrate on the lyrics, then she opened them and slowly raised her head to look in our direction. I gave her the thumbs up, not knowing if she could see me against the glare from the spotlight. Then, for a heart-stopping moment, she seemed to lose the air of the song; thankfully, it was like the momentary slip of a bicycle chain, and she quickly recovered.

I looked around me. Some patrons were listening, even intently, but others seemed to be only half-interested. At one table a group were talking among themselves, not loudly, but still it was chatter. I couldn't help but wonder why Johnny had given her such an early slot in the program. He'd managed to get the crowd behind them with a rock number, now there was a chance of losing them. I looked again at Teresa who seemed oblivious to everything but keeping in time with the band and putting her heart into the mysterious story that the song told.

Viv leaned across to me and whispered, 'It has three hundred and fifty words – she's on the last verse.'

I nodded back to her, amazed that she knew that. On stage, Johnny looked happy. For the final part of the song, I felt that Teresa was looking in my direction, yet I suspected that she probably couldn't see me. Then it was over. We clapped and whistled and the crowd close to us, infected by our noisy reaction, joined in and the response quickly spread throughout the pub and Teresa looked shocked. Johnny took her hand, held it up high, as if she were a winning prize fighter, and invited her to take a bow, which she clumsily did, then she picked up the tambourine and, clearly relieved, retreated to the back of the stage. Johnny was now singing the blues song, 'You Gotta Help Me'; I picked up my pint, at long last able to enjoy the drink.

We had to wait until the interval before we could talk to Teresa. As she came off the stage, Celine ran to her, like she was meeting a long-lost friend arriving off a flight and hugged her. I grabbed Hugo's arm and dragged him out of his seat. 'All she has is us,' I said. 'C'mon.'

When Teresa saw us, she broke from Celine and flung her arms around Hugo, then around me. As I felt her against me, I was reminded of the good times we'd had. It only lasted a moment; Johnny came along, and she turned and kissed him on the mouth. I stood apart from them and listened to him tell her how well she'd done.

'Thank you, Johnny – thank you. It's all down to you. I was so nervous...'

'I must look for the guy from the label,' he said, moving away, his eyes scanning the pub.

The Jamaican – I discovered his name was Opera – and Billy the bass player had joined our group. Viv seemed to be flirting with Opera, but he was only showing her mild attention; instead, he was looking with interest at Celine. Billy had fastened onto me, but it didn't take me long to realize that he was the type that stood beside you, holding a drink, and made no further effort to speak. I edged away from him and found myself talking to Hugo. When I jokingly suggested that the two of us were part of Teresa's new fan club, he gave me a trace of a smile and said that he thought we were two sad fuckers. Johnny returned, long faced; it turned out that the guy from the label had left before the interval. The band returned to the stage for the second part. As the night went on, the music became secondary and drink on the table became the main interest. Then, the gig was over, and the pub started to empty, bodies going on to clubs or parties or simply heading home. At that moment, I was feeling comfortable, the place suiting me like a glove. Johnny and Teresa were the only ones not drinking; nevertheless, you'd never have thought it, for they were both in high spirits. As for Viv the cousin, there wasn't much hope of her being our guide for the rest of the night. She couldn't form her words and had propped herself against Celine. Opera and Billy had moved in on two women at the far end of the bar and we didn't see them again. Hugo was looking at a pint, like he was staring sin in the face.

Teresa came to sit next to me. 'I hope the bedroom's okay for you. I wasn't sure…Celine and you…you know?'

'It's grand, but you didn't have to give up your bed for us.'

'That's nothing compared to what *you've* done for me. And coming all this way from Dublin, just for one song. You and Celine are true friends, that's all I can say. It's a real pity you must go back tomorrow. We'd have loved to have shown you around London.'

'Another time, we'll do that.'

There was a moment of silence. I was tipsy, she was sober. Then I remembered the photographs that we'd discovered under Ma's mattress, and I asked her why she'd left them there.

'I knew you'd find them, sooner or later.'

'Wasn't there another photo…of us?'

Our eyes met, and I was thinking of those frivolous brief moments in the photo booth. Although, what *she* was thinking, that was a mystery. And it remained so. For just then, Johnny said it was time for them to go.

We took a black cab back to the house, lucky to be able to get the address out of Viv, who by then only wanted to sleep. Celine and I helped her inside, thought better of getting her upstairs and instead laid her on the couch that was losing its stuffing. Her orange dress had come up, showing her knickers and Celine, giggling, ran for something to cover her up.

'Not bad pins,' Hugo said, staring from the chair opposite.

Celine came back with a bath towel you wouldn't dry a dog with and restored Viv's modesty. I'd a wino's thirst and went looking in the kitchen for a drink. All I could find was some gin. The next challenge was something to drink it from; I settled for some half-clean, chipped cups and returned to the others and found Hugo was dozing where he sat, Viv was curled up in the manner of a sleeping child and Celine – thankfully, awake – was sitting on the floor with her back resting against the couch. I held up the bottle and cups, like a returning prospector. 'It's all I could find.'

'Anything will do – it'll finish off the night,' she said. She took a mouthful, but the neat gin went against her breath, and she took a fit of coughing. Hugo stirred, looked briefly round him, then reclosed his eyes. Celine was careful after her coughing episode and only sipped at the gin. She looked content; for my part, I was certainly relaxed. But I never expected her to say, 'Mark, it must have been hard for you seeing Teresa and Johnny together like that?'

'You're seeing it the wrong way,' I said. 'She's a friend, just like you are. And what she does with her life is her business.'

'You look at things in such a broad way.' She hadn't finished her gin and put it aside. 'I'll fall asleep like the others if I don't go to bed.' At the foot of the stairs, she turned and looked back at me. 'Try not to wake me.'

I was left on my own, Hugo to one side, Viv to the other. Although gin wasn't my drink, I drank one more cupful. Then I followed her to the bedroom. A bedside lamp, with a rose-coloured shade, gave the bedroom a dreamy, comfortable light. She was asleep, wearing pyjamas, and lying to one side of the bed, almost to the edge. The bedclothes had been pulled back for me on the empty side. I removed my shoes and removed the pillow from what should have been my side of the bed. Then I found an overcoat of Teresa's and laid it on a rug and using some of her carelessly discarded jumpers to cover me, I eventually fell asleep in my clothes, the smell of Teresa all over me.

The first time I woke, I thought I heard sobbing from the bed. Then I didn't hear it anymore, and I must have drifted off again. The next time, I was awakened by urgent shouts from downstairs, and I sprang from my makeshift bed and went to look. Viv was off the couch and standing in the middle of the room, looking upset. She saw me and shouted, 'You keep this creep away from me!'

The colour had left Hugo's face, and he was holding his hands up, palms facing outward. 'I did nothing... The towel had slipped, and I was just covering –'

'Yes,' she interrupted, 'and what about your sneaky hands? They were all over me!'

'I'm telling you, there was nothing...'

'I'm going to my room and I'm locking my door!' She stomped off, leaving him looking shocked.

'She's got the wrong idea,' he said. 'I woke up and her knickers were showing again. I was sitting here looking at a cheek sticking out and went over to cover her, and she woke up...'

'There's no point in telling me,' I said. 'You'll have to convince the others.'

'But you believe me, don't you?'

'I wouldn't share a drink with you if I didn't.' I divided the last of the gin between us.

'I don't drink gin,' he said, like a spoiled child.

'Friend, there's nothing else.'

We sat quietly for a while, as if we'd nothing in common. It was the middle of the night, in a terrace house in London, in a room that had suddenly become an ugly place, with naked light bulbs, old-fashioned wallpaper, and no sign of homely touches, except the extravagant cane chair with wings that probably had come from a junk shop. Hugo was now sitting back on it, staring with contempt at the empty couch, like *it* could be blamed for his trouble. Without warning, he brought up a completely different subject. 'I never meant to come between Teresa and you,' he said.

I told him that she no longer mattered to me and that I didn't want to talk about it. However, that wasn't going to stop him. There was a choice of either listening to him or leaving the room: I stayed to listen.

'I was up in Dublin on a training course, and I just happened to bump into her. We got on well, which surprised both of us. Then we started going out and it went on from there. Of course, you were off the scene at that stage, and I'm telling you this because you're a straight-up fellow and you deserve to know. I don't want you thinking that I went behind your back. Now, it doesn't matter anyway, although I can see that you still carry a wee torch for her.'

The effect of the night's drinking had suddenly worn off me; I felt too sober for such a serious conversation. He was now an annoyance, spinning his own version of the story and leaving out that last night in Douglas, when I saw them kissing through the back window of a taxi. I could take no more of it. 'I want you to drop the subject!'

'Mark, here we are sharing a civilised drink, even though it's disgusting gin, and Teresa shouldn't be coming between us, especially now she's with this Johnny fellow.'

'I asked you to drop it!'

'We've so much in common. You've already said it yourself, that we're now reduced to making up her fan club. That's what we are, her bloody fan club. Yet, it's nothing for her to parade that Englishman in front of us.'

'I think it's you, Hugo, that's still carrying a torch.'

'Haven't I every right. Legally, she's still my wife. Not that that seems to matter…'

'Why did you come here then?' I asked.

'I came because my young daughter would have wanted me to come. I can't have her turning against me down the road and saying that I never supported her mammy.' He paused for a moment, took a swig from his cup, and continued. 'Isn't it funny the way things work out? I'd never have met her if I hadn't first bumped into you that day in Douglas. Later, when I saw her in Dublin, I recognised her from the Palace. And now, here I am with you and we're talking about her as if she were the centre of both our lives.'

'That's a bit over the top.'

There was a wariness in his look now; signs of drink and sleepiness were leaving him. 'I'm only trying to be friendly.'

'Maybe you should tell it as it *really* was.'

'I don't understand,' he said.

'Do I have to spell it out? I know you spent that last night in Douglas with her. So, your story doesn't wash with me.'

'And where did you get that notion?'

'You were seen,' I said, pleased to have caught him out. 'That morning, the day we left, you dropped her off in a taxi. So much for your story of you and her not getting together until much later.'

'That's crazy!'

'I saw it with my own eyes,' I said.

'Man, you're out of your mind. Don't you remember those nights at the Palace? She made it clear that she was disgusted by me. And, to tell the truth, I wasn't too enamoured by her either. But it changed later when we met in Dublin. But *only* then.'

I didn't want to hear what he was saying. Because from that humiliating moment when I'd had to spy on them from a telephone box, I'd always assumed it was him I'd seen in the taxi at the seafront in Douglas. Now, a doubt was in my mind. I hadn't seen a face that morning, that's true. Was it possible that I had jumped to the wrong conclusion? In my mind I relived the moments. A taxi pulls up, its engine left running; I see the kiss, the car door swings open; I see Teresa step out, the taxi pulls away. Although my conviction of what had happened had been dented, I wasn't going to admit that to myself, nor to him. Not yet. We drank in silence for a while, then went to our respective rooms. Celine must have slept through the earlier commotion, I thought, as I tiptoed past the comfortable-looking bed and lay down on the coat on the floor, arranging Teresa's jumpers again to cover me.

I awoke to the smell of frying bacon. When I went downstairs, I found that Teresa had come back early from Johnny's place to make breakfast for us. 'Sleep well?' she asked.

'Like a log,' I lied.

'Good,' she said. 'I worried about you not being comfortable.'

'And you?

'It took me ages to come off last night's high…guess I did in the end.'

Celine appeared soon afterwards, still in pyjamas. She wanted to strip the sheets and pillowcases from the bed and put them in the washing machine.

'Not at all,' Teresa said. 'They're just on clean and I certainly don't mind lying between the sheets of friends.'

CHAPTER TWENTY-TWO

Celine was quiet on the train back to Holyhead; a childlike excitement seen on the journey over had changed to a matter-of-fact attitude. I guessed it was my fault, even though she hadn't accused me of anything. Nonetheless, I'd bought her a magazine before boarding and ferried tea and sandwiches to her and tested her from time to time with harmless remarks or self-answering questions, like sometimes I'd seen Da have to do with the Mother.

When we reached the port at Holyhead, we queued in a shed where our boarding tickets were checked and then we were signalled to move forward to a police desk. There were two men in plainclothes, with a uniformed stocky policewoman standing behind them; she had the air of a hunting dog. They examined our tickets and asked for identification; luckily, Celine had decided that we should bring our Social Welfare cards, just in case. I could see the first plainclothes man running his finger down a page of names. Turning up nothing, he then looked at me, and I could sense his suspicion. 'Where did you stay on your visit, Mr. O'Bride?' he asked.

Celine pulled an envelope with the address on it from her handbag and handed it to him. He studied it and showed it to his companion, who read it and demanded to know what our business had been in London. It seemed simpler to say that we were visiting friends rather than saying that we were there for a gig, which might have sounded a bit extravagant. I felt that we were being scrutinised and realized that

I was beginning to feel nervous. Even though there was no reason to be.

The second plainclothes officer turned his attention to Celine. 'And you...' He took a moment to consult the tickets. 'Mrs. Culmane, were you with him?'

'Yes.' Her voice sounded unnatural to me.

There was a pause, then an exchange of glances between the two men.

'What's your address in Ireland, Mr. O'Bride?' the first plainclothes man asked.

I told him.

'And yours, Mrs. Culmane?'

'It's the same,' she said, getting flustered. 'We live at the same address.'

'How come, you've different names?' the second man asked.

'She's my girlfriend,' I said.

He looked around at the policewoman, who shrugged her shoulders, giving the impression that she'd no interest in making moral judgements. But then she threw a question of her own at Celine. 'What date is Mr. O'Bride's birthday?'

'It's July 2,' she answered promptly.

It was clear what was coming next. The question came from the first man. 'And you, sir, when is the lady's birthday?'

I had a moment of panic. These people had all the control. There had been stories of Irish people being picked out of a line and then whisked off to a barracks for questioning. They had the power to do that, and I didn't have the answer to the question. I was saved by Celine. 'How many times have I told you, Mark – think of your mother's.'

'March 19,' I said.

'Fairly typical,' the policewoman muttered, as if to her all men were the same.

The queue was building up behind us, and the police decided that we weren't terrorists and waved us through. Onboard, Celine said her nerves were in 'bits' and she needed a stiff drink and added, 'When they started asking those questions, they made me feel that I was hiding something.'

'They're only doing their job.'

'So why then did you feel you had to lie? why did you have to say I was your girlfriend?'

'To save us from more questions – I had to think fast.'

'You could have landed us in real trouble.'

'At least, now I *know* your birthday,' I said, giving her my best smile.

It didn't stop her worrying and she kept looking about her, nervous that she could be taken off the ship at any moment. She only relaxed when we were well clear of Holyhead. Later, somewhere in the middle of the Irish Sea, she asked, 'And what if we'd been arrested?'

'We weren't, and there was never any reason for us to be arrested.'

'You hear stories – how would Anthony have managed if it *had* happened?'

'But we weren't, Celine. If it makes you feel any better, we'll go straight to Stella's as soon as we're off the boat and pick him up.'

'Yes, we'll have to do that. I can't wait to see him.'

When we finally got home to the apartment, Celine undertook to read the bedtime story to Anthony, a job that I would normally do, when I was around. Later, she came out and sat watching the television. I looked at the clock and thought of going to the pub for a nightcap, then dropped the idea and went into the kitchen, made some tea for supper, and brought it out on a tray with a doily and biscuits.

'What's this about?' she asked.

'It's nothing, really,' I said.

'It's pretty, not something –'

'No, not my usual form.' There was a long pause, then I asked her if she was glad to be back.

'Yes. It was great getting away – but London wouldn't be for me.'

'You're a home bird.'

'You *could* say that if…if I were in my own home,' she said.

'What do you mean? This is your home for as long as you want it.'

'Thanks, but you know what I mean.'

'No, I don't.'

She hesitated, then said, 'I thought that there was more to us than that.'

Suddenly, my head started to pound. I wondered what had brought this on. Was it because I hadn't slipped into bed with her in London? This was now a serious conversation. It had crept up on me. A joke or banter had no place here. The person sitting across from me had stripped away all the veneer from herself, like the old-timers in the trade who had stripped paintwork with a blowlamp. What was revealed was a woman in a pink twinset, who stared in the direction of the television, eyes filled up, unconsciously twisting the doily. I tried to think of something to say, but my brain had seized. We sat in silence for a long time, watched I felt by the family photographs, my jury.

Finally, I got up and switched off the television and faced her. 'Celine, I want you and Anthony to feel that this really is your home.'

She looked at me, her face telling me nothing.

'Don't we get on?' I asked.

She nodded.

'It's so important for me to have you here,' I said, and reached for her hand. It curled into a resisting fist, and all I could do was gently place my palm on top of it. Her free hand wiped a tear. 'Please don't be like that,' I urged.

Desmond Gallagher

'I won't…I'm being silly,' she said. Then I felt the fist uncurl and my hand rushed to fully clasp hers, our fingers mixing.

'There, that wasn't too hard, was it?'

A fresh tear came, I offered a handkerchief. And, as she dabbed her face, a faint smile appeared. Being close to her like that was a new experience. Her hand was warm; my arm rested on her black skirt, the shape of her leg beneath it; the pink twinset suddenly seemed like a beautiful covering for her upper body; there was a slight smell of perfume. I knelt and lay my head against her. She stiffened for a moment then relaxed and I felt her fingers in my hair.

I realized that all this had raced ahead without my thinking about it. The simple wish to provide shelter for her and the boy was now on the verge of changing to something much more personal. There was still time to draw back if I wanted to. But my body made the decision for me, for rather than reverse me out of the situation, it contentedly stayed put. For how long we stayed in that position, I can't be sure; however, it ended when I got a cramp in my leg and had to fall away from her and lay sprawled on my back on the floor. We laughed, and I propped myself up on an elbow and took a long look at her. She was sizing me up. Her mouth was slightly open, revealing those china-like teeth. I lazily reached out for her hand. As I rolled her fingers in mine, I felt her rings and remembered Jimmy. He had lost his rights when he had raised his hand to her, or so I told myself. And, as if she were reading my mind, the rings were tugged at and placed on a side table. An unofficial act of separation. But who am I fooling? I thought. She's still Mrs. Jimmy Culmane; they could easily be put back on again in the morning. Yet, that would have to wait, and be a worry for another day. At this moment, both of us knew what was coming next. I suggested that I carry Anthony from the Mother's bedroom into mine.

'You'll disturb him,' she said.

'I'll be careful.'

The boy was so deep in sleep that there was never any danger of him waking and, although he shifted and flung his arms about while being carried, he settled back into his dream world as soon as I placed him in my bed. When I went back out to Celine, I saw that she'd been crying again, but she quickly gathered herself, patting her hair into shape.

'He's fast asleep,' I said.

'You *do* like Anthony, don't you?' she said. Next moment she was sitting on my knee. I placed my arms around her and sunk my nose into the warmth of her back.

'Of course, I like him. He's a grand little footballer...'

Later, as I followed her into the Mother's bedroom, I saw myself in the hall mirror, following in the Da's footsteps.

CHAPTER TWENTY-THREE

The apartment remained Celine and Anthony's home for four years, at least. The neighbours of old, including the eternal Mrs. Mulligan, smiled at us when we met them on the stairs or on the street. Little escapes the notice of people in this close-knit community, and it was common knowledge that Celine was married to one of the Culmanes from the flats. I could imagine the talk that went on behind our backs and it made me smile to think that we were probably notorious by now. Meanwhile, I found a simple lifestyle: work, home for a wash, then dinner, and later – on most nights – it was out for a quick nightcap. Anthony started school; Celine and I shouted for him on the annual sports days; we even went to Mass during his First Communion year, which wasn't easy as both of us hadn't been regular Mass-goers.

One day, my boss came out to the job I was on and told me that a man describing himself as a pastor had phoned the office, looking to speak with me.

'How does he know me?' I asked.

'He didn't say. Here's his telephone number'.

It was written on the back of an old envelope. On the way home, I popped into a call box and dialled the number.

'Hello, Pastor Smith here,' a man answered. He had an ordinary Dublin accent.

I pushed the button and was connected. 'You were looking for me,' I said.

'Is that Mr. O'Bride?'

'Yes...Mark O'Bride.'

'Mark, thanks for returning my call. I always think that it tells a lot about people when they ring back, even if it's a caller they don't know. God will bless you for that. Now, Mark, I want to arrange to meet you, just for a chat.'

'There must be some mistake, Pastor...'

'Smith.'

'Pastor Smith, I think you must be mixing me up with someone else.'

'No, Mark. I'm confident it's you I want. When would be a good time for us to meet? I'll leave it to you to name the time and place – I can go anywhere you say.'

'Hold on there,' I said. 'What's this all about?'

'Mark, I'd rather we wait until we meet.'

'Sorry, I don't know you, and don't know what you're on about.' I hung up.

However, the man called Pastor Smith was persistent. He called to the office a few days later and the nice, obliging Mrs. Kelly, who did up the wages, told him where I was working on that day.

I was alone on that job, busily getting on with the work, and my transistor radio was playing loud in the hall. It drowned the front doorbell, and it was only because I opened an upstairs window to air a room, that I realized someone was at the door. There was a man on the gravelled front, and I shouted down, 'There's nobody here.'

'Are you, Mark?'

'Yes, who are you?'

'I'm Pastor Smith. Remember, we spoke briefly on the phone.'

I felt ambushed and was tempted to tell him that I was too busy to talk to him; however, he'd stirred my curiosity. He had grey hair, combed back smoothly, with ripples from the hairline to the crown of his head, and he was smartly dressed in a brown suit and tie and his appearance wasn't as I'd imagined from his telephone voice. From the doorway I saw it was raining and that he was getting wet, so I led him through to the customer's kitchen and put on the kettle. 'It's time for my break, anyway,' I said, just to make sure he knew that I wasn't going out of my way for him. I found mugs and we sat on stools, making small talk. Although not sounding posh, I felt that his way of speaking had been changed to sound better than his normal way, like he didn't want to show where he came from. So far, he'd said nothing important and eventually I had to ask him what it was he wanted.

'We have a church member that you know, and I'm here on his behalf.'

'And who's that?'

'James Culmane – he would like things between you and him to be patched up. We think highly of James, and I would like –'.

'I don't want to be rude, but I really don't want to hear any more. End of discussion!'

He sipped his tea, as if I hadn't spoken. I swallowed the rest of mine, washed the mug at the sink, then turned to him, clearly showing that I was waiting for him to finish up and go. He went to the sink and spilled out his unfinished tea and then looked at me, and I could see he was sizing me up. He then said, 'If Jesus can forgive all who come to Him, surely, Mark, you can at least spare the time to listen to a brother's story?'

'Pastor, I'm not one of your lot, and I'm certainly not like Jesus. I've told you I've no interest.' I went to the hall to open the front door and said something about work to be finished upstairs.

He followed me out and stood at the threshold. Although he said that he was sorry for keeping me from my work, he still didn't leave, like an obstinate piece of wallpaper you're trying to scrape off a wall. He said that coming to my workplace had been the only sure way he'd had of meeting me.

'It should show you the importance I place on talking to you.'

'Well, it won't be today, Pastor,' I said, then went to close the door.

He was half in, half out, in such a way as to block the closing, a debt collector's trick. 'When will it be then?'

'Saturday.' (I told him that just to get rid of him.)

'Where will we meet, Mark?'

I thought of a bar, then I figured that a pastor mightn't want to be associated with alcohol. 'Bewleys Cafe, Saturday at ten o'clock?'

He hesitated. 'Mark, I normally prepare my Sunday sermon at that time; nevertheless, if that's good for you, it'll be good for me, too.'

He offered me his hand and I shook it, soft to the touch, with excess skin and large freckles on its back, then he glanced at the grey and black sky and hurried down the driveway. I heard a car start beyond the hedging and went back to work. Although I had no intention of meeting him, I found that the visit had unsettled me, left me with no concentration.

That night I sat down with Anthony and helped him with his reading. This was because Celine had come home in a panic from a recent parent-teacher meeting. 'His reading ability is a year behind!' I told her the school was being dramatic and that I would read with him. My plan was a fifteen-minute daily session at the dining table, but the boy tired easily and had to be bribed with the promise of a comic on Saturday mornings. Celine was happy. I'd taken the pressure from her (when she had tried in the past it had ended in tears). It wasn't an easy task and I thought at times that he could be taking after Jimmy, who'd never been promoted from the back row of the class.

Saturday came around, and Anthony swung between Celine and me on the way to the newsagents to pick his 'reward' and afterwards we went to the park and sat on a bench while he did his first scan of the comic. I checked my watch. I imagined the pastor on his way to keep the appointment with me in Bewleys. But what was he anyway? Who had given him that title? I guessed it hadn't been a traditional church. Maybe it was a cult? A pigeon walked close to my shoe, as if it knew I was too distracted to kick out. Celine must have noticed how quiet I was, for she touched my arm and asked me if something was the matter. I shook my mind clear, like you'd shake out a paintbrush when cleaning it, and smiled at her. Anthony was lost in his comic. I ruffled his brown hair and playfully pulled him close to me; however, he wriggled free and escaped back to his private world. I checked the time again; only a few minutes had passed; the pastor would be well on his way. When I was a teenager, I had stood-up a local girl with whom I'd arranged a first-time date and the Mother had found out and ripped into me – 'I thought we were rearing you to be a better person than that?' Her look of disappointment as she spoke those words has remained with me. I glanced again at my watch.

'Celine, I just remembered I told a man I'd meet him.'

'Are you sure it's a man you're off to see and not another woman?' she said, in mock jealousy.

'It's to do with work,' I said. 'When I get back, we'll go out.'

I walked smartly, there was enough time. He was still there, dressed in a blue suit, shiny from use. He showed no surprise that I had turned up, and never commented on my being slightly late. We brought our coffees to a table among the quiet men reading the Saturday newspapers, away from the chatting women shoppers who seemed to be carefully placing their Switzer or Brown Thomas shopping bags in full view of everyone else. I wondered if the pastor thought that I regularly came here. We spoke about the weather, admired the café's stained-glass windows, and drank coffee. I sensed that he was waiting for the right moment to bring up the subject of Jimmy, and it came in an indirect sort of way.

'Let me tell you about our church,' he said. 'We call ourselves Spirit Reborn – simply put, we use the Holy Spirit as our compass.'

There he goes again, I thought. He thinks I'm someone tuned in to these matters. Spirit Reborn. It sounds like the name of a pop group. I noticed that the pastor had a small piece of paper stuck to his jowl, where he had cut himself shaving.

'Mark, we come together once a week and you're welcome to come and witness with us at any time. Because we're still small, we manage to run our church with a team of volunteers who are dedicated to the Lord, including your friend James Culmane.'

I nodded, like one of those novelty 'nodding dogs' you'd sometimes see on a car dashboard.

'James met us through one of our brothers,' he continued, 'who'd urged him to come along to a meeting. When I first met him, he was a broken man who'd lost all hope. He openly confessed before the congregation that he was an unfit person who hated himself. And, as no one knows better than you do, Mark, he'd hit rock bottom. He had lost his wife Celine and his son Anthony. Now he talks of them all the time.'

'And?'

'He wants to try again, wants to get back with his rightful family. Our church has given him its backing and we pray that he'll succeed.'

'Pastor, did Jimmy confess that he'd beaten his wife? Only a coward would do something like that.'

'We can all change, Mark. The Holy Spirit can do that for us. And, as well, he has the full support of our congregation.'

There was something about his language that irritated me. Church. Congregation. Holy Spirit. The more he spoke, the more I disliked him. Furthermore, he was wasting my Saturday morning. It was time for me to be on my way. 'I think we're finished,' I said.

He didn't resist and came out of Bewleys with me and as we stood on Grafton Street, he pressed upon me a printed card. 'All our details are on this. Come to one of our services and see how James has changed. I'm not asking you to take my word for it – see for yourself.'

I didn't answer him and walked away. When I got home, Celine looked at me in surprise. 'You finished early?'

'There wasn't much to talk about, really.'

'Will we get ready then?' she asked.

'That's what I'm here for.'

We made our way along Meath Street – from the St. Luke's Avenue end – until Anthony complained of being hungry and we went into a cake shop. There were stools at the window, and we sat over our cakes, sucking cream off our fingers, gazing at the people passing on the street. Celine and the boy loved the excitement of Meath Street. It was a family moment, even though they weren't exactly my family. Yet, it was still a moment to hang on to. Celine caught me looking at her and placed a sticky palm on the back of my hand. We grinned at one another and for me it was the grin of the contented – there was no other place I needed to be at that moment.

CHAPTER TWENTY-FOUR

Pastor Smith tried to contact me again through the office; however, Mrs. Kelly was now on her guard and didn't help him. Some weeks later a solicitor's letter arrived for Celine. The very sight of the headed paper made her nervous, and she stopped reading after the first formal paragraph. 'What are they on about?' she cried, shoving it towards me. Although the way it was put together was far from plain language, its demand was blunt, and from her point of view, heartless.

'Jimmy can't do this,' I said, not knowing whether he could or not, unlike the solicitor who'd sent the letter. They wrote:

Under the instruction of our client, James Culmane, we are writing to advise of his intention under the Guardianship of Infants Act 1964 to process his right as a Guardian to his son, Anthony Culmane, under the said Act.

The client views your Guardianship as being one that fails the moral criterion required by the said Act.

This notice of proceedings will affect in 21 days unless you present to this office in the interim.

I tried to console her by saying it was a ploy to frighten her.

'They want to take Anthony away from me! What are we going to do?' she said and began to cry. I hadn't seen tears from her since the night we came back from London. I held her and felt her sobbing going through me in waves. Anthony came into the room, and she broke from me and turned away to hide her upset.

I had never asked the boss for advice on personal matters before but felt he could help me this time. The type he was, he hadn't spoken of his own broken marriage to any of us, his workers, the plebs. However, for a period we'd seen him carrying around a bucketful of worry. There'd been children in the mix, too; this was what made me ask his advice on the letter.

'I thought *you* knew everything?' he joked, putting on his reading glasses.

'Give me a break, I'm out of my depth here.'

He read the letter, let out a thoughtful 'hmm', then re-read it slowly. When finished, he carefully folded it and handed it back. He took out a pipe and stuck it between his jagged, stained teeth, lit up and sucked in the smoke. I was hoping it would give him inspiration. He angled his head, let out the smoke, and pointed the pipe stem at me. 'Mark, there's only one thing you can be certain of with a letter like that.'

'What's that?'

'It'll cost you – the winners are always the legal people.'

'What can we do?'

'I can't help you with your personal life. That's for you and your lady friend to sort out.' He puffed furiously on his pipe to stop it going out, his eyes staying on me all the time. 'Why don't you talk directly to this fellow Culmane, it could save you a lot of money.'

'Thanks, but no thanks. Can't you come up with something better than that?'

'You asked for advice, Mark. That's the best I can think of at this moment.'

I put the letter in my pocket, picked up my brushes and went back to my work. With the transistor radio at high volume, I painted at speed, trying to take my mind off the problem. When the room was finished, the problem was still there, with still no solution to bring back to Celine. At least, no solution she would like.

~~~

I looked along Pearse Street, almost empty on a Sunday morning. The directions on the card that Pastor Smith had given me pointed to a turn into a side street. I saw terraced houses, but no building that looked like a church. At that moment, a man and woman with two children in tow, all in Sunday best, came along and went through the doorway of what appeared to be a disused small factory building. I listened outside and heard singing. The door opened with the slightest touch and next moment I was standing almost alongside Pastor Smith, and in front of me was the singing congregation. All eyes were fastened on me, or so it felt. Pastor Smith smiled and signalled to a man who guided me to a plastic, stackable chair and handed me some hymn sheets. People to my left and to my right smiled at me. We were sitting in an open, draughty space, and the only natural light came through dirty narrow windows high in the walls. There was no ceiling, but a steel framework that supported a corrugated metal roof, which showed the tell-tale signs of rain getting in. Fluorescent lighting tubes hung from the framework and new wiring that fed them told me that they were newly installed. The solid concrete floor had been painted a grey colour, like you'd sometimes see in a car repairer's workshop. Two small blower heaters were placed on either side of the congregation, a feeble attempt to bring cosiness to the space. I noticed that each adult carried a Bible, not pocket-size ones but significant things, stuffed with handwritten notes written on slips of paper that acted as bookmarks. I looked at the rows (plastic seats couldn't really be called pews) ahead of me, searching for Jimmy, but couldn't see him. I didn't look behind me as that would have been *too* obvious. The singing stopped and the pastor looked out over his congregation, slowly going from row to row, as if he were counting heads. Then his eyes came back to rest on me.

'Brothers and sisters, we've a new face amongst us today. Let us welcome Mark to our act of praise.'

Everyone clapped and the people next to me shook my hand. Then the sermon began. The pastor's manner was the same as when I'd met him before. No sign of drama; no raised voice to make a point; yet, still, the congregation seemed to listen to every word he spoke. Every so often someone would cry out, 'Amen!' or 'Hallelujah!' All around me the Bibles were being used, for as soon as Pastor Smith mentioned a biblical reference, the pages were thumbed, and the relevant passage found. They were working hard with their books.

It was during the collection – the pastor called it 'giving of tithes' – when I spotted Jimmy. He was wearing a suit, as were the other stewards. I avoided looking at him as he passed a basket in my direction. It was a silent collection, no clinking of coins. And I wasn't going to let myself down; my crisp pound note landed on a bed of notes, and I moved the basket to my neighbour. Pastor Smith spoke again, calling on the Holy Spirit to protect the members during the coming week, then, the congregation sang a final hymn, accompanied by eager guitar strummers. Then it was over and the man who had guided me to my seat went around collecting the hymn sheets. A pleasant-faced woman with prematurely silver hair in a bun approached me. 'Mark, you're so welcome to our church. I do hope to see you here again.' She gave me a silver-coloured lapel pin of the Holy Spirit, and I smiled and thanked her.

'Put it on, it'll protect you,' she urged.

As I pushed the pin into my lapel, Pastor Smith came along. 'I see you've been enrolled.'

'It's only a pin...' There was an awkward moment, then I said, 'I only came to try and sort out this mess...'

'Whatever you may think, I'm sure you've been guided here by the Holy Spirit, even though you mightn't realize it now.'

'You're right, I don't realize it, nor do I think it.'

The woman who had given me the lapel pin had overheard us and looked puzzled, then she ran after someone else she had spotted.

By now, the congregation had begun to disperse. 'There's James! I'll call him over,' the pastor said, then he hurried away; his 'flock' would have to be seen to the door, thanked for their attendance, thanked for their donations.

Jimmy had certainly changed on the outside. He looked clean: suit, shirt and tie, trimmed hair, even combed in a new way. His smile was like the pastor's, almost glued to his face. We shook hands. There were no bear hugs from him, no messing, no banter (as in the old days), but the friendliness of an encyclopaedia salesman.

'What gives with the suits?' I asked, nodding towards Pastor Smith and the steward who had guided me to my seat.

'The pastor believes that to serve God and our church we must look the best we can. But you're looking well, too,' he added.

He seemed to be even *speaking* differently. I wanted to say something nasty, words that would rile him, chip away this new exterior and reveal the lizard beneath. But my bag of put-downs was empty.

'I hoped you enjoyed the service,' he said.

'It wouldn't be for me… Anyway, that's not why I'm here.'

'This church is my family now,' he said. They found me a job, and I could be a foreman at the site soon; they really believe in me and I'm so grateful.'

'Jimmy, that's all good and –'

'I'd prefer it if you called me James,' he interrupted.

'Why? Is Jimmy not good enough for you anymore?'

'James is a strong name, Jesus' apostle. Why use a weaker version?'

'As long as you know who you are.'

'That's the thing, it's only now that I've come to truly know who I am and what I'm meant to be. Pastor Smith has shown me that.'

'Has he also shown you how to get a solicitor to frighten the shite out of Celine?'

I hadn't noticed that Pastor Smith had returned and was standing next to us. 'Mark, Mark, you've got this all wrong,' he said. 'James is only looking at all his options.'

'This is between him and me! Why are you putting your oar in?'

'Mark, we're all one in the Lord here. James's family is part of our family.'

I couldn't believe the gall of him. 'You can't separate Anthony from his mother. That would be a catastrophe!'

'That, I believe, will be her decision,' he said. The friendly mask had slipped; he was trying to outstare me.

It was clear to me what they were up to. They would brand Celine as an unfit mother, because she was living in adultery; they would paint Jimmy as the wronged husband, who'd been deserted by her when times had become tough; furthermore, it would be shown that he was a man with a strong Christian concern for his son's future. And even though he'd struck her in the past, he would claim to be a changed man, and these misguided people would back him up in his claim.

'Any judge will come down on the side of the mother,' I said, without any grounds to know that.

'That'll be a job for our barrister then,' the pastor said, moving on with the air of a factory floor manager who had just made an everyday work decision.

Jimmy and I were left on our own. He seemed uneasy, and readjusted his shoulders within his suit jacket, as if its shoulder pads were annoying him. 'I'm sorry, Mark, I thought that we could be friends again…that we could sort this out.'

'Me too, me too,' I muttered. I was thinking that the boss had got this one wrong. So much for his advice! I left the building knowing that I had achieved nothing, and on the way past Trinity College I dropped the Holy Spirit lapel pin through the railings, more in annoyance than in disrespect. Anyway, I didn't think that God would mind, seeing as it hadn't come from a proper church. Before heading out that morning, I'd told Celine that I was going to a union meeting. Later that day, she asked me how I had got on at the meeting. The question startled me, because for a moment I thought she'd discovered where I'd really been. Then I realized what she had meant.

'The usual boring stuff,' I said.

CHAPTER TWENTY-FIVE

Another solicitor's letter arrived, piling the pressure on Celine. 'Not to worry, I'll find an answer,' I said. She was leaving it to me to sort out, yet I hadn't made any headway in solving the problem. The strain was affecting my work. My concentration was shot and when the boss remarked that my work was unusually sloppy, I told him about my visit to the church meeting and the second letter from the solicitors. To his credit he kept off my back from then on and didn't offer any more advice. Often, while at home, I found myself stealing long looks at Celine and at Anthony. On one occasion she was standing over the cooker and she caught me in the act and challenged me over it and I told her that she was beautiful. That night, she was avid for sex, as if she'd read a dirty book and wanted to put it into practice. This only made me feel worse. And when I looked at Anthony, I found myself thinking of his future, of him as a young man, whom I would protect and guide and bring to a point of self-responsibility. While it felt good to let my mind wander like that into the future, I was haunted by a question. Does it feel real?

Days passed, and I began to have a new shameful thought, which made me mad with myself for even thinking like that. It would creep up on me, and I would bury it, then it would climb out of somewhere and annoy me again. Now, it was permanently camped in my mind. It caused me to hunt in my pockets for Pastor Smith's phone number. I was sure that I hadn't thrown it away and found it in a trouser pocket at the bottom of the laundry basket. Rather than have Celine overhear me, I rang him from a phone box.

'If you're so sure that Jimmy's a new man, why not put it to the test?'

There was a pause before he asked, 'What do you mean?'

'Let Celine meet him…let her decide. If she's swayed and wants to go back to him, then I won't stand in her way.'

'And if she doesn't?'

'Then, everyone will know where they stand.'

'Has she agreed to this idea?'

'No, not yet. I have to run it past her.'

'Okay. What's next, then?'

'I'll get back to you.'

We were closer now to the deadline threatened by the solicitors, for after that date they would make official Jimmy's demand for guardianship. The sunshine was out of our lives; Celine no longer believed that I could shoo the problem away. That night, dinner was just over when Celine started to nag me over it. I listened patiently, but after a while I felt the walls closing in on me and said that I was going out to the pub.

'Oh! Anthony will miss his reading…'

'He'll manage.'

'Will you be late?'

'You'll see me when you see me.'

'Alright, then…'

I was determined to get drunk to the point of numbness, but it didn't happen that way. Yes, I did have a few pints, but instead of enjoying them, I was engrossed in the problem of getting Celine to go to a meeting with Jimmy. It was a matter of finding the right moment, of putting it to her in the right way. Only, I still hadn't figured out how to do it. I left an unfinished drink on the counter and, as I was leaving, the barman remarked, 'Mark, are you slowing down or something?'

When I arrived home, I found that Celine had been crying. She was silent and didn't offer to make supper, instead she kept her head stuck in a magazine, not to read but to dodge my eyes. I sat across from her, behind the pages of the evening newspaper, the words of which were floating before my eyes, meaningless. When I could stand it no longer, I asked, 'What is it?'

At first, she didn't answer, as if she hadn't even heard me. Then she raised her head and looked at me, her face smudged with black patches where her eye makeup had run. 'You *know* how you spoke to me.'

I asked her to explain.

'Hard. You spoke hard to me… Like you were trying to hurt me.'

'It's the pressure,' I said.

'If there's pressure, it's on the two of us. Why take it out on me?'

'I don't know. Did you read to Anthony?'

'Yes.' At that she stood up, placed the magazine under her arm and sighed. 'I'm going in.'

I watched her go to the bedroom and sat for a long time, hearing the clock yet not hearing it, looking at the gallery of photographs yet not seeing them. It was like being in a trance, but at the same time being completely alert. Sometime later, I realized that I had work to go to in the morning and went to bed. She stirred when I got in beside her. I moved close to her and put my arm across her shoulder. She had her back to me, yet she didn't pull away. We lay like that for some minutes, then she said, 'Don't you love me?'

I fell back onto my side of the bed and looked up into the dark. 'How long are you here now, and you still have to ask me a question like that?'

'It's a fair question,' she said.

'Have you and Anthony wanted for anything? This is your home if you want it to be. We've been over all this before.'

'I know,' she said.

'I don't say things, I do things. That's the type I am.'

'You wouldn't have spoken so hard to me if you really loved me.'

'Celine, we're all on edge now, both of us.'

'It still doesn't give you the right...'

'It's not like me, you know that.'

'That's what got me,' she said. 'I'm now wondering if there's another side to you. Jimmy would hurt me and then be full of apologies afterwards. I don't want to repeat my mistakes.'

'You know I'm not like that.'

She turned in the bed and, in the gloom, propped herself on an elbow, and studied me for a moment, then her hair brushed my face as her lips found mine. 'What's that for?' I murmured.

'We're making up,' she said.

'I didn't know we'd fallen out.'

'Well, we had, sort of...'

Suddenly I wanted her. There was something teasing about what she'd just said. Our lovemaking was urgent, like the first night we'd shared the mother's bed. I shut my eyes when we were spent and she had gone to sleep, but I couldn't quieten my mind. The meeting between Jimmy and Celine would happen on the following Saturday morning in the park. It would have to look like a casual encounter. He knew that and was prepared to take his chance. But I hadn't had the heart to tell Celine of the plan and felt guilty at going behind her back.

I was beginning to dread the thought of what could happen.

CHAPTER TWENTY-SIX

Celine and I were on a park bench, sharing the morning newspaper, she with the guts of it and I with the racing supplement. I was marking my selections for the day, and every so often I looked up and yelled words of encouragement to Anthony, who was chasing a football, back and forward, imagining himself to be the 'bestest' player ever, but kicking it more times with a shin than a foot. Then I glanced around the park to see if I could spot Jimmy. No sign yet, he was late. I returned to reading the form – good or soft ground – left-hand or right-hand tracks – weight being carried, then I heard Anthony shout, 'Kick it to me! – To me!' I had a second of panic. I saw Jimmy tossing the ball into the air, like a First Division player running on to the pitch, then he trapped it with his foot and stroked it back to the boy.

Celine had also looked up. 'What's *he* doing here?'

'It's a public park; we can't control that. Hopefully, he won't bother us.'

'But he's playing with… Now he's coming this way!'

He had left the boy and was strolling towards us; he had swapped his Sunday-suit look for a sports jacket, a blue shirt with the neck button open, and a slightly hanging knot in a green tie. He kept glancing back at Anthony.

'Don't talk to him! Pretend not to see him!' she hissed.

He was almost upon us.

'Fancy meeting you here,' he said, and offered me a handshake.

Celine was restraining my arm, but I pushed my hand out only managing to touch his.

'We come here for Anthony; he loves it here,' I said, nodding in the boy's direction.

He looked for a moment at a scuffmark on his shoe from where he'd kicked the football, then he tried to make eye contact with Celine. 'How are *you*?' he asked her.

'We're fine,' she answered, hunching her shoulders, crossing her arms, and dodging his look.

'Good. I'm glad to hear that.'

'Are you, now? That makes me feel *so* much better.' She was speaking to him but looking elsewhere.

'Can't we be civil?' he said.

'Civil! You weren't very civil with your bloody threatening letters!'

'That wasn't me… It's the way these people work.'

'And who put them up to it? Huh? Who put them up to it?'

'You can't blame me for fighting my corner? This is the way I was advised by my church.'

'What church? What are you on about now?' she said.

I became nervous when he looked to me. Was I expected to spell out what he had meant? I kept my mouth shut; otherwise, my part in the chance meeting would be out in the open. There was an anxious moment, then he seemed to find the confidence to explain himself.

'I'm with a church, now. It's where I get my guidance.'

'You? A church?'

'Yes…it's a Bible church.'

She looked away to check on Anthony, then turned to me. 'This is a joke! That's it – it's a joke! Isn't that it, Mark?' She let out a high-pitched, almost hysterical laugh. Then it stopped; her face took on a fierce look, like a cornered dog facing a sweeping brush. I felt her grip my arm with such a force that it threatened to stop the flow of blood.

Playing my part, I said to him, 'That's rich coming from you!'

'A man can always change,' he replied, as if I had given him a cue. 'I've been shown a different way, the Christian way.'

At that moment, Anthony came running up, looking puzzled. 'Is nobody going to play with me? I need somebody in goals.'

'Son, we'll be going now,' Celine said. 'There's no time.'

'Ma, we're only here a few minutes, stay longer for the game,' he pleaded.

I took pity on him and took up the football. 'Here, I'll kick with you for a while.'

She was startled. 'You're not leaving me...?'

Jimmy reached out and ruffled the boy's hair.

Her back arched. 'You've no right to be doing that!'

He stayed composed; unlike how he would have reacted in the past. 'No harm meant. Listen, I'll be on my way. If you're here next week, perhaps we might run into each other...?'

'What about the solicitor's letter? The date on it will be passed by next week,' I said.

'Don't worry, I'll tell them I've met you.'

'What does that mean?' she said, sharply.

He had bent down to rub the scuff mark from his shoe. 'Nothing other than what I've said. Let's just wait and see what happens.'

Anthony was tugging at my jacket. 'What about the game? Let's play! let's play!'

Jimmy was walking away, the sports jacket removed and slung over a shoulder.

Celine sprang from the bench and snatched the football from my hands. At first, I thought that she was going to march us home; instead, she kicked it across the grass. Her wild kick caused a shoe to come off and it flew, and she hobbled after it. Once she'd recovered it, she ran after the ball, in a moment of abandon, followed by a shrieking boy. I followed them; the racing page stuck into my jacket pocket.

I had no idea of what would happen next.

CHAPTER TWENTY-SEVEN

On Monday, Celine had another one of her regular letters from Teresa. She left it on the table for me to read when I came in from work. It was like that now, we read each other's letters. Teresa wrote that she was doing more gigs with the band and felt less nervous about performing, despite an occasional bout of diarrhoea before a show. She said that Ruth was staying with her, and that she was likely to have her for another six months. She also wrote that Hugo had changed his ways after a stern warning from the police over a breach of the peace incident; for a time, he'd been in danger of losing his position at the school over it. As well, she mentioned that his parents were poorly. She invited us to come to London for a short holiday, painting a picture of Ruth and Anthony at play, together. I told Celine that we should accept the offer, that we needed the break.

Later, when we were lying in bed, she said, 'It's wonderful to have London to look forward to.' She was quiet for a moment; I felt she was living it in her imagination. 'It'll take our minds off this solicitor business,' she added.

She hadn't brought up the subject since our meeting with Jimmy in the park.

'Did you think he'd changed?' I asked.

'He looked tidier if that's what you mean?' But that wouldn't have been too hard to do.'

'If he *has* changed, does it make a difference?' I said.

'How do you mean?'

'I don't know, really. Just asking.'

'Mark, you're not one to say something without a reason.'

'Honestly, there's nothing… It was a stupid question.'

She switched off the lamp on her side of the bed and lay back. Suddenly, she put the lamp on again and sat up. 'I get it! You're afraid that I'd take up with him again. Isn't that it?'

I stared at the ceiling to avoid looking into her eyes.

'Don't you know me, at all, you adorable man?'

'I'm sorry I said anything; it was stupid of me.'

'No,' she said. 'It's so like you. After all you've done for me, do you really think that I'd pack up and go back to him? Even if he's become a saint, I wouldn't want to leave you.'

She was in a slip, and I caressed her back with my hand. 'Will you put out that light, woman, and let's get some sleep.'

In the dark, she fell back down beside me. 'You're such a dope,' she said, then snuggled up to me.

Saturday morning came and Anthony was bouncing the football all around the apartment, like it was cup final day, and he was a centre forward.

'Son, I don't think there'll be any footy today,' Celine said.

'Ah, Ma!'

'What's up?' I asked.

'We shouldn't have to endure this. I really don't want to meet Jimmy again.'

'But it's bought you time.'

'Time for what, tell me? I can't see where this is going to end, can you?'

'No…but, at least you're talking and not traipsing in and out of the court.'

'Regardless of that, it's not right that you should be put through this, too.'

'Let *me* worry about that,' I said. 'C'mon, let's get ready.'

Anthony started shouting. 'We're going! We're going!'

We were sitting on our usual bench, and I was watching for Jimmy and spotted him as he entered the park. He strolled across to Anthony and they began to kick to one another, and it looked like he was showing him how to direct the football. Celine had also seen him; she tensed up beside me. 'I don't want him with Anthony! I don't want him worming his way back into our lives!'

'Let's give him some space and see what happens.'

After about ten minutes, he left the boy and walked across to us. Today he was dressed in a smart, red jumper, a shirt and tie, with the knot peeping out at the neck, and he carried a brown paper bag. 'Hello, again,' he said, as if it were an everyday encounter.

I nodded back – Celine looked away.

He handed me the brown paper bag. 'Anthony said last week he likes comics. I bought him these, but he doesn't know about them, and I'd wouldn't give them without your say-so.'

I looked in the bag. Three comics.

'We don't need your comics,' Celine said. 'You come along here and think you can buy his affection…'

I could tell that he was hiding his disappointment.

'A mother knows best. I won't let him see them… I'll take them away with me,' he said.

Strangely, I felt sorry for him. 'Celine, there can't be any harm in giving him just the one. It won't change anything.'

She had crossed her arms and was looking into the middle distance.

I picked a comic from the bag and put it inside my jacket. 'I'll pass it on later, but I won't tell him who it's from.'

'Thanks, whatever's best…' He looked back towards the boy and added, 'It's amazing how quickly they grow. You've done a great job with him, Celine. And you, too, Mark.'

Knowing Celine, I felt that his compliments would madden her. Before she could let loose, I got in first by asking, 'Have you called off the big guns?'

'Big…you mean the solicitors? Ah, they're waiting on instructions from Pastor Smith.'

'Who's *he* when he's at home?' I asked, pretending to be innocent.

He seemed surprised at the question, then he must have remembered my snake-in-the-grass predicament. 'He's the pastor of our church. He knows all about Anthony – and of course, about you too, Celine.'

He was looking at her now, yet she was still avoiding eye contact. 'Every week, at Sunday service, he says to me, "James, when are we going to meet your family?" Then he asks the congregation to pray for us.'

She turned to face him, looked for a moment as if she were about to speak, then seemed to think better of it. Instead, she stood up, straightened her skirt, and went across to where Anthony was playing.

I was on the point of following her when Jimmy held my arm. 'Will you be here next week?' he asked.

'That depends on her,' I answered. Then I pulled away and ran to join the others.

Our post-mortem on the meeting in the park happened a few days later. I hadn't said anything and, as before, had waited for her to raise the matter. She asked if I thought that Jimmy was being brainwashed by a cult; she had read how these groups can get a grip on people, pressurize them. I told her that she was letting her imagination run wild, and she then criticised herself for even allowing herself to think about him. She added, 'If we had divorce in Ireland, like they have in England, I'd be a free woman by now.'

'Unfortunately, there isn't, not unless you're richer than I think and prepared to spend a lot of money.'

'Where does that leave *us*, Mark?'

'What do you mean?'

'Are you happy living the way we do?'

'Of course, I'm happy. I'd live in any way or in any place with you and Anthony, you know that.'

She thought for some moments, then said, 'I wish this threat weren't hanging over us. Then we'd know we could live in peace, forever.'

'Do you want me to do away with him?' I said, laughing.

She smiled. 'That's a bit too drastic. There must be a simpler answer.'

Over the following weeks – unless rain ruled out playing football – the Saturday meetings in the park continued. Celine never dropped her guard and Jimmy, despite the occasional request that we call him James, didn't comment when we failed to use it. But she did relent on the weekly gift of a comic, as I had said that it would at least help with the boy's reading. As for Jimmy's kickabout with Anthony, I always felt that it would pain Celine if I were to run up and join in with them; instead, my soccer time with the wonder boy came by getting to the park early or staying on when Jimmy had left. Coming up to the weekend of the arranged trip to London to see Teresa, I told him of our plan and that we wouldn't be at the park on that Saturday. I saw a look of mistrust and felt him studying me. Was the old Jimmy going to surface and row with me over it? Then the look disappeared, and he said, 'We *should* keep our friendships up. That pair were almost sisters at one time, always going around together, dressed in the same clothes.'

During the week, he posted a sterling pound to Anthony. Celine didn't want the boy to have it, but I convinced her to let him have a splurge. A two-line letter that came with it was signed 'Dad'. The boy glanced at it, however, he only had eyes for the money, and the letter was dropped like torn wrapping paper, which must have pleased

Celine. I gave him an old wallet and matched the pound with one of my own and, during the trip over, he never stopped checking that his treasure was intact.

~~~

Teresa had left her cousin Viv's place and moved in permanently with Johnny. It was a rented house in a neighbourhood lined with trees and had a garage at the rear. Inside, you had to watch your step – the place was mined with band equipment (on the first night, needing the bathroom and not wanting to disturb anyone, I struck out into the dark and fell over an amplifier and bruised a shin.) Next morning, I got no sympathy from Teresa and Celine. 'Poor Mark!' they giggled, nudging one another.

I grabbed a cup of coffee and lounged on a sofa, while they talked in the kitchen. Johnny appeared in a tracksuit which revealed the start of a paunch. To me he seemed excessively cheery, and I wondered was he always like this when at home. He downed an orange juice, pulled a red sweatband over his long hair, and went out for a jog. The children were having a lie on, the calm before the storm, for when they woke it soon became clear that Ruth didn't like the idea of sharing her turf with someone who wanted to kick the head of one of her precious dolls about the floor. The two mothers came between them, like UN negotiators you'd see on television. Ruth looked defiant, unhappy with being told off. Teresa raised her hands in the air, saying she got her bad traits from her father, Hugo. At the same time, Anthony was behaving like the child invited to a birthday party who didn't want to hand over the present, and no matter what Celine said, he continued to scowl. The two mothers went into a huddle and came up with the solution; we would all go to the zoo. Instantly, peace broke out and the children ran to get ready.

Johnny came back from his jog, the colour of beetroot. He was lukewarm about the trip to the zoo and was unconvincing when he suddenly remembered that he *had* to go to a venue to collect money owed to them for a gig. As for me, I always liked the zoo; I had happy memories of family visits to the one in the Phoenix Park. The Ma and Da shadowing us younger ones while we ran to each new discovery. Now, today, I was doing the same. 'Uncle Mark, look at the size of this fellow! Uncle Mark, why does he smell of pee?' Meanwhile, the two mothers were carefree, hanging back and chatting to one another.

It wasn't my fault, but later in a spurt by the children to reach the reptile house, Ruth tripped and fell flat on the ground. I ran to her, and she came up sobbing, pointing to blood from a grazed knee. Celine took over, sparing Teresa the job, and steered her off to the toilets to wash the pain away. Anthony had dismissed the wound as minor and gone ahead to see the snakes; I realized it was my first time alone with Teresa since our arrival.

'She has told me all about what's going on with Jimmy. Solicitors, and all…it's so messy,' she said.

'He's pushing her, and I've no idea how this will end up.'

'No idea, at all?' She was watching to see if Celine and Ruth were returning. 'What do you want to happen?'

'I want the whole thing to disappear, to go away and leave things as they were. But it won't be that easy, I'm afraid.'

'You don't have to tell me about it,' she said. 'I've been through it all.'

'Sure. But still, Ruth has turned out brilliantly.'

'You always liked her, Mark.' She quickly added, 'Johnny loves her as one of his own.'

'That's as I imagined it.'

'And Hugo is easier to talk to now too, so there aren't constant rows over sharing Ruth. I've heard there's someone new in his life who seems to have mellowed him, which I never thought was possible. So, things are looking up.'

She went quiet, and I wanted to reach out and move a stray piece of hair that dangled in front of an eye. She surprised me by what she said next. 'But what about you, Mark? I feel you're struggling…'

'Huh?'

'You like things to be a certain way. I know you.'

I held her eyes for a moment, wondering what had made her say that. A part of me wanted to sigh and tell her that she was right, but another part of me wanted to hold back. While I was deciding, I heard the others returning. Under royal command from Ruth, we had to inspect the tiny wound on her knee; she held the leg out for us, as if she were doing ballet exercises. I dropped some loose change from my pocket into her small hand, an instant cure. She ran to the reptile house to show her money to Anthony.

'Let's go to the tea rooms next,' Teresa said. 'I'm dying for a cuppa.'

We took up two tables, as they were small and round. The children seated at one, scoffing cake, fighting all done with, forever; the grown-ups at the other, the females talking to one another, and I left to be the bystander. I tilted my chair back and spent some moments studying them and it dawned on me that I was captured by both women. It wasn't long before the children complained of being bored and we abandoned the tea rooms and set off again, wondering what type of exotic creature was to be found around the corner.

Back at the house, we found Johnny loading the band equipment into a van. There was to be a gig that night. Teresa said we should all go – they had a regular babysitter who, they were sure, would also take Anthony under her wing. However, I knew Celine wouldn't leave Anthony with someone she didn't know, no matter how dependable Teresa claimed the babysitter to be. 'You go, Mark,' she said. 'I'll stay here with Anthony and Ruth.'

But I didn't go; the babysitter was cancelled. Instead, when the children had finally settled, I went to the local pub, downed two quick pints while watching *Match of the Day* on the television; then I asked about takeaway drink and left carrying large bottles of beer in a paper bag. To someone else, it might have seemed odd. Go all the way to London and spend the night in, but we made it as best as we could.

'Do you think Teresa will stick with Johnny?' Celine asked me.

'What makes you ask a question like that?'

'Well…he's a bit over the top, isn't he?'

'She seems settled,' I said. 'I certainly can't see her heading back to Dublin.'

I could tell there was something else on her mind. She drank some more beer, then said, 'What were you two talking about earlier on?'

'Nothing, really… We talked about the situation, you know, Jimmy and all that. However, she said that we must be strong, that everything will work out in the end.'

I had lied to her – a white lie – thinking that it would keep her spirits up. But it was a mistake to think that Celine could be taken in so easily.

'Then, why did she tell me that I should be prepared for anything?' she asked.

CHAPTER TWENTY-EIGHT

At Holyhead, Anthony was asleep and wouldn't wake. I struggled to carry him to the security control point, where we were met by a uniformed constable. Thankfully, he must have been a family man, for he took pity on us and waved us through. We made for the saloon where I laid Anthony on a long, upholstered seat and covered him with my jacket. The sea crossing was rough, and the boy woke and was sick. It didn't miss the jacket. I took it to the toilets to try and clean it; the rough weather had made white-face passengers congregate in the area and already its floor was swimming in vomit. I ran a tap on the jacket but knew it would have to be taken to the dry cleaners when we got home. When I returned to the saloon, I found the boy fast asleep, using Celine's lap as a pillow. I offered her my shoulder because she looked exhausted. Soon she was snoring, not loudly, but like a small dog. I was afraid to move in case I would disturb her. With no chance of a trip to the bar, there was plenty of time to think.

~~~

For the next month, our Saturday mornings at the park continued and each time the formula was the same as before – Jimmy had some kickabout time with Anthony and then he made at stab at further conversation with ourselves. I noticed, with each passing meeting, Celine's claws were showing less and less. Then, one Saturday I cooked up a story about having to finish an emergency job at a diplomat's house in Ballsbridge; the wife and children were due to join him in Dublin the following week.

Celine looked stunned. 'What about the trip to the park?'

'It can't be helped... You take Anthony.'

'*Me*? On my own? No thanks, I couldn't face that!'

'The boy will go nuts if you don't take him.'

'I'm not ready for that,' she said, 'you know I'm not.'

'You can do this. Why else would I say it? Just go along and do as before. There's nothing to it.'

'Mark, you're pushing me into this, into something I don't want to do.'

'Listen, you've got this all backwards. Hasn't it kept Jimmy off your back? You still have Anthony all the time, what more can you ask for?'

'An end to the whole thing,' she said.

I went out that morning in my working clothes, a pair of painter's white overalls under my arm, and took a bus to Sandymount; the tide was out, and I walked along the strand. Later I found a bookmaker's shop and spent the afternoon there in the company of its hopeful regulars, their ears cocked to the results coming across the speakers. I headed home after the last race, after the last docket was torn up.

She didn't speak about the trip to the park, as if it weren't any of my business. I knew that they had met because Anthony's head was stuck in a new comic. She'll come round in time, I thought. When she's ready, she'll tell me all. During the week, she finally brought it up. 'James asked about you, last Saturday. He praised you to the heights – said you're a giver, not a taker.'

'It went alright then?'

'Nothing I couldn't handle, like you said it would be. But that doesn't mean that I'll do it again.'

'Let's hope it doesn't come to that.'

She wanted sex that night; it was noisy, and I was sure it would set the neighbours talking; however, there was no fear of Anthony wakening, for he usually slept like a hibernating animal. 'Love me,' she urged. I thought of how Jimmy had described me as a giver, not a taker and felt such a cheat. We sat up in bed afterwards, like cross-country runners who had crossed the line and were now drained. I would have smoked a cigarette, like you see in the films, but because the Ma and Da's bedroom was sacrosanct, and, to my knowledge, had never been smoked in, I instead occupied myself with fingering her hair, my mind empty, at one with the night silence of the building, and the casual sight of her breasts. She fell to the pillow first, holding my hand. For a while, I watched her as she slept, then lay back and closed my eyes.

On the next visit to the park, Jimmy looked self-satisfied. 'How's it going, Mark,' he greeted, and then said, 'Hello, Celine.'

She nodded to him. 'Hello, James.'

So, it's James, now! I thought.

'I'm so thankful to have this time with him,' he said, looking back towards Anthony. 'We get on well together...'

Neither of us replied. He reminded me of a canvassing politician, a cheesy smile to distract you, while a foot is edged forward to stop the door shutting.

'I want to put a proposal to you both. What would you say if I stopped the solicitor's letters and you never got them again?'

'And?' I said.

'We make an agreement about Anthony.'

'What type of agreement?' Celine and I had said that together, like two Alsatian dogs growling at an intruder.

'Pastor Smith and the congregation have all prayed that my family will be brought together again. Now, I think I might be asking too much, too soon. Instead, let's take it one step at a time. The idea is that Anthony comes to me for one day a week.'

'No way!' Celine cried. 'I knew I shouldn't have gone along with these meetings! This has been a *big* mistake!'

I was unsure of what to say, frustrated. She was looking at me, blaming me, but I hadn't caused the problem in the first place. Yet why did I feel like a Judas?

'Fifty-two days out of a whole year isn't much to ask,' he said.

'We can add,' she said, with a tone as corrosive as paint stripper.

'Pastor Smith says that I have rights…'

'Smith should mind his own business.'

'Celine, you don't want to test me, do you?' he said.

'How do we know it would end at that?' I asked. 'One day could become more days... it's wide open to abuse.'

He looked at her. 'It will only happen if *you* want it,' he said. 'If this ends with us being back together again, then I'll be a happy man, but I know you still don't trust me and it's up to me to change that.'

'That's a fine speech. It seems you're looking for everything, and forgetting that Celine is now with me,' I said.

'Sure. But she's still my wife.'

'Legally,' I answered. 'That's all.'

I saw that Anthony was dribbling the ball towards us. 'Listen, not in front of the boy. We'll have to stop.'

'You'll come next Saturday, then?' he said.

'We'll see.' I broke away from them and ran with my arms outstretched and waving, like a defending goalkeeper against the best centre forward in the entire world.

CHAPTER TWENTY-NINE

I had begun to think about the Da a lot. So much so, that one day, I took his old bicycle from the pram shed, cleaned the dust and cobwebs from it, then found the air pump and blew up the tyres. My plan was to cycle the same route that he had taken to and from his place of work. He had done that for over forty years. Out the same time in the morning, back the same time in the evening. Except on Fridays when he rewarded himself with a pint or two on the way home. I can still see him coming up the street, a broad smile betraying his visit to the pub, pushing the bicycle. He would pass it to me, pat me on the head, and press the price of a comic into my palm. I can imagine the simple pleasure he would have got out of that. Then I would put the bicycle in the pram shed for him. I remembered Ma telling me that in their courting days he had once taken her to Sandycove on the crossbar. It had scared her so much that she'd never got on the bicycle again, yet when he died, she had treated it as if it were a prized ornament. It lived in our narrow hall for years, until the day it was placed in the pram shed. Now, I was going to give it an outing.

I hadn't realized that I was so unfit and had to stop for a breather along the way. When I got to the building where he used to work, I found that it was now disused, with a developer's board showing an artist's impression of an apartment block. I rode home and, saddle-sore, placed the bicycle back in its home. Walking away from it, I realized that I'd been so busy concentrating on the trip, that I hadn't had time to think about the problem of Celine and Jimmy; however, as I climbed the stairs to the apartment it came back to me in spades.

The first day of the new arrangement happened on a Saturday – the plan was that we would meet in the park where we would hand Anthony over. Jimmy would have him all day and return him in time for his weekly bath. He had wanted to have the boy every Sunday, clearly keen to show his son to the church congregation, like a Gaelic football team would return with a trophy to its parish; however, Celine couldn't get out of her head the idea that his church was one of those cult places. Nevertheless, because of his persistence, she agreed to giving him one Sunday a month. Anthony had been told of what was to happen and seemed neither hot nor cold with the idea. His mother, of course, would have preferred it if he had kicked up a racket and bawled that he didn't want to go, but he hadn't lain on the floor and refused to budge, instead, she and I were now walking towards the park's exit after handing him over. The further we went, the more his cries – 'Pass it! Pass it!' – became distant and weaker. And it seemed cruel that other park users that we met on the pathway could look carefree.

Celine said she couldn't face going back to the apartment and wanted to walk for a while. The streets were busy with Saturday shoppers, all going about their lives, none of them aware that this woman beside me was down a dark hole, that I was only there to offer a weak lamp to stop her stumbling. We walked for a long time, aimlessly. She turned down an offer to go into a bar, but later agreed to go into a café. I ordered for both of us. She never even sipped at her tea and played with a triangle of thin, white bread, as if it weren't meant for eating. Her gaze went over my shoulder and out the window. When she finally looked my way, she said, 'I wonder how he's getting on?'

'He'll be fine.'

'I'm sure Jimmy's gloating. He thinks that he's getting one over on me but he's in for a big letdown, I tell you.'

'I should hope so,' I said, reaching out my hand to touch hers. She didn't pull away, but she didn't hold it, either.

'It would be impossible to go back to him. I'd jump every time he'd raise his voice or make a sudden arm movement. The fear would be there, even if nothing were to happen. I would never want to live like that again.'

'I know. Remember, there's a place with me for as long as you want.'

'I know that.'

She looked away, and I had the impression she was staring at nothing. We sat like that in silence. Then she met my eyes again.

'Mark, I've come to a decision you won't like.'

'What do you mean?'

'I've decided to move out.'

I'd heard her, understood what she had said, but still my thoughts were darting about in a state of panic, like a person who heard a fire alarm but needed to smell smoke to be sure.

'It's been on my mind for a while,' she continued. 'And I think you *know* why…'

'Celine, I haven't a clue what you're on about! For God's sake, tell me!'

'You'll probably deny it, but I'm sure you've been testing me.'

She could have thrown her tea in my face or kicked me hard under the table, but neither of those acts would have surprised me as much as what she'd just said.

'*Testing* you? What put that notion in your head?'

'It's more than a notion. It's exactly what it is. And don't try to squirm your way out of it. I told you I wanted nothing to do with Jimmy, but no, you wouldn't listen. You're the one that wanted me to meet him, you even pushed me to meet him without you.'

'Anything I did, I did for you and the boy.'

'I just don't buy that, Mark.'

'Tell me why I would do such a thing?'

'Who knows what goes on in that head of yours? But I think that you don't see a future for us.'

'What are you on about?' I was trying to be calm. But I wasn't sure if I'd spoken too loudly and glanced around to see if we were getting stares from the rest of the café – nobody seemed interested. Then I searched her eyes, they told me nothing.

'Haven't I treated you well,' I said.

'You know you have.'

'I thought you loved me?'

She was quiet for some moments. 'I loved you more than you will ever know,' she answered. 'I never told you this, but some months ago, I came off the pill to give you a child, one of your own; unfortunately, nothing happened.'

This was a piece of information I didn't need to hear. Is she deliberately trying to hurt me? No, not her. It isn't in her to be spiteful.

'Where will you go?'

'I'm not helpless.'

'I deserve a better answer than that.'

'Mark, I may owe you, but you don't *own* me.'

As we walked home, she had a stony look, and I felt it was useless trying to get her to change her mind. At the same time, I worried over how she would manage.

She was so anxious to see Anthony again that we waited outside the building, scanning the street. When they sauntered along, father and son smiling, the boy didn't run to Celine until the last moment. She buried him in the folds of her skirt, and he had to twist himself free to breathe.

'I'll see you next week,' Jimmy said, and turned away.

There was a dam burst of information from Anthony as we climbed the stairs to the apartment. Later, Celine listened to more details of his day while she got him ready for his bath, although, as she went to the hot press to fetch his clean underwear, I could tell she was swallowing her hurt.

When he'd gone to bed, I said, 'Celine, you and the boy belong here. This is your home. Can't you see that?'

'It's not the same anymore, Mark.'

'Why? Tell me what's different?'

'It's different because you've fucked it up.'

Later, as we lay in bed, I was surprised when she rolled into my outstretched arm. I kissed her, half-expecting her to pull away. But she responded gently, as if this were the first moment's pleasure she'd felt in a trying day. To tell the truth, I thought it could also have been one of her last acts of kindness to me.

I came home from work one evening of the following week and they were gone. I looked in every room, chasing ghosts. Where there should have been a cheerful table setting and her humming to herself and a boy chattering and the smell of cooking, there was only furniture and photographs that didn't speak back to me.

That night, I moved out of the Mother's bedroom and back into my own room. The sheets hadn't been changed and I smelled the boy. It brought me back to a day when I would be stuck to the bed, where from a fog of teenage sleepiness, I could hear the radio and the Mother moving round outside. 'Get up, son, or the day'll be gone on you!' she would shout in.

Now, the apartment was in silence.

CHAPTER THIRTY

Early 2000s

A text arrived from Celine, and I had to move from the strong sunlight into the shade to read the screen. *Happy Birthday Mark! Have a great day and don't drink too much sangria!* That's her all over, I thought, she never forgets me. I looked around the swimming pool while I formed the reply in my mind and decided to give it a Spanish flavour. *Muchas gracias Celine. I'll certainly kill a few beers later! Marco.*

I returned to the sun lounger and closed my eyes. Spanish pop music came from somewhere; it was soothing, the meaning of the words was beyond me. There was a danger of falling asleep, a nasty trap to make me look the colour of a tomato. Sensing the enemy, I sat up and spread more cream on my flabbiness.

'What's up?' the Yank said in a lazy voice from the neighbouring sun bed.

'A text from Celine.'

'Oh? What gives?'

'Birthday stuff…you know.'

'Doesn't she realize that we're trying to forget birthdays?'

'You can't stop nature,' I answered, lying back down, angling the peak of my cap against the sun.

He farted. 'That's what I think of your philosophising.'

Batchelor Row

'Sweeney, you're as crude as ever.'

Paul farted again and chortled. 'That's what you get for filling me with Chinese.'

The night before, we had accepted the challenge of an all you can eat buffet and afterwards had headed for the bars at Cabo Roig, then saw the dawn as a taxi returned us to our hotel. Now, it was recovery time, poolside, with Costa Blanca sun thrown in for good measure. We were like the fictional Don Quixote and Sancho his sidekick, just who was the knight on horseback and who was the guy on the mule was sometimes difficult to figure out. In truth, we probably swapped roles, whenever the mood took us. Loyalty to friendship was our cement, and our travel trips together were what kept us sane.

Our last trip, taken three years before, had been in America, when Paul's daughter Marina had volunteered to be our driver and had suffered the company of two early retirees for a fortnight while driving us along the byways of New England in her old Toyota. Marina is a looker, like her mother was in her day; also, you couldn't be feeling down in her company, as she shone like a lighthouse in the dark. In addition, she revered her father in a way that had made me think that she was making up for time lost. Yes, she's the type that you'd want to take home in a suitcase.

This trip – our European trip – had been left up to me to plan. I had chosen Spain when I heard that Teresa and Johnny were gigging in bars to expats on the Costa Blanca. When I sent a text to Paul in the States, he'd replied, *Not another Derry?* (You have to know him to know his sense of humour.)

We were going to Johnny and Teresa's gig later that night.

'Do you think she'll have changed much?' he asked.

Earlier, I had been thinking about the same thing, but I wasn't going to reveal that to him. 'In what way?' I asked.

'We all change, and it's been a long time...'

'You're talking looks?'

'Looks, beauty – whatever.'

- 257 -

'So superficial of you,' I said. I opened my eyes and looked through my shades at the sky, probably not a cloud between here and the eastern Mediterranean. Somewhere, within feet of me, was the edge of the swimming pool. But getting in the water would take effort. Later, he asked me what I thought of Johnny.

'He's an okay type,' I commented, 'and they've stayed together, which must account for something. And I hear he does a great impression of Elvis.'

There was a pause in the conversation. He was humming 'Wooden Heart'. Then, unexpectedly, he said, 'You know, Mark, I don't regret a moment of the time I spent with Maria, nor the time spent with Shirley, the second wife.'

'That's good,' I said. I'd never met Shirley. He now had the experience of splitting from two wives.

'In a way, I owe them.'

'You say that about everyone.'

'I guess I do. Bet you feel the same.'

'Paul, unlike you, I've managed to keep my bachelor stripes.'

'Tell me, seeing that Celine's still sending you birthday wishes and all, whatever happened to *her*?'

'Celine – I thought you knew all about it. After leaving me, Jimmy kept at her, wore her down. Foolishly, she gave him a second chance, but all that new image and Christian stuff soon slipped away. The time he broke her arm finished it between them. He claimed it was an accident, but she said he'd flung her down the stairs in a temper. A shelter for battered women came to the rescue and while there she was encouraged to go to the guards and, eventually, to court. He was given a suspended sentence and was ordered to stay away from her. As if it were meant to happen, the garda that investigated the assault took a shine to her and she and Anthony ended up going to live with him in County Offaly. I suppose he offered her more protection.'

(I didn't tell him that she'd refused an offer to come to my place.)

'Although,' I added, 'as you can see, every so often we text one another; the boy is now a man trying to make it as an actor in London.'

'And Jimmy, what about him?'

'I see him around, now and again. I nod to him, that's all, and going by the shabby clothes he wears, you'd give him a penny.'

'What about this church he was involved with?'

'I haven't heard anything about them in years. They could well be gone by now.'

Behind my sunglasses, I let my eyes close. Talking of the past, of things connected with what had happened decades ago, had stirred up many memories for me. Faces floated in front of me. The Mother, the Da, and the family when we were all young. And in my mind, I was reliving those times. Somewhere around that point I fell asleep and only woke when Paul flicked me with a towel on his way to the bar. I unpeeled myself from the sunbed and sat for a while with my legs dangling in the pool, then followed him inside.

It was dark when we took a taxi to the gig venue, which was an Irish bar called Patrick's Well. It had a large space outdoors, rather like a garden, with lanterns suspended above us, and away to one side, I saw a fountain in an illuminated swimming pool. Loud music was coming from speakers in the trees and there was the smell of food coming from an open hatch at the side of the building. Johnny and Teresa had spotted us as we came through the arched gateway and came to greet us. She insisted on kisses the Spanish way, three times to the sides of the face. She looked unchanged to me, although I suspected that the soft light was being kind to any lines that might be there. Johnny's long hair had been replaced by a tanned bald head, yet he looked very fit, like a triathlon man. They had reserved a table for us in front of the outdoor stage. A young English girl in shorts and tee shirt, waving a tray, pranced up to us, and drinks were ordered.

'I can't believe it,' Teresa said. 'I can't believe you're here.' She reached across the table to squeeze our hands; the gesture seemed to startle Paul.

'She's been so excited over your coming,' Johnny said, sitting back, clearly pleased that she was happy. We talked for some minutes, then he looked at his watch and reminded her that it was time to get ready for the show. He stroked his bald head and said, 'It takes so much longer now – for me, anyway.'

I knew what he had meant when he came on stage, for he was dressed in an Elvis-type suit, studded, winged at the collar, and he wore a black wig that rose from the front like a Hawaiian surfing wave. Her outfit was a country and western fringed suit, complete with western boots and a cowboy hat that sat on her back, held by a loosened cord. In duet they sang 'Suspicious Minds', then cowgirl Teresa bowed out, promising to return later. The stage was clear for 'Elvis' to gyrate his way through all the standards. The customers, many red from sunburn, became more excited with each familiar song. Some got up and started to dance and we had to guard our pints against one stout woman, who was wildly chasing her teenage years and threatened to knock over our table.

Then Teresa came back on stage, neatly stamping her heels as she sang 'Take Me Home, Country Roads'. Under normal conditions, I would have thought her act to be dated, but beneath a Spanish night sky, with a crowd determined to enjoy themselves, determined to drink dry this bar called Patrick's Well, it was hard to stop yourself from tapping along. When she was singing her next number, a song about lost love, I saw her give Paul a lingering, almost intimate look. I glanced round; his eyes were also fastened on hers. What's going on here? I thought. Then the moment between them was over. I couldn't stop myself thinking of the boat trip of many years ago, when we were returning home from the Isle of Man. He had convinced me that day that it hadn't been him in the taxi. He'd denied passing the night with her and had even quoted the marine motto *Semper Fidelis* as if he were swearing on the Bible. But now I wondered had he lied to me?

Teresa wound down the song to its end, and he turned to me and smiled; his face was flushed, and he looked as happy as a boy counting the rich pickings of his Confirmation Day. I asked myself, Why should I spoil a night like this? a good friendship like ours? I cleared my mind of what I'd just seen and jumped on to the crowded dance area. A thin, young thing backed towards me, shaking her bottom, and I closed my eyes, searching for my own rhythm.

Later, we went back to Johnny and Teresa's villa. We sat in a lounge that was painted all white. It was a large echoey room with a tiled floor, and we were seated in an area with a large couch and easy chairs which were grouped around a long coffee table. There was a formal dining table and chairs at the end of the room, a kitchen ran off to one side, and a marble staircase led to the upper part of the house. There was a framed poster of Bowie hanging on the wall behind us. I noticed that there were no family photographs – they must be back in their London home, where they lived when the season on the Costa ended, I thought. Teresa disappeared into the kitchen, saying that she had a light supper prepared for us. We were chatting and relaxing when a car pulled up outside and Johnny shot up from an easy chair and cried, 'The taxi's here!' Teresa reappeared from the kitchen, wiping her hands, and Johnny rushed outside.

'Mark, you won't believe who's arrived,' she said.

There were excited voices, first at the gate, then in the garden. I heard a female voice but wasn't sure who it was. I looked to Teresa – she was giving nothing away. Then the screen door was pulled open, and Ruth came in carrying a sleeping young girl. Johnny stood on the threshold behind her, holding her luggage, enjoying the look of surprise on my face. She was struggling with the child and Teresa ran to her and, between them, they placed her on a couch; it was only then that Ruth found time to catch her breath and as she straightened herself, a hand movement swiped her fair hair back into shape. She came towards me, arms outstretched, and she was so like Teresa in the photo captured years before in a photo booth, in Douglas, the photo which had been discovered under Mother's mattress and kept safe by me ever since.

'Uncle Mark!' she said.

I insisted on the three kisses, the Spanish way, as Teresa had taught us earlier in the night. She looked towards Paul, and he also demanded the same treatment.

'You don't remember me?' he said, holding her by both hands. 'I met you in Derry when you were a child.'

She looked puzzled. 'You know my Daddy?' she asked.

'We met once or twice, some years ago.'

I knew she didn't remember the Yank, yet I guessed that she'd probably heard of him. When the excitement of Ruth's arrival died down, Teresa encouraged us to eat the food she'd prepared and then, casually, settled herself on the armrest of my chair. There was so much for everyone to catch up on, and the conversation went around the room, and then the child woke up and Ruth took her on her lap. 'And this is Anne, and she's a big girl and she's going to school next year – aren't you, sweetheart?'

The child was sleepy, and she stared at Paul and me and took her time about accepting us. Eventually, she came to life and began to run around the room. Ruth looked at her watch. 'It's way, way past her bedtime,' she said.

'I've the room ready,' Teresa said.

The child resisted, and Ruth lifted her and brought her upstairs. Then Teresa called up to her, 'I'll send Mark up to read to her. He's good at the bedtime stories.'

I wondered how she knew that, then I remembered the letters that Celine used to write to her from my place. Paul and I exchanged looks; I hoped that the beers I'd taken earlier had worn off. I finished the coffee that I'd been drinking, gave myself a shake and climbed the stairs. Ruth pulled a chair over beside the bed and handed me the story book, then disappeared from the room, and the child looked at me, full of expectation. I cleared my throat and began. The book had large letters and well-spaced lines, and I was only on the second page when she fell asleep. I stayed for some minutes to make sure that her sleep was deep, just as I used to do with Anthony. Satisfied that I could leave the room without disturbing her, I tiptoed away.

I re-joined the others, and all five of us took our drinks out onto the patio. We sat talking, the whiff of anti-mosquito candles in the air. Teresa was sitting across from me; I had seen her now in her grandmother role; yet, for me, time hadn't seemed to change her. I noticed that Paul was quiet and that he had a look of contentment; Ruth and Johnny were laughing and joking over some incident that had happened to her at the airport. A moth was banging against the glass of a lantern beside us. The Spanish sky was so clear, the stars so sharp, and the shutters were down in all the surrounding villas, and our voices must have carried far in an otherwise still night and we ended up by talking until dawn, a close-knit family of sorts.

Also by Desmond Gallagher

WATERFORD STREET
(*An Irish novel inspired by actual events*)

Set in Dublin during the early 1900s. Ordinary people
living their lives in extraordinary times, mostly unaware
of the history happening around them.

ISBN 9780951156520

www.kingfordpress.com

info@kingfordpress.com

Available on Amazon
and selected retail outlets

www.ingramcontent.com/pod-product-compliance
Lightning Source LLC
Chambersburg PA
CBHW031105260626
47172CB00001B/231